Lock Down Publications and Ca$h
Presents

A
GANGSTA'S
KARMA 4

Trap House Confidential

WRITTEN BY

FLAME

First Edition 2023

Printed in the United States of America

This is a work of fiction. Names, characters, places, and incidents either
are products of the author's imagination or are used fictitiously. Any
similarity to actual events or locales or persons, living or dead, is
entirely coincidental.

P.O. Box 944
Stockbridge, GA 30281
www.lockdownpublications.com

Like our page on Facebook: Lock Down Publications
www.facebook.com/lockdownpublications.ldp

Stay Connected with Us!

Text **LOCKDOWN** to 22828 to stay up-to-date with new releases, sneak peaks, contests and more…

Like our page on Facebook:
Lock Down Publications

Join Lock Down Publications/The New Era Reading Group

Visit our website:
www.lockdownpublications.com

Follow us on Instagram:
Lock Down Publications

Email Us: We want to hear from you!

Acknowledgements

If you've read any of my previous acknowledgements you know I first thank GOD, the BENEFICIENT and MOST MERCIFUL. He is my foundation, and I cannot be shook because HE is the rock I stand on.

Now, to make this short, I want to thank my immediate family for all they've done to assist me with my books. Next, I want to thank Amiyah Bertrand, Jessie Bitiou from PBC, Cameron B. Harris from Fair Hope and Lunch P. from High Point . These people are sources that gave me the essential information needed that helped me see my idea for this book through.

As for the storyline in this book, I did my best to think outside of the box. I strived to change the formula of what readers of urban novels think hood books should be. This book based on voodoo is not meant to offend ANYONE! Charge this book to my imagination and not my heart. Just like with other religions, voodoo practices differ from one group to the next. I incorporated as much confirmed info on the whole religion that worked best with the things I fabricated in this story. I pray all my supporters and fans enjoy this one-of-a-kind urban novel. GOD BLESS

Prologue

January 23, 2020 - 5:52pm
Somewhere in Martin County, FL

"...God blesses all da trap niggaz/God blesses all da trap niggaz," the thug rapped along to Future's lyrics to calm his nerves.

CT was several eye blinks away from his doom, and he was none the wiser. His thirst for power - and his insatiable greed - had him burning rubber straight down a stretch of unfamiliar road.

Although his gut instinct proactively tried to talk him into cancelling the exchange at his destination, he simply couldn't stop the odd first encounter that ultimately brought about this deal from reprising itself in his mind. The events of that unusual day, where he *heard* the excessive number of commas that resulted in him clairvoyantly seeing himself drowning in a torrent of blue cheese, were providing the mental energy he needed to psych up the belief that all would go down without a hitch. Otherwise, he would've been more than just a damn fool if he hadn't jumped on the latest "play."

The play itself had been too unreal, too sweet - a quart-of-tea-mixed-with-five-pounds-of-sugar sweet - to pass up. And because of that, CT's upsurging stomach didn't slow him down. In fact, he sped up, ready to button this matter up as quickly as possible, so all he had to do afterwards was roll back to Delray Beach weighed down - literally.

CT, once again, found himself lost in a pipedream, and in it he'd become the plug that supplied every Coke Boy and Pill Man in the region. He'd have the most marked down prices for the wholesalers, and he'd be able to lift his foot off the dope and quit bilking pharmaceuticals from his clientele. *It's not exactly free bands I'll be raking in with this power play. I would've dealt directly with the devil himself on this one if he had presented himself,* he recklessly thought with a daunting smile as he navigated text-by-text toward the inevitable.

CT was completely homed in, even with the persistent intuitive warnings that were irritating him. It didn't matter anyway because the trouble he went through to get to this point wouldn't let him turn back, not now.

But little did CT know that his morally corrupt soul would become number sixty-two, bringing him closer to fulfilling the indebted servant's mission.

CT picked up his brand-spanking-new Samsung Galaxy 8 from his lap. He instantly noticed his phone's signal had dwindled, registering just one bar now, and his GPS hadn't started working again. With today's extensive cellular networks, he found it unbelievable how his phone suddenly ceased to function properly not long after he entered Martin County. At the moment he was only able to send and receive text messages from the connect he was on the way to see.

One-handed, CT began thumbing a message, periodically looking up at the deserted road ahead and back down at his phone. *jus past water tower. where 2 now?* he texted.

Bing

CT's phone chimed. He'd received a text and proceeded to read it. *turn left when u c da no trespassin sign. Can't miss it. da street a dead end. im da last stop on da rite.*

No trespassing...Dead End...Last Stop? CT internally questioned before digesting how it was a hell of a coincidence to be meeting up at such a place. And it didn't make it any better when he finally took notice of where he was: in the middle of West Bubbafuck, surrounded by literally nothing. On top of that, it was sundown now.

Again, CT checked his GPS and signal strength, and the indicator was flickering between one bar and blank. "All this 4G, 5G bullshit is worthless," CT said aloud to himself. "These crackas know how ta gas shit up ta get 'cha ta buy it fo' da high-high then months later they strong-arm ya ta download an upgrade or return ya shit becuz its defected."

Still, CT's cash fever motivated him to overlook all the bad signs and keep course. Money had a magical way of turning the most logical, cautious person against their better judgment, and he was no different. *In and out like a bank robbery, then it's back to the city to watch these M's jump in my pockets*, he optimistically thought as he finally came upon the designated street. *Me and baby will be laced up and dripped out by the time we hit the Super Bowl in Miami Gardens ten days from now.*

Upon turning left at the sign, CT immediately speculated that the sprinkling of residents in this remote rural area had to be living in hellish conditions. He'd trafficked work all over Florida, but he'd never came across a street, road, byway, or back alley like the one he was on. The unoccupied homes were in ghastly shape. They were uninhabitable, boarded up and starting to fall in on themselves. There were also rusted and wrecked automobiles parked in yards overgrown with weeds. The area looked long forgotten, without a single living thing in sight.

Taking in the haunting landscape while travelling down the barren two-lane street caused CT to let out a thundering fart unexpectedly. *Am I nervous? Uh-uh, I have to be having a nightmare, and this is where Leatherface lives now,* he concluded before reassuring himself that he wasn't having a bad dream by giving his arm a good hard pinch.

CT winced from the sting.

Suddenly, five yellow light reflecting signs, with the central one reading DEAD END, came into view. An instant afterwards he was at the road's end. As he began turning into the driveway of his destination, inch by inch, his trucks high-grade halogen bulbs bathed the nonconforming residence in a seemingly supernatural light. Once in full view...

Well, let it not be said that the house illuminated before CT belonged amongst all the other tumbledown places he'd just passed. The obvious thing that struck him odd was the house's color. *Why black?* he wondered. *And why does it look...wet? As if it were literally just done.* Even with the knowledge that the person inside the house was, by any standard, a zany individual, CT remained perplexed by the choice of color. He subsequently surveyed the manicured lush-green lawn. Since he knew he was very much awake and alert, his only explanation for being at this location was the plug wanted to make the exchange in a nonpublic setting this go around because of the large amount of work he was purchasing.

The gritty CT shrugged, for he was more determined than ever to make good on the lower-priced promises he'd already made to his loyal clientele, despite the strangeness of the entire situation. He finally hopped out of his gunmetal gray Chevy Silverado on 34s. He readjusted the lightweight FN on his waist prior to reaching into the truck and grabbing the extra-large custom-made Goyard duffel bag crammed neatly with one-point-eight M's worth of sad Franklins. Next, he checked the scenery: Still no hint of movement whatsoever. With measured diligence, he stepped past a jet-black futuristic Jag backed up in the driveway.

The "schmoney" to be cleaned up ahead caused CT to ignore all the red flags that were manifesting in his mind.

Bing

door open. come in, the text read on CT's phone.

Moving in double-time, because the deserted area without streetlights appeared to be swallowing him whole with each passing second, CT twisted the freakishly warm doorknob. Slowly, he pushed in the solid wood door. A burning aura radiated from within, ridding him of the winter chill he felt. Once the door was opened halfway, he reluctantly stuck his head inside the warmth and yelled, "Yo', Fiend! It's CT!"

CT's voice bounced off the walls eerily.

"C'mon in, big dawg," the familiar voice shouted back from somewhere in the rear of the ill-lit house. "You gotta homie wit 'cha? Or ya slidin' solo?"

At last, CT felt relief after hearing Fiend's voice. With the duffel bag over his shoulder, he took his first unshaken steps inside of the house. "I'm double-oh-seven." Bringing one of his shooters along had crossed his mind, but he ultimately chose secrecy over support.

"Me, too, big dawg. Walk toward da back. I'm in da master bedroom finishin' up wit'cha package. Er'thang copacetic, big dawg."

CT chuckled. "I met alotta niggaz from all ova F-L-A but 'chu by far da...I'd call ya crazy but 'chu have ta get better ta be considered that. You burnt out!"

CT had originally met Fiend by chance nearly four months ago at a strip club named *GODDESSES* in West Palm Beach. He'd been in VIP with his entourage during one of their frequent, sometimes daily, visits when he noticed the unknown Fiend, who had turned up all by himself.

As that night advanced, Fiend got drunker and cockier, eventually announcing he was buying the bar for everybody to get lit, and that utterance led CT to begin taking careful stock of this Fiend character. CT had understood that accurately appraising Fiend would be challenging since most out-of-towners be putting on and capping. However, Fiend's wicked chain and charm had been what compelled CT to coolly approach him to shrewdly seek if they were in the same field of work. And indeed they were. After learning that Fiend's stomping grounds were in neighboring Martin County, they'd exchanged numbers, and CT had deviated from his normal procedure by leaving his clique in the dark about the dealings he had with Fiend.

And up until this exclusive meeting, in order to feel each other out, CT had conducted all previous business with the personable hustler in various semi-open locations not too far from the Palm Beach County/Martin County line. His rapacity after securing this one-of-a-kind deal with Fiend was what guided his decision to keep their collaboration hush-hush. He didn't want another 561 Dope Boy coming nowhere close to competing with his impending numbers, so Fiend would remain his "imaginary friend" as long as he had a say so.

"But fo' real, let's Usain Bolt this," CT added, with the nearly sixty pounds of banknotes on his shoulder. Although padded, the strap was beginning to dig into his flesh, feeling as if it would lacerate him if he didn't put the duffel down soon. "I gotta drop some of this work off at diff'rent niggaz traps befo' it gets too late. I gotta date wit my ol' lady tonite, too. I'ma be runnin' late already becuz, fo some strange reason, I ain't gettin' no serv--."

Without warning, CT went limp...

...And he officially became trapped - making him victim sixty-two.

Chapter 1

January 24, 2020 - 2:03pm
Lake Worth Beach, FL

Another year past, another year older.

Plus, again, another year invalidating all haters.

His longevity had disappointed multitudes of people, from swindlers to statesmen. *Another year survived. Yet another year to strive to survive*, he thought as he opened one of the two windows in his room.

His modest bedroom was instantly inundated with the smells and sounds emanating from outside. He closed his eyes tight and focused on the familiar ambiance. The loudest most distinguishable noise he heard was a lawn mower, followed by light construction work, scores of birds chirping, water spewing, hearty laughter, and music playing somewhere off in the far distance. Then he took a big whiff of the air, his wide nostrils inhaling and recognizing different kinds of aromas, and exhaled.

Scritch

He tossed the lighter on the unmade bed.

His very next breath inflated his lungs with a "normalizing" vapor. The full-bodied smoke replaced all of the oxygen in the breathing organs enclosed by his ribs and sternum. Ten seconds later, he masterfully blew out a plume of smoke before rapidly sucking fresh air up his expansive nose once more until he was unable to fit any more air in his chest cavity. Another ten seconds elapsed before he aggressively expelled the air from his lungs with a grizzly bear-like growl.

At last, he eyes shot open. He was officially up now, not yet forty-five seconds after he'd first rose from the bed.

As the wake-and-bake high took hold, all the sounds and aromas that flowed into his room finally gained significance. He now recognized the loudest noise was just Gotcha Pa and his time-tested, sputtering Toro lawn mower. Gotcha Pa was cutting somebody's yard nearby, most likely without approval, in hopes of getting money to buy a rock.

The minor construction noise was nothing but the mover-and-shaker Tukan across the street overseeing the prep work for his rinky-dink inner city home repair company. "Homie Depot," as it was known around L-Dubb, was on call twenty-four hours, with Tukan employing a crew of local panchos to do the third-rate work for tightwad customers.

Ms. Franklin, she was the true-to-life Bird Lady in the house next door. The widow's ghetto aviary chirped, cheeped, tweeted - and reeked - non-stop.

Either bad-ass Pudge or E-Wok was the culprit behind the unscrewed fire hydrant. And now a wild bunch of truant half-pints were in the flooding street roughing each other up. Though Truman Street was largely travelled by locals, because of the area's shady activity, traffic began to congest as the goons-and-goonettes-in-the-making kept playing around the outraged motorists with reckless abandon.

And the booming music that was once playing in the distance...

Car alarms blaring, dogs howling and windows rattling

...was Dimez flaunting through the hood in his unrivaled Infiniti Q45 on 34-inch Ashantis with twenty ten-inch competition speakers loud enough to be registered on the Richter scale. Make no mistake, he was a rolling earthquake.

He stepped back from the wobbling tempered glass window he had installed, with a Bubba Cush-filled blunt dangling from his lips and his deadly hand on his rod, which, by force of habit, was the first thing he latched onto every time he awoke. After a few mellow drags on the blunt, he put it out in an ashtray crammed with roaches. Then, in unvarying order, he brushed his pricey weeks-old ultra-white porcelain implants, washed his well-groomed face, and rewrapped his long wicks of dissimilar lengths. Once finished, the next thing on his mind to do was to...

Phone rings

"Just like clockwork," he mumbled to himself as he returned to the bedroom to fetch his iPhone. As soon as he pressed the green telephone icon, the caller went postal.

"Nigga, why I always gotta call you first, huh? You that occupied caterin' ta da latest thot that 'chu losin' track of time? An' I ain't tryna hear that bullshit 'bout you just gettin' up eitha. You ain't no damn vampire. Frontin' like you Blade or sumthin'."

"Ha! If I'm Blade, you my evil white witch... Broomhilda."

"Nigga, puh-lease! Quit da antics." Momentary silence. "So, when you brangin' ya dawg ass ova here? Lemme guess, after you stop by ta holla at 'cha triflin' ass homeboyz on Ray Street first, of course. I don't even know why you continue socializin' wit them clowns. They too irrational, which keeps 'em in da back of trol car. They asses lunatics. An' you—"

"Cotton, shut da hell up. I ain't gonna keep tellin' ya to stay in ya lane. You getting'outta pocket mo' an' mo' now." He paused for her backtalk. When she remained in check, he added, "An' FYI, it's GANG GANG fo'eva. Ray Street Savages, we hungry an' lurkin'."

"Honestly, you... you doin' too much. That Gang Gang bushwah you on gonna cause me ta run off wit da kids an' ya scratch, especially if ya Haitian ass get jammed up one mo' time."

"You got jokes, lil' white girl." He laughed some more. "But ta answer ya only non-rhetorical question, I'll be around there in a while. As you guessed, I gotta check in wit my bros ta make sho' they on point an' da inventory full enuff ta' make it through da nite. Y'know da drill by now.

"Whateva, Sosa. Bye!" She hung up.

Unbidden laughter burst out of him. "Befo' Anybody Else...My BAE, Cotton."

The notorious Sosa absolutely loved his loyal, off-the-chain snow bunny. They'd known each other for more than half their lives. They'd grown up a stone's throw away from each other amongst the immigrants, mostly zoes and guats, as they were locally known, on E Street between Lake Avenue and First Avenue South. However, they didn't officially hook up until they were Lake Worth High sophomores because her father blatantly hated all border jumpers and banana boat riders.

With Sosa being a descendant of Haitians and Cotton being Jewish, they were the odd couple, no contest. He was a first generation Haitian-American and a beefy five- nine, while she was one-inch shy from being classified as a little person. By all means, she wasn't white bread, which attracted Sosa to her. She was a mini knockoff of Iggy Azalea, and so she was duly guilty of "blackfishing", which was when a white person tried to make themselves look black. She wore dark spray tan, put on makeup lavishly and styled her hair synonymously with black culture. Basically, she copied anything tied to black customs since seventh grade, which further enraged her shyster father.

While Cotton had been pampered all her life, Sosa grew up stone broke. He'd evolved into a Swiss army knife in the streets. His ambition had landed him behind bars as a juvenile and as an adult many times for various charges, mainly doing petty time for scrambling to get by. During all his little stretches laid up on ice in the PBC jail on Gun Club Road, Cotton stuck by him dutifully. She'd dropped him lines and money on his books with the cash she'd squeezed from her parents before ultimately supporting him with the "Free Bandz" game she'd learned from her meth-head aunt a dozen years earlier. By age twenty-two, he had reached Big Dawg status in the drug game off of Cotton's profitable racket. His ascent allowed her to fall back and pursue only the most well-paid scams. And before long, his dogged hustle spread beyond the south side of L-Dubb, while she gradually withdrew from seeking unlawful ventures in order to preside over their household.

Despite them currently living luxuriously with their kids in the slums where they'd come of age, they were still inclined to take part in achievable capers together like they'd pulled off during their wildest days.

Sosa quickly dressed in a cream-colored Balmain silk button-up shirt, khaki Balmain cargo shorts and desert camo-themed Jordan Vs. In his dresser mirror he inspected his facial hair again for any imperfections before grabbing his bankroll of spare C-notes, his Gucci shades, his unique G Shock watch and the keys to his Polaris Slingshot that was parked under the car port. Lastly, and most importantly, he made sure he had his rod with him.

As he opened the door to leave the crib, he said, "Dinky, Mondo, *annou ale!*"

Almost instantly, his fur buddies responded to his "Let's go" command. They appeared by his side more hyper than a toddler that wolfed down a two pound chocolate Easter bunny. He locked the door and walked over to the car port. With Mondo taking his coveted place in the passenger seat of the three-wheeler, Dinky ran alongside him once he pulled off.

After checking up on his bros on Ray Street to see if the trap house needed to be restocked ahead of the evening rush, he was parking at Cotton's location.

"What took you so long, nigga? You usually get here in no time," Cotton fussed, flouncing out of the house in a pint-sized halter top sans bra and immodest hoochie-mama shorts. And on her hip was a chubby child nearly as big as her.

Though he had no time limit for his arrival, he took a quick glance at his G Shock. "From da time I woke up ta da time I pulled up here, only fifteen minutes or so went by."

"Nigga, yo' connivin' ass can do alot in that time. So, which dirty bitch face you was all up in this time on ya way ova here, huh? Was it that eater Lydia? Or that thot Boo Yada?" Cotton let the accusations fly, all while her precious daughter giggled gleefully because it was as if she were riding a bucking bull. She then got face-to-torso with Sosa once he clambered out of his twenty-seven grand toy. "You sellin' that house today, nigga, or I'll burn it ta da muthafuckin ground. Period. Try me."

Having fell behind a little, Dinky, the hundred-ten-pound Cane Corso, was just running up to the yard when he removed his shades and replied in short, "I ain't getting' rid of the man cave."

Cotton sucked her teeth purposely. "I knew I shouldn'ta agreed ta yo' bullshit man cave cuz it ain't nuttin' but a hoe house fo you an' ya dawg-ass friends. Not too long after you got that spot you been slowly goin' back ta ya old triflin' ways. So, if you don't get rid of it, say goodbye ta ya family...fo' good." Once the last word left her lips, the teacup Chihuahua, Mondo, trotted up and collapsed next to her small bare feet. "Unh unh, hell no! Nigga, I told you 'bout not puttin' Mondo in ya... in ya... whateva you call that thing. He ain't as fast or intimidatin' as Dinky. He can get lost or

16

ran ova, you ass. But 'chu wouldn't care if that happened, would ya?"

None of what she said fazed him. He'd adapted to her attitude and learned to live with her insecurities a long time ago. Besides, he understood that her handling him harshly was justifiable. His past slipups created the scorned woman she became.

"Look, when I be ready ta dip from Ray Street, sumtimes Mondo hops back in, sumtimes he don't. When he don't, I figga he wanna run wit his sista so I let him." He shrugged. "Plus, that crib ain't nuttin' but my nap house. An' on top of that, it ain't too far from here ta there. It'll take ya ten minutes, if that, ta walk ova--"

"Me, walk!? Nigga, you got me all da way fucked up. I ain't walkin' nowhere. Period. Not the future, Mrs. Saintus."

"Drive then. You gotta brand new Lexus that 'chu ain't drive yet."

Her face contorted further, expressing extreme disgust. She then snarled, "Just becuz you buy me a new car every otha year isn't gonna miraculously get me a driver's license, alright."

"Well, why ya won't send J-Mill or Jerri ova ta da spot if ya so worried 'bout me doin' sumthin'. They went wit me ova there befo' so they know how ta get there."

"Boy, bye. Ain't no way in hell I'm lettin' Jerrika or Jenario walk or bike around there by themselves. One of these predatory niggaz or guats ain't gon' get da chance ta abduct my babies."

He instantly got mad at the thought of somebody touching his kids. "I wish a muthafucka would. These muthafuckas 'round here know they part wit they life fo' fuckin' wit my fam. An' if they don't know, they gon' bad wish they had." He plucked his little girl from Cotton's hands. He then asked

17

the animated four-year-old, "Who da king of these streets, Kia?"

With a beaming smile, she replied, "You, daddy. You da kang." She hugged his neck and kissed his cheek.

"I know that's rite, baby. An' da *kang* loves his Fat Mama." He kissed her back, then placed his shades on her. "Now…who's da queen of these streets?"

"Me…Kia!" The smile that followed her answer was queen like, regardless that her two front teeth were missing. "I'm Queen Kia 'cause you said so, daddy."

"So, who is mommie then?" He asked as if he were truly clueless while looking at Cotton asquint.

Kia's regal smile faded, and she became diffident. She laid her head in the crook of her father's neck. Yet, compliantly, she uttered, "Daddy, you said that mommie is the Wick…Wicked—" She struggled enunciating the word. She took a few seconds to collect herself. "You said mommie is the Wicked Witch of the West."

Sosa smirked pompously.

He may have been an uncouth gangsta through his upbringing, but his three kids with Cotton were equally street and book smart. It sure as hell wasn't his parenting know-how that led to his nine-year-old twins and toddler to blossom into the precocious, technology-savvy kids they were. He had no doubt that their intellect not only came from the latest electronic or digital doodads, doohickeys and gizmos he bought them, but it also came from Cotton's meticulous tutelage. He was glad his kids were ahead of their time; therefore, he didn't have to worry too much about them falling for cons and scams.

Out of the three, however, he couldn't be prouder of his little lady, Qunkilya, seeing that she sided with him no matter what.

"Lil' heffa," Cotton growled, "you listen here, tryna hide behind those big- ass shades. Ya daddy is full of shit, okay?

18

In this family there are three queens an'...an' if I ever verify that 'cha daddy is doin' me wrong again, Jenario gon' be da only kang in da house." She gave Sosa a brief icy look. "So, I ain't no damn witch. I'm that *bitch*. Period. I'ma queen just like you, if anythang, undastood?"

Still clinging closely to her father, she retorted, "But my daddy said I'm special because I'm brown-skinned like Princess Tiana in *Princess and The Frog*."

The iceberg that sunk the Titanic was in her eyes when she looked up at Sosa again. Slowly, she looked back at Kia and said, "Da color of ya skin don't make you special, Fat Fat. You special regardless, got it? Ya daddy be talkin' foolishness, so don't pay him mind. Ya daddy a psycho, he cray cray fo' real, okay?"

Kia shook her head no. "My daddy no cray cray. He da kang. Period."

A big snobbish smile took form on Sosa's mug. "Da one true queen has spoken."

"Qunkilya, go take a nap. Right. Now!"

Her mother's tone conveyed how serious she was, prompting Kia to shinny down her father's body and dash off. She wasn't the slightest bit sleepy. But she was going to be deep under covers for the next thirty minutes or so, pretending to be asleep to avoid her mother's fury.

"Uggghhhh...Stop fillin' her head up wit 'cha bullshit, nigga. Just da otha day she called me a harlot. I know it was you that taught her that word. I almost whooped her ass fo' callin' me that."

"She don't even know what it means," he responded. "It was a joke, by da way."

"It's a joke until she finds out what it means," she countered, turning away from him slightly. "Y'know like I do that da kids gon' learn 'bout our past one of these days. An' like I said, it's a joke now until they find out how toxic our relationship has gotten becuz of you." She paused momentarily.

"Also, stop fillin' my children head up wit all that Black Power, Black Lives Matter, Farrakhan shit, too, nigga. You gon' make 'em racist. My babies gon' love *all* people."

"That, I won't do. Becuz at da end of da day, they black in an extremely racist country. My kids ain't gon' be green when it comes ta how da *real* world function an' feel 'bout 'em. I know I ain't at home a lot ta educate 'em like you do, but I'ma teach 'em ta love themselves fo' who they are first, then ta love their own kind, then how ta love othas that treat 'em rite wheneva I can. That Hebrew in 'em only gon' get 'em so far, mainly wit paperwork wit 'cha name on it, cuz it ain't visible like their blackness is."

He sighed, a rare happening. "Our kids, y'know they gonna always love you, too, Anjelica, even if they learn 'bout our past. Ain't nuttin' like a mother's love. Kia an' da twinz love me, no doubt. But they run ta me only becuz I give 'em all da material things they want." He thought twice about what he just said. "Wait, I'm cappin' ...they run ta me all da time ta cook fo' 'em, too, cuz yo' white ass got no taste buds." He smirked. "Seriously tho', becuz they mutt asses know I'm their personal ATM machine, I'm da king. But any otha time than that, they dart they punk asses ta you cuz you a great mom. I'm Boo Boo da Fool while you kiss they booboos an' all that...an' overfeedin' em wit junk foods, microwaveable foods, an' Uber Eats." He shook his head in mock disappointment.

"Also, fo' da time bein', Queen Kia thinks you black becuz I carefully explained ta her a while ago you albino."

"Nigga, that's why she—" She caught herself from fully snapping. Instead, she gave him the side eye while biting on her bottom lip. His unbridled silliness, which she knew was a dynamic component of his individuality, moved her to let it go...until the next time he said or did something out of line.

Switching subjects seamlessly, she asked, "So, what 'cha got planned tonite fo' ya 35th birthday ol' man? I know ya planned sumthin' wit 'cha dawg-ass pot 'nahs."

"Like da last couple, I'ma spend this B-day wit y'all…an' y'all pamperin me like a kang!"

"Bye, Felicia! You gettin' treated today like any otha day, nigga, 'cept you gettin' a gift this year fo' good behavior." She rolled her natural grayish-blue eyes. "Anyhow, since you been on a roll, wit no smokin' gun provin' you been sneakin' around, I can sign off on you goin' ta a club this year."

"C'mon now, CC, y'know damn well I don't fuck wit clubs no mo'. They death traps fo' niggaz that's drippy like me. But…" he trailed off.

"But what?"

She fell for the flimflam before she recognized it.

Quick on the draw, he said, "Cano did suggest that we hit a strip club tonite. Maybe GODDESSES or Sugar Daddy's."

"His fat, ugly ass always up in da strip club I heard. That's da only place his lil' money moves hoes ta show his low-down, disgustin', up-ta-no-good ass some attention."

"Hold up now, you gonna get off my dawg. An' I never said I was goin', did I?"

"Who you foolin' nigga? I know ya wanna go, an' you can. As long as you share ya location."

"How 'bout we drop da kids off at my mama house an' you go ta da club wit me? Fo' old times sake."

Silence.

"Oh, you gonna gimme da silent treatment now while lookin' at me all crazy?"

She remained mute.

Since they were mere inches away from each other, Sosa swiftly scooped her off the ground with little exertion. He tossed her lightweight body over his shoulder like a lumberjack hauling a log.

"Put me down, Sosa!" she screeched. Consequently, she started to flail her short arms and thick legs. "Julius, you got my ass on display fo' everybody ta see! An' my titties 'bout ta pop out!" When he refused to unhand her, she proceeded to pound on his back and added, "Sic 'em, Dinky! Get him off momma!"

Laid out sideways at rest in the driveway, Dinky simply lifted her gargantuan dark chocolate head, looked at her owners suspiciously for several seconds, then planted her dome back down on the pavement.

Little Mondo, on the other hand, leapt into action. He snarled and snipped at Sosa's ankles ferociously. He was undeniably Cotton's champion, while Dinky was easily Sosa's alter ego.

Both dogs may have played favorites in the house, but they never seriously injured Sosa, Cotton, or the kids. Strangers or people with threatening presences, however, couldn't get within ten feet of Sosa and his family without potentially being ganged up on and ripped to shreds.

There was just one exception where Dinky wouldn't reconsider taking a sizeable chunk out of that ass - Sosa, Cotton and the kids included. That one condition pertained to *ANYBODY* irritating or roughhousing with Mondo relentlessly. She wasn't with anyone antagonizing her smaller playmate, having gone to bat for Mondo since Sosa brought them both home as puppies five years ago.

"Shut up all that fussin'," Sosa demanded as he marched toward the house. "An' if ya titties pop out, so be it. That just means less work fo' me ta get 'cha in ya birthday suit once we get inside cuz 'I'm bout ta blow da candles out on this Easy-Bake cake an' cut this ass ta pieces fo' my G-day."

With the expectancy of oral sex and hardcore fucking in the air, her "cake" moistened. Even with the stress, anxiety and ulcers he caused her after the birth of their twins, she had a lot of trouble cutting herself off from his freakish dick game. The thought of what was about to go down caused her to loosen up.

"Well, put some damn pep in ya step an' get me inside so you can stain this cotton all nite long."

Using her nickname in a naughty way was a running gag between them. And once it was initiated, they tried their best to one-up each other.

"Don't trip cuz y'know I'ma harvest that ass like da cotton-pickin' nigga ya pop sprays me as," he declared.

"Yeah, baby, an' I'ma look just like a Q-tip while I 'm bouncin' this phat cottony ass on that dick."

"Damn, you got that," he admitted in defeat. He opened the door, and said, "Now it's time ta K.O. this pussy ...so I can hit da club wit my squad."

Catching on to the last part of his sentence, she shouted, "Oh, hell ta da--"

Door closes

Chapter 2

January 25, 2020 - 6:30pm
Boynton Beach, FL
Knock at door

"Good grief! Your desk, Harden, it's inside out still," the unexpected intruder yapped after entering the office without consent. "This is my fourth time ever coming into your workplace and not once has it been in shipshape order."

Encroaching upon the reclusive Detective Harden in this fashion had long become acceptable in the station. If it wasn't allowed, he'd just flat-out ignore every visitor that rapped on his office door, including the POTUS himself, that tangerine colored liar-in-chief.

The hard-bitten gumshoe went on with riffling through the contents of the file he'd been reviewing prior to being rudely interrupted. Responding to his colleague's annoying drivel about the essential clutter on his desk was a waste of his precious time. He was fed up with trying to make all of his tactless coworkers understand that the collection of paperwork on his desk was simply his tenacious desire to crack the unfinished case.

Detective Harden had an axe to grind, and all the veterans in the department that knew him well understood why. However, the zealous greenhorns that were new in the station had to be enlightened by superiors about the mysterious ongoing case he'd been toiling over for the last seven years. Some took longer than others before they grasped his urgency and left him alone. But still, he knew he couldn't avoid being occasionally barged in on by an old-timer or rookie, so early on, he learned to pay irrelevant hogwash no mind.

Hopefully, this brief interaction will finally spell out to the tenderfoot officer that I'm all work and no play... PERIOD! Just like the bumper sticker says that some jerk put on my door, he said to himself.

"You know, on your tombstone it's going to read...Worked To Death."

"What do you want?" Harden said stoically because his patience was wearing thin by the second as he continued scanning through the file.

The first-year cop closed the door. He sidled up to the desk with a folder in hand. There was no chair for him to sit, so he stood. As Harden carried on browsing through the papers without regarding him, he faltered trying to locate a suitable place on the desk to set down the folder he held. After a while, he cleared his throat and said, "Sir, here is the report you requested." He then extended it toward the higher-up.

Harden finally looked up. He glowered between the carrier and the file in his hand quizzically. "Where's Karen?"

With the folder still held out, the first-year officer answered, "Mrs. Gwynne had to leave the station. Supposedly, she had a family emergency to see about."

Even then, Harden refused to take the file he'd specifically asked Karen for. "Did you look in that?"

"No. But should I have?" The rookie took a second to reflect, then said, "From the name on the tab however, I know what the contents concern."

At that, Harden snapped the folder out of his hand in a flash. "You're dismissed," he said in a cold manner before placing the newest report down on the desk and resuming leafing through the previous papers. After several seconds of waiting for a specific confirming sound, he looked up conspicuously and found the newbie fixed in place. "What now?"

The rookie adjusted his stance until his chest stuck out in the uniform. "Since you set yourself apart from others by working alone and avoiding off duty functions, we haven't got the chance to formally become acquainted with--"

"What do you want Noah Schwarzkopf?"

Caught off-guard by Harden's direct rudeness, he stammered, "Uh...okay." He cleared his throat again. "I realized, sir, in good time through my own observation that you were one tough nut to crack. Then I recognized your aloof demeanor was tied to your compulsion with the egregious *RISING SUN* case." He relaxed his posture. "We share something in common...No, not our charming personalities, of course." He sniggered, stopping immediately once he saw Harden's expression become more forbidding. Next, he sighed wearily. "Sir, I'm looking for answers in that case, too. My mother's sister curiously vanished four years ago…"

"Phyllis Kohlker from Greenacres."

"How…how did you know?"

"I can see a definite resemblance." Harden finally stopped what he was doing to scrutinize Noah. "I know what you want, kid, but I work solo in the department. I'm pretty sure you've already heard that...and observed it."

Not one to surrender without a fight, Noah bent forward and braced himself on the sliver of exposed edge of the desk. Looking fixedly into Harden's baby blues, he countered, "I've been interested in this case since I was fifteen, sir. I'll be twenty-two soon." He inhaled and exhaled before bringing up a traumatizing matter." When my aunt disappeared, I became...It haunted me because I knew she was gone forever. Her disappearance has deeply and adversely affected my family, and it's the main reason I applied to the police academy.

"Then once I became aware you were totally absorbed with the *RISING SUN* case as well, I tried to subtly gain your attention, which I clearly failed to do. I was just hoping to stand before you to offer my assistance. So, I'm here to help you anyway that I can, sir."

Staring back into the pleading eyes, he replied, "You have a promising, yet migraine-inducing, career ahead of you, kid. But no thanks. It's aggravating enough that the U.S. Marshals have decided to abruptly step in." He paused. "Sorry for your loss but know that I'm working methodically and diligently on all missing person cases in the county. Now, will you kindly excuse yourself. I have very important research to sift through, and every second counts."

"But sir, I—"

"Piss off!" Harden exploded as he pounded the desk with a fist, causing the six or seven teetering stacks of files to rattle.

Flummoxed by the sudden outburst, Noah recoiled and departed hastily.

At last, the comforting sound of the closing door filled Harden with a sense of relief. The tranquility that followed was what he demanded. He could once again be at peace in this sanctuary away from home.

But first, he opened his desk's top drawer, pulled out an essential pill bottle and promptly popped off the top, shook two high blood pressure pills directly into his mouth and swallowed them. He replaced the bottle and closed the drawer.

Not too long after he became a member of the Boynton Beach Police Department, Carol Harden, named as an eccentric tribute to Johnny Cash's song "A Boy Named Sue" by his British father, had autonomously and systematically alienated himself from department protocols. Because of his unpleasant childhood, he didn't give a flying fuck whether his peers of eighteen years related to him or not. Since his first day on the job, he'd been a zealous peace officer. But once tragedy befell his family, he quickly developed tunnel vision and began utilizing the department's resources extensively in his quest for unexplainable answers.

While he knew chances were slim that he'd ever find out the truth of what happened to his sister in 2013, he was determined to grind daily on the harrowing case, not just for himself, but for the families of all the missing. Despite all the legwork and hours he'd put in, he'd also shot down as much outside help as possible. He firmly objected to working with others on the multijurisdictional case because he didn't need anyone, not even the formidable U.S. Marshals, leading him away from his focal points or muddling up his expansive investigation. However, when he experienced occasional burnout from overwork, he readily accepted help from the select few colleagues that had *earned* his trust.

As far as the current case assignments in his jurisdiction, he was always mindful and diligent of his oath to serve and protect. For the most part, though, only a small percentage of his immediate cases were time-consuming to solve. But once those cases were cracked, or he was no longer needed, he spent every spare tick of the clock on the case that mattered to him the most.

Harden gently set the file he'd been reviewing on a stack. He then opened the latest folder that had been laid on the least untidy portion of his desk. It took him roughly ten minutes to read over the pages of the recently filed report. In conclusion, the four pages contained all the material information on one Charles Trotter, a twenty-five-year-old black male from Delray Beach that was a prolific, dangerous drug dealer.

According to the fiancée, Rhiannon, the filer of the report, Charles, aka CT, was last seen forty-eight hours ago leaving home to go visit an unknown acquaintance.

When CT failed to return home later that night as planned, or to answer her influx of phone calls and text messages, Rhiannon grew concerned because CT reliably communicated hourly, at the least, while he was out and about. Twelve hours after Rhiannon had called the police non-emergency line to report CT missing, the police waited an additional twelve hours, in case he returned by his own volition, before a countywide BOLO was finally issued for CT's customized gray pickup truck.

With no helpful leads or witnesses mentioned in the report, CT's disappearance became like so many of the other cases preceding him: unsolvable at the moment.

Slowly, Harden closed the manila folder. He placed it on top of a mound of files to look back on later. His fellow officers were unaware that the stacks were systematically arranged, and CT's file was now momentarily resting on the tallest stack he dubbed "Nearly Hopeless." He'd been working the current case long enough to adequately determine from the initial report which pile the newest one belonged to.

He then went into his desk's top drawer again. Instead of retrieving his pills once more, he opened an etui that was half-full of colored pushpins. Once he removed the appropriate pin from the plastic case, he stood up and moved mindfully toward the wall next to him. Affixed to the wall was a nine square foot area map of Palm Beach County. Dozens of multi-colored pins were tacked to the poster. He adeptly pushed the selected pin into its likely permanent place, which was CT's last known location - his home - before he disappeared. He stepped back a few feet and observed the infuriating visual aid. He knew the chart lacked some pins due to people having gone missing without ever being reported. However, over ninety percent of the pins in place were colored red, so a majority of the unreported would've also been deemed nearly hopeless too.

Among the sea of colored pins there wasn't a single white one. He sure as hell craved for the day he'd be able to use the designated pin: FOUND ALIVE! He swore to God he'd not only tack a pin on the board before he retired, but he'd also secure the etui's lone black pin to the map. Adding the black pin meant his elusive, mysterious perp had been captured, and hopefully on the fast track to be lethally injected and buried near the earth's core under the Florida State Penitentiary in Raiford. *Death is really the only befitting thing for this diabolical piece of crap,* Harden determined as he stared at the layout in a trance.

Harden remained confident he'd simultaneously place a white and black pin on the poster. He awoke every morning optimistic, although the likelihood of him adding another red, blue or yellow tack to the pin-up was high. Just like all the family members of the vanished, he was positive he'd personally see justice and get closure.

In all honesty, though, he prayed he was the one to collar, or better yet, kill, the evildoer that primarily preyed upon the underclass in the county. And not having the arrest powers because of lack of jurisdiction wouldn't obstruct him either.

Regardless of his sister being one of the first abducted in the current spree, Harden sincerely believed it was the same demented vigilante behind the rampages in different cities and the recent one in PBC. Most of his colleagues maintained that the latter-day kidnappings were just the work of a coalition of abductors involved in sex trafficking, however, and not tied to the horror in the nineties. Low on evidence, what he assumed was simply inadequate and unacceptable to the others. And due to the fact that the rare witness in various reports of all the rampages all described someone different with the victim before they disappeared, he theorized it was the same person the reporting witnesses saw on each occasion. He presumed "the male", self-appointed server of justice, would just masquerade as either man or woman, then allure his victims with their personal weaknesses before spiriting them away.

God, what sense does it make knowing this hellion's pattern for all these years if nothing useful is to come from it? Harden invoked while fiddling with the rosary beads he'd pulled out of his pocket. *I'm not second-guessing you but please bestow me with the solution to end this gloomy reign of terror once and for all because too many families have no closure.*

Phone rings

Harden grabbed his vintage flip-phone, which was both his personal and work phone, off the clip on his hip. "Yes...As usual, I'm looking over case files, but no, I'm not busy...I know you wouldn't have called unless it was relatively important, so what is it I can do for you? ...Really? How'd you come across such a list?" He sighed. "Well, I have a commitment this evening I must prepare for so I can't stay very long... See you in thirty minutes, Bojanski." He put the outdated cellphone back on its clip.

God sure knows how to keep me engaged with these breadcrumbs, he thought as he took his blazer off the coat tree in the corner and donned it, *because He knows I have no choice at this point but to pursue every crumb until this nightmare is over.*

He looked at his TAG Heuer watch, a gift from his now ex-wife. In less than three hours, he was scheduled to meet his son and his former spouse at the Cheesecake Factory to celebrate a special occasion. The drive over to Bojanski 's office would take fifteen minutes, on average, and that was if traffic conditions were perfect. And depending on Crime

Scene Specialist Lou Bojanski's finding, he was hoping to make it to the dinner early...or ten minutes late at the very least.

As a precaution, however, he dispiritedly pulled the phone from the clip. He toggled buttons until he found the saved number. He finally pressed the call button with trepidation.

Just as he was walking out of his office with the phone to his ear he ran into Karen.

"Jeezus!" Karen shrieked, bouncing forcibly off Harden's chest and almost falling. "Oh, gosh, I'm sorry, Harden. I-I didn't see you."

"It's fine, Karen. Are you okay?"

"Yes, I am." She straightened herself swiftly. Just about good as new, she said, "Well ...I see you're on your way out, but I was just stopping by to let you know I received that file you requested from Delray PD. Unfortunately, I seemed to have misplaced it somewhere. After I used the ladies' room, I was going to bring it to you. I just don't—"

The balls on this rook, he thought with a partly suppressed laugh. "It's fine, Karen. Don't worry yourself over it. Someone took care of it."

"Don't worry about what? And who took care of what?"

Distracted by the encounter with Karen, Harden forgot he'd placed a call, and that person was now on the line. "Hey, sport. I wasn't talking to you. Anyhow, I'm just calling to let you know that I'll be running a little behind. But not too late…"

Chapter 3

February 12, 2013 - 9:16pm
Riviera Beach, FL

He laid his prowling eyes on her.

By that time, she'd spotted the car's headlights at least a half mile away. She was strolling towards him alone in a cold drizzling rain as he contemplated on how to approach the situation at hand.

He was uptight, and he had every devil-be-damned reason to be, since this girl was in the makings of becoming his numero uno. His first three attempts earlier in the day had backfired terribly. But those fiascos presented different unfavorable conditions that made it difficult to be successful.

This opportunity, however, was golden.

Broadway, the revamped boulevard once known for its sinful liveliness, was virtually empty, giving him the confidence required to make his move. He must get a move on it, too, because he was a goner himself if he missed his given twelve o'clock deadline.

He slowed down the beat-up Sonata to a crawl as he closed in on her. He verified that his surroundings were devoid of police, or any kind of potential witnesses, before he came to a stop alongside the curb just in front of her. Disregarding the chilly fine rain, he rolled down the passenger window, and his prey unheedingly walked up to the vehicle.

"Hey, handsome. Are you looking for a good time this lovely nippy evening?" she solicited.

"How much?" he said directly, wanting to get straight to the point so she'd get in the car as quick as possible.

The standard response prodded her to jump into the vehicle. It had been a slow day, and the evening so far wasn't any better because of the awful weather, so she was elated to have come across a trick that would give her the money to fuel her meth addiction. It had been quite a while since she last used, thus she was anxious to get this over with quickly so she could score.

Before she could name her price, he happily pulled off from the curb.

In an hour or so, I'll finally see firsthand how the pots in this house works, *he thought before turning towards his hapless, soon-to-be condemned victim and rendering her unconscious with a hard-packed right hand to her jaw.* Immortality, here I come!

***

January 25, 2020 - 11:58pm
Miami, FL
The homestretch.

Four more to go, then he was off the hook.

A quartet of unaware no-goods was all he needed to officially fulfill his end of the tedious, yet occasionally enjoyable, contract. And he couldn't have been happier with being so close to the last act. He couldn't wait to be granted what was promised to him as a bonus upon completion of the agreement. He'd put up with countless snags, and two very close calls, over the years in order to redeem his unrestrained power and to take back total control over his life.

Above all, though, he'd finally have the capacity to restore his afflicted mother's condition.

It was near midnight now, and he was just entering the bowels of Miami. The section he was rolling through was swarming with people; he could see so much of his country of birth in the squalid community. He was on his way to pay an unsolicited visit to the person that saved his life a little more than seven years ago.

To say the least, he wasn't in any way thrilled about seeing the one that delivered him from an early grave.

His unsung savior was the individual that exploited the grave situation he was in back then. That fateful day, he was deceived into accepting an ominous, spur-of-the-moment, verbal pact while in severe distress. He'd incoherently said yes to the peculiar hero's terms without delay. And by doing so, he ended up changing his life permanently.

Once he was good as new, he was in disbelief and unsettled about what he'd agreed to. But, in hindsight he was glad he cut the deal, especially since he was close to meeting his objective.

Because of his unwritten deal with whom he ultimately learned was an infernal priest, cruising through the former Zoe Pound controlled territory on NW Second Avenue at such an hour in his sable Jaguar was no problem. Ever since the dark shaman gifted him a supernatural amulet, which he always kept on his person, he intensely felt the hedge of protection it provided. He mostly felt the protective force, however, whenever he reached Little Haiti's sinister boundaries to answer a summons. It felt majestic being recognized and left untouched in an area he had plenty of refugee kinfolk and friends that were from Hispaniola. *But it's going to feel even better becoming somebody that's bowed down to and felt in one's bones everywhere I step,* he pondered as he pulled up to the well-known unholy house. *I*

*also can't wait to no longer need to use this silly charm for
my supernatural powers.*

"And more importantly, I can't wait to reunite with the
people I was instructed to cut loose when I complete this
mission and safeguard them from what's coming," he uttered
to himself.

Specifically, he yearned for the day he'd be able to hug
and kiss his mother again.

He whipped onto Sixty-Third Street and pulled over
seconds later. With the perilous Edison Projects not very far
away, he exited his vehicle unafraid. He noticed the hood
was buzzing with immoral activity as usual. If this hood's
depraved residents weren't forbidden to snatch up, he'd have
met his target number in less than a year. But since these
menaces were off limits, just like any other time he visited
his lifesaver, he strolled up to the house impervious to the
nightly excitement.

He was dressed in designer label, and his impeccable
custom gemstone-encrusted charm milly-rock'd enchantedly
around his neck as he moved toward the hideous dwelling.
He was seen yet unseen, and he attributed his juice to the
rotten soul inside of the residence he was about to enter.

He opened the ramshackle door without knocking. There
was no need to make his presence known since his every step
was tracked spectrally by the *bokor*, a male voodoo priest
that was prepared to use black magic to attack and hurt
others. Once he crossed the threshold, the door, whose
hinges needed a good oiling, shut slowly behind him on its
own. The interior was just about absent of all light. However,
like a feline needed just a small amount of light to see in the
dark, the darkness instantaneously activated his acquired cat-
like eyesight. The living room illuminated in an odd green
color as if he were a commando wearing night vision
goggles.

Set against a wall was a primitive table made of worm-eaten planks of wood placed on bricks. There were grapefruit-sized rocks spaced out on the platform. In addition to the jagged rocks there was a smudged glass bowl with liquid in it, two cracked glass candleholders, various frazzled feathers and fossilized bones, a rusty medieval machete, an old rattle, a tarnished mason jar of graveyard dirt, and a corroded small black iron cross. Several of the aged objects on the table represented four elements: Fire (candle), Water (bowl of spirits), Earth (stones) and Air (the space itself).

ZooMan drifted up to the altar. He picked up a black candle that was coated with soot and rubbed it with crude oil from the middle to the top, then from the middle to the base. Thereafter, he placed the anointed candle in a glass candleholder and lit it.

The next bat of ZooMan's eye, on cue, the person he'd come to see emerged from the shadows in his peripheral vision. *They* slinked towards ZooMan.

"*Kisa'k nouvo la, zanmi'm?* I know you just love stopping by to see how your old partner in wickedness is doing, right?"

The inhospitable stench in the air overran his nostrils, and the stagnant broiler-like heat blanketed him. If he hadn't become used to it, he wouldn't have been able to tolerate the horrid conditions for no more than a few seconds. But since he was accustomed to the setting, and close to never having to come here anymore, he haughtily advanced past the *bokor* and said, "Again and again I tell you I am not your friend, Francois. We'll *maybe* become friends once I meet my end of the grim deal and you deliver what you promised. And what's new is I've just about achieved the goal, as you should know. So, you should know also why I'm here then."

"After all these years of developing our brotherhood, you still don't trust me, not even a little?"

"To begin with, I'm basically a contracted bounty hunter. We're not comrades." He paused. "I'm not a fool though, because I know with the help of Baron Samedi you bailed me out twice before. You did so seeing that I mastered my tasks in no time at all. I meant more to you here than in one of those damned pots.

"And secondly, you know damn well I don't trust you. I trust you just as much as Haitians trust each other... and we're both Haitian. I'll only trust you somewhat, and possibly befriend you, once I trap the final victim and you petition Baron Samedi to grant me my abilities, with no strings attached, as promised.

"Do you wish to talk to Baron Samedi himself then? To square this up once and for all since the end is at hand."

The proposal surprised ZooMan. After some thought, he said, "Oh, what the hell? It's been a while, so go ahead and call him up."

"Because you don't have with you his favorite rum, cigars, or the other things he adores, he's going to be irritable."

"I know. I'll make up for coming around empty-handed my next... As a matter of fact, I'll bring a boatload of his preferences because we're going to celebrate my exaltation."

If you can wrap this up, the next time you stop by isn't going to go as you'd like, the old *bokor* Francois Gedeon concluded as he prepared to open the gateway between the human world and the spirit world. After he lit a red candle on the altar, he used his spiritual power to call upon the *lwa* Papa Legba. The invoked *lwa*, who was a spirit that served as the gatekeeper for the other *lwa*/spirits, was then asked to open the doorway between the worlds so the head of spirits and the Master of the Cemetary could enter.

While slipping into a trance, he grabbed the machete and knocked on the ground three times. Next, he took some of the graveyard dirt and created three *x's* on the floor. Suddenly, his body was possessed by the Ruler of the Dead.

Following a bit of uproarious howling and indecent dancing around the sparsely furnished living room, the *bokor* Francois drew near to ZooMan. Controlling Francois' body, the *lwa* Baron Samedi looked around for a while prior to speaking in a primeval accent.

"Where is my fowl?" He looked around some more. "Neither my rum with chilies nor my cigars do I see." He groaned. "Since I do not see my provisions, explain to me the meaning of this imprudent session at once. And your reason better be worthwhile."

"My apologies, Oh Father of the Dead and Controller of Spirits," ZooMan replied with sincerity, not looking straight into those possessed eyes. "I didn't expect to see you face-to-face today, which is why I'm without my offerings. But I'll bring—"

"What is it you seek?" he growled, clearly agitated.

Having learned early on to be straightforward and confident when conversing with the wise and forthright Baron Samedi, and to not mention certain things about his and Francois' arrangement, he stated, "My Master, with four more souls to capture, it's only a matter of time before you come and punish the world. I just wanted—"

"Devoted one, don't worry," an annoyed Baron cut in. "Soon, because of you and my other adherents, the final phase of my plan will begin. This scheme of mine has gone on for far too long as it is." He gnashed his teeth. "But once you confine the last four souls, the ritual for my reincarnation can take place at last. And once I harness the energy of those wretches and assume physical form, you and the others will help me purge this atrocious planet."

Cackling.

"Now, when you come again, be in possession of a box of *real* Cuban cigars, a bottle of Barbancourt rum - bear in mind to include exactly twenty-one chili peppers in it - and domestic fowl. None of that oily Church's or unsavory KFC defilement, either. Preferably Popeye's."

And with that, some more air-humping and laughing ensued before Baron Samedi slipped back to the spirit world to regulate the deceased.

The flames on both the black and red candles went out. The room was pitch black thereupon.

Francois Gedeon exhaled wearily. Then, "Have you finally been put at ease?"

"Once I'm deified with no restrictions, then and only then will I be satisfied."

"You didn't mention the bonus I promised you to Baron, did you?"

Skeptical since the first time Francois instructed him not to speak to Baron Samedi about specific matters, he just said, "No."

"Bon. Sa bon anpil," the bokor acknowledged in Creole while slinking a few feet away. "Once all is square, you can trust me to appeal to Baron to grant you the boundless power you thirst for."

ZooMan frowned. "I don't like your condescending tone. I never did. And soon you'll never talk down to me again without repercussions." He looked at Francois with a dead-eyed stare. "By the way, I thirst for it because I earned it. I'm—"

Interrupting him, Francois fired back in an unworldly pitch. "You earned nothing, *malpwopte, ti kras kaka!* You should be enduring the most abysmal suffering in a realm that's frigid and damp as I speak. You only exist in the human world because I responded to your plea for help and restored your despicable life. If not for me, you'd have died full of holes on a hot pavement. And if not for me feeling a little empathy after you talked about your mother's ill health, I wouldn't have transferred a portion of my power into a charm and entrusted you with it." After unloading on ZooMan, he switched back to his regular voice. "The bottom line is you owe me... forever. I owe you nothing. Don't get that misconstrued. I only added the bonus of persuading Baron to fully empower you once you've concluded your mission because, like you said, I saw how quick you learned to kidnap with finesse. You became like no other I had under obligation. You've exceeded all of my expectations. And because of your speedy work, you're now a couple of souls away from freeing yourself from the contract and becoming an immortal being that's revered and worshipped. What's more, your productiveness and timeliness will strongly move Baron to empower you once I fully recommend it."

Now was the time ZooMan asked the bothersome question. He deserved an answer here and now, inasmuch as he 'd felt something wasn't right when Francois directed him to not disclose the promised privilege to Baron Samedi. "Why is it you don't want me to bring up what you promised me to him?"

Francois started to respond. But before uttering the second syllable the bokor stopped. He pondered for a spell.

Finally, he said, "I've dealt directly with Baron for over three decades. I'm one of the select few he possesses these days. So, I know to only ask him for something once the deed is done. Receiving what you desire will be much easier once you please him by getting the job done."

ZooMan laughed subtly at the indirectness of Francois 's response. Rather than press him for a clear-cut answer, however, he said, "Well, I intend to *get the job done* ASAP... possibly tommorow."

"I've warned you, don 't be careless. I'm aware of your recent activity, and it's insulting to take notice of how impulsive you've become the closer you've gotten to the end. You used to choose your targets wisely, play their game for a little while, then take them. But lately you went back to your old risky technique of 'see 'em and seize 'em' on the spot." Francois skittered up to ZooMan.

"Need I remind you, I will *not* be invoking Baron, or any *lwa* for that matter, to extend you any more lifelines. Therefore, the next time you're in a life-or-death situation or you're in deep, hot water, it won't matter that you're great at what you do, you'll be on your own." He began to slowly circle his best abductor. "You've almost completed your marathon. So, why sprint recklessly towards the finish line and risk breaching the contract? Unless the prospect of living in eternal damnation doesn't bother you."

With swagger, ZooMan stepped away from the evil priest. "The sooner I can wrap this up, the sooner I'll get from under your manipulative thumb. I'm ready... I've been ready a long time now... to be back in total control of my life."

"My promise of giving you dark powers has got you full of yourself. Tsk tsk. Your self-interest has you unable to see the grand scheme of things, and that's a shame." Francois glowered. "Hopefully, what I'm about to say next will help you concentrate while you're out there being a daredevil... If worst comes to worst and you end up rightfully surrendering your soul to me, I'm not only going to imprison you in a *govi* forever, but I'm also going to find a way to pack in with you the most reprehensible spirits for failing to pay your debt. And as for this insolent attitude you've acquired, I'm going to command those *djabs* to maul you eternally. Got it?"

"Hmph. Hopefully, what I'm about to say next will prepare you for the day we become coequal... I'm a natural now. I no longer fuck up. How I been moving recently may be fast and loose to you, but I know what I'm doing. I cleaned up my method so much over the years that its now foolproof."

A sudden thought struck ZooMan, and he decided to share it right away. "Say, I have one victim lined up already. I met her on the dating app *Woo'd* about a month ago. She's a gutta rat and a cakewalk. I should bag her tonight. As for the other three, I'm going to resort to my favorite hunting ground. And the icing on the cake, my final victim will be full of vileness, guaranteed." He prepared to end the visit.

"You'll be seeing me in two days max. At that time, you should have done more than persuaded Baron to give me what you know I've earned. Now, give me five keys of coke and ten pounds of weed so I can be on my way.

You're going to get everything you want, but let's see if you want everything you're going to get, Francois determined after listening to ZooMan's boastful response. While sneering, he retorted, "I assure you, I'll give Baron no ground to turn my request down. When we meet again, at the trap house, you shall have your power. And get the drugs yourself. You know where it's at."

Then, the unholy priest that had been there a second ago faded swiftly into the darkness.

Instead of mulling over Francois' words, ZooMan got the work and slipped out of the house focused on one thing. Unconcerned with the steady nighttime craziness in the area, he pulled his phone from his pocket as he dawdled back to his vehicle with the Hefty bag full of dope. He placed a call and awaited an answer. "Wassup, boo?" he said, turning on the performance once they picked up. "My bad fo' hittin' ya up so late but I couldn't get'chu outta my mind… I'm fo' real, no cap. I don't play no type of games. Not only do ya look like Jill Scott in da face, you gotta phat, round ass like her too… What I want is ta finally see ya tonite. We texted an' FaceTime'd a lot already. So, lemme slide through,

Qa'Deejha, an' scoop ya up... Ta Denny's first, then ta my lair... I'll pay ya sista ta babysit... You ain't gotta put on nuttin' fancy cuz I hope our chemistry through da phone leads ta us bein' naked in my Cali King.

A minute or so of freaky talk transpired before he ended the call with, "I gotta go now. I'll call ya when I'm a exit away. By da way, I got some new gas ta twist up. We gonna get faded tonite... Ai'ight, I'm gettin in traffic now, Big Sexy. See ya soon."

Just as he ended the call...

Blum-blum-blum-blum

The shots fired were resounding, and extremely close by.

A split second later, a male with a blood-stained white tee hobbled past ZooMan in high gear. A few seconds behind the wounded man, an armed male was in hot pursuit.

Better him than me, ZooMan thought while hopping into his black Jag and cranking it up. *It's just too bad I'm unable to offer him a new life... that would belong to me.* He revved the engine, causing the quadruple exhaust to roar like the powerful beast the car was named after. *But you hold on, mama, because I'll be able to fix everything in a couple of days,* he reassured himself before throwing the snarling wild cat into gear and blackening the pitted asphalt behind him. "And whoever was involved with incapacitating you will pay for what they did."

Chapter 4

January 26, 2020 - 5:43pm
Lake Worth Beach, FL
Thunderous snoring
Out of the blue...
Dogs barking
As a consequence...
"Femen bek ou," Sosa grumbled at both Dinky and Mondo from under the covers.

Even after giving his dogs a common command, the intense pounding on the front door incited them to resume barking.

Since he had just emerged from being lost in the land of Nod, the disorder had yet to fully register with him. He was beyond hungover from a night of raising hell. He'd hardly ever turned up for his birthday since he turned twenty-five, but he'd chugged so many different liquors last night that he should've perished in his sleep from alcohol poisoning. And he'd blown such an excessive amount of gas that he ought to have overcooked his lungs.

The awful physical fallout from rowdy drinking and smoking lifted a little as what sounded like G-men attempting to break down his door persisted and his fur buddies' continuous frenzied barking helped him overcome his grogginess.

"Shut up!" he repeated himself in English. "Lemme sleep."

45

Phone rings

He flung off the high thread count sheets. "Shit just got real!" His vision was out of focus due to heavy eyes and his coordination was out of sync when he rolled out of bed. Although he was getting up for the first time today, his ritual of waking-and-baking and spiffing himself up was ignored as he stormed out of the room. He left his phone chiming on the nightstand by his bed as he marched towards the door clutching his rod on rickety legs. He massaged his forehead in an attempt to alleviate the pummeling in his dome, which was aggravated by the pummeling at the door. *"Deplase,"* he ordered the excited dogs. "I said MOVE!" He roughly pushed the dogs aside with a leg. Still very much woozy, he opened the door without determining who it was.

A pair of look-alikes stood on his stoop. And behind them on his lawn was a mid-size ATV.

Impulsively, the manic canines barreled by him and leapt at the visitors. The animals' rush caused the guests to drop their helmets.

"What y'all doin' way 'round here by y'allselves, bangin' on this door like y'all gotta warrant or sumthin'?" he asked once he'd surveyed the scene.

With Mondo rollicking around his legs, J-Mill said, "Mama sent us over here… "

"… because you haven't answered her calls or called her back," Jerri closed out while straining to keep Dinky from knocking her over.

"Mama would've come herself… "

"… but she said she didn't want to kill a bitch if she found one here with you," Jerri finished.

Sosa let Jerri's expletive pass since he knew she only quoted what Cotton said. Instead, he tucked the hollow-point loaded Heckler & Koch nine-millimeter in the back of the snug Amiri jeans he'd slept in. "Y'all go on back home. An' tell y'all mama I'll be there in…" He lifted his left hand to check the time on his brand new flooded Datejust Rolex. His wrist was bare, however. He shook his head to clear it. "Umm... Tell Cotton I'll be there in an hour or two. Now, take off an' take Mondo an' Dinky wit y'all. Y'all drive slow an' stay on da sidewalk, too. An' don't stop fo' nobody till y'all get home, not even fo' da police. Ya hear me?"

"Yes, daddy," they said at once. The twins picked up their helmets and put them on. Since J-MiII drove their shared four-wheeler there, Jerri took over for the trip back. Once J-Mill climbed on and hugged his sister tightly, they pulled out of the yard with the dogs in tow.

Sosa shut the door. His phone could be heard ringing in the bedroom. In no hurry to be verbally skinned alive by the obvious caller, he first moseyed to the bathroom. With the effects from going all out last night still fucking with him, he took his precious time washing his mug. He couldn't thoroughly enjoy the stimulating cleansing, however, as long as his phone was ringing relentlessly.

Becoming more sober-headed by the second, he walked into the dungeon-like darkness of his room. He moved with precision to the nightstand where he normally put his phone. When the phone went silent, he groped for it but found it misplaced. Rather than cutting on the light or letting in some sunshine by opening blinds, he waited patiently for it to start ringing again; it didn't take long for that to happen. He set about blindly searching for the buzzing phone. It eventually turned up in his bed, tangled in the covers. He expected to see Cotton's name on the screen but was surprised when he noticed it was IronHead calling. He fingered the green telephone icon.

After a short exchange, he hung up. Next, he slipped on the same shirt and shoes he had on last night and headed out. In his 2019 Maserati Ghibli S Q4, he took a left followed by two rights. He rolled to the end of Ray Street and turned into his partner's driveway, ending the one-minute trip.

"Goddamn, ratchet-ass nigga, that's how ya rockin' now?" Pressure blurted out as soon as Sosa climbed out of the car. "We ain't jits sellin' dope on da corner no mo'. We got pull, an' ain't too many drippin' harder than us. Sportin' da same fit two days in a row is shameful an' tacky, just in case ya ain't know."

Clearly, Pressure was referring to the clothes Sosa had on last night.

"Bro, now ain't da time," Sosa said monotonously as he saluted the pack. "My head still spinnin' like a muthafucka, so miss me wit'cha bullshit. Clothes da last thing on my mind."

"It's been a long time since I seen yo' ass that lit, *baz*," Yak declared. "You took a whole bottle of D'usse ta da head by yo'self in a lil mo' than fifteen minutes, stingy nigga."

"An' you smoked 'bout five grams of Gelato," Edson inserted. "You wasn't on *one* last nite… you were on TEN!"

"I bet I was, an' I'm payin' fo' it now," admitted Sosa.

"So, I guess you straight on this then," Huff insinuated, gesturing toward the fired-up jay in his hand.

In desperate need of a pick-me-up to bounce all the way back, but not his preferred herbal medicine at this moment, Sosa respectfully shot down the offer. Saying no to something he'd become dependent on was difficult but necessary right now. He had urgent matters to address at once, according to IronHead's call.

Edson, Huff, Pressure, Yak, TP, Cano and IronHead were Sosa's partners since their schooldays. They all were born within a year of each other, and all of their parents had emigrated from Haiti, the poorest country in the western hemisphere. Although only Pressure and TP were not U.S. citizens, they all became Americanized through school. They had a blast while attending Barton Elementary. But it had been at Lake Worth Middle where they, along with other Haitian kids, had to band together against bullies.

While a few of them had known each other from living in the same area, the eight of them, specifically, became tight after a huge free-for-all in middle school between Haitian kids and their tormentors. They served a ten-day suspension for the brawl and formed a solid bond once they returned to school. Over time they emerged as a modernized Top 6, a bygone clan of young Haitian thugs from L-Dubb whose music in the early 2000s sparked a transformational movement throughout PBC for new age zoes. When they entered their high school years, only Sosa, IronHead and TP would move onward with their education, for they'd looked forward to hooking up with junior and senior thots since middle school. Huff, Cano, Yak, Edson and Pressure began trapping full time instead, strengthening their street reputation beyond the southside of L-Dubb. Before long they became equally dangerous in the trenches. They 'd cemented themselves as distinguished dope boyz, having built up their operation while stepping on all opps that tried to choke off their campaign. In due time, they regulated the best parts of the southside, but Ray Street had remained their center of operation.

"Where Head at?" Sosa asked.

Yak answered, "Lampin' at his BM Shirley crib by now. Y 'know that corny-ass nigga be tryna cock-block an' keep a eye on that hoe."

"What? I just talked ta that fool. He told me ta pull up pronto. He said there was smoke in da air."

"He headed toward Latona a couple minutes ago." Pressure said. "I'm surprised ya ain't pass by him on ya way ova here. He was on foot."

"Naw, I ain't see that mammoth-head nigga. He prolly took da cut ta her crib." He groaned because his headache was mounting in the evening's surprising heat. "Cano inside?"

"Y' know it," Edson warbled.

Before seeking cool shelter inside of Cano's mama house, which was the second-to-last residence opposite a church on the short street with no outlet, he looked up the block and said, "Who slider that is next ta da spot?" He pointed out the raspberry Dodge Stratus that was curbed by their trap. The peculiar car gave him a crazy vibe.

"That's Kentucky," Huff replied. "He down there wit TP. He came through wit da pack we needed ta keep da spots hummin' fo da week. They breakin' it down togetha."

Phone rings

Sosa knew there was no ifs, ands or buts about who was calling him this time. Even so, he simply tuned it out. "One of y'all remind me ta holla at Kentucky befo' I clear it. But first, let's fall off inside so y'all can fill me in on what's poppin'."

They crowded into the house that they'd hung out at regularly since they all became friends. Without missing a beat they were welcomed with a nonchalant *bonswa* from Ms. Woodlene, who was watching television in the living room while looking after Cano's rowdy younger siblings and her unruly grandkids. Collectively, they greeted her back. They then moved casually through the small house that became more cluttered and more cramped as the years passed. They soon filed into the tricked-out den. As Kodak Black boomed in the room, they snuck up on their homie as he played *NBA 2K19* against an opponent on-line.

"You can't stop da Greek Freak! I don't care who ya try ta guard him wit," Cano shouted into the headset. "Tuh... Ayton? HaHa! He can't fuck wit a baby picture of Geeannis Anti... Antitoe—"

"It's Giannis Antetokounmpo, dummy. That's *Yan-nis Ahn-tee-uhn-koom-po*," Sosa set Cano right on the pronunciation of the superstar Milwaukee Bucks player's name. "You illiterate ass nigga."

Startled slightly yet still fixated on the best LED television that money could buy, Cano said, "I know you ain't tryna set nobody straight, nigga, becuz... Get that shit outta here! I told ya, lil punk-ass white boy, da Greek Freak swattin' er'thang CP3 an' Booker put up... Anywayz, back ta you, Mr. Know-It-All, you shoulda known yo' lightweight ass couldn't hang wit da big... Middleton wit da trey ball! Hands down, man—"

The screen went black.

And the reason for the outage was Yak cutting off the PS4.

"Stupid nigga, that was a season game. That counts as a lost fo' me now," Cano shouted in the process of slamming the headset on the floor. "There was two minutes left in da fourth an' I was up by nine on that cracka. You fucked up my stats." He made a deep throaty sound out of frustration. "I was bustin' his ass fo Kobe too. R.I.P. G.O.A.T."

"What?! Kobe dead?" Sosa bellowed.

"You ain't heard Da Black Mamba, his daughter an' some othas died in a helicopter crash earlier today," replied Yak.

Boy, this turning out to be a fucked up day, Sosa thought as he shook his head, *and I have a feeling it's only going to get worse.*

"Fuck all that," Pressure began, "it's time ta let Sosa know what went down a while ago."

The wrinkles in Cano's forehead from frowning retreated. A smile swiftly took over his look of fury. With a roly-poly physique that was molded from years of eating unhealthy creole dishes, and a voice similar to the sound of a defective garbage disposal, he said proudly, "I called a play on them wannabe goons outta H.O.L."

"You did what?" said Sosa, shocked.

"See, you were so fucked up last nite that'chu don't rememba nuttin'," Huff retorted. "While up in VIP at GODDESSES, a group of them suckas tried ta flex on us. Da frequency in da club was turnt when they made their way ta our section. Then, fo' no reason, they started talkin' big shit 'bout us in front of da hoes that were hoverin' 'round."

"Shit really got real when that nigga Urnge told them hoes we were fakers an' that they were Big Steppaz wit big bags," Edson declared, getting mad all over again at the memory of the episode.

"So, y'all mean ta tell me that becuz them lames talked a lil' shit an' lied in front of some eaters y'all sentimental asses ran down on 'em witout holla'n at me first?"

"Eva since I toted ya into ya crib you been outta commission. We couldn't reach ya da last twelve, thirteen hours," Cano contended. "So, how could we let 'cha know what da play was?"

"Not ta mention, if ya hadn't slipped outta VIP wit some bitch befo' they showed up you woulda heard exactly how reckless they were bumpin' they gums," Pressure chipped in. "They tried ta lil' boy us in front of beaucoup people, not just some hoes. We gotta defend our character. An' if you were on point, you wouldn'ta went fo' that rah-rah eitha."

Yak then stepped to Sosa. He had his phone in hand. "But what really set da play in motion was when Peezy posted this story on da Gram." He handed Sosa the phone.

The approximately thirty second video showed a few of Da HOL Boyz somewhere, presumably in their hood, not long after they left GODDESSES. With the first light of day visible in the background, they were hooting and hollering so much for the first ten seconds of the clip that what they were saying was incomprehensible. Once they stopped shouting over each other, HOL Boy Peezy took the forefront. While his homies flaunted stacks of rubber banded hundos and brandished several rods and poles in back of him,

Peezy's opening claim was that Sosa and his squad were only shown respect in L-Dubb. Peezy made some other trivial claims before ending the video with the most egregious allegation: He and his inner circle were purposely dicking down their sisters, BMs and homegirls, supporting the claim by providing the names of several females.

"That's it?" Sosa asked. Truth be told, he was unaffected by the ludicrous video. He was sure of himself, and his bros, and no zeros could discredit them. "Once again, y'all got at 'em ova that? C'mon, they nonfactors. They just loudmouths. They ain't makin' no noise outside of lil' known H.O.L." He took a moment to think. "On some real nigga shit, I think you tender-dick niggaz got in y'all feelings cuz they claimed they fuckin' some bitches we know. If that's da case, that's pitiful cuz a hoe gon' be a hoe anyway. Y'all merked—" He broke off his sentence to ask, "How many of them niggaz y'all slumped by da way?"

When not one of his boys immediately spoke, he added, "Don't all y'all speak at one time."

Volunteering to speak up, Cano swallowed and grumbled lowly, "None."

Frowning, Sosa went on. "Where y'all hit 'em at?"

"We saw some niggaz posted at that lil' hut in front of their hood," Cano replied. "We rolled past 'em, bust a u-ey, then dumped on 'em on our way out their hood."

The lowdown left Sosa torn. He was unsure about how to feel regarding the news. Even though he didn't *p-l-a* with the *y* when he warred with the opposition, he was on the fence because he was good friends wit HOL Boyz Wes and 360.

He originally befriended Wes at Barton Elementary. They'd been cool from second grade until Wes moved to H.O.L. during their sixth grade year. They hardly ever crossed paths from then on. However, they'd ran back into each other their senior year at Lake Worth High after Wes got expelled from Santaluces High for fighting. It was then that Sosa met 360, Wes' homeboy that also got kicked out of Santaluces High for the same brawl. Sosa willingly took the two under his wing. They built a rapport through playing double-six dominoes and joking around during lunch period. After high school ended, Sosa occasionally bumped into either Wes or 360 around the county, and there remained nothing but mutual respect between them. The mutual respect eventually led to Sosa and Wes combining their bags and buying work from a plug Wes knew at the time.

Fortunately, Wes and 360 weren't participants in the video Sosa just saw.

Although they weren't in the video, the imminent hot war between the two sets created a dilemma for Sosa due to his high regard for both Wes and 360.

Now instead of leveling up, I must decide if I'm going to try to defuse this petty beef or gear up for their retaliation, Sosa said to himself as he walked out of Cano's rec room. *And I also must decide if I'm going to try to smooth things over with Cotton or surrender without a fight and risk being put out of my own house.*

Once upon a time, friction with the "other side" fired Sosa up. But ever since he got his weight up with his team, he wasn't as thrilled as he'd once been about beefing, especially over foolishness with niggas making slave wages. Conflict costs time and money, and the only thing he wanted to spend time and money on lately was living his best life.

And as long as his good name rang all over L-Dubb now and forever, Peezy's initial claim in the video, which was the only thing that got a reaction out of him, really didn't matter. Whether or not his name went beyond L-Dubb was irrelevant because making his name known in his hometown meant something to him.

As Sosa was passing through the raucous living room again, he asked Ms. Woodlene, *"Eske ou genyen aspirin oubyen Tylenol, manman, oubyen nenpòt sa ou genyen banmwen'l pou yon tét fè mal?"*

Ms. Woodlene, affectionately called Mama by   Cano's bros, said she didn't have aspirin or Tylenol or anything else for a headache.

Her response let him down. He was hopeful that she could give him something to lessen the headache that was doubling back in full force.

Phone rings

His aggravating phone was taking a toll on his mind, too. He held back from answering Cotton's call. He knew that stringing out the inevitable was simply making it worse for him. But he didn't give a damn right now.

"Aye, Sosa, wait up," Huff called out. "We gonna stroll wit 'cha ta da spot."

With his thoughts being in a scrambled state, Sosa wasn't surprised he'd forgot about going to the trap to chat with Kentucky. For real, he was ready to head to his main house, although he could guarantee he was going to end up with a migraine - or a brain aneurysm - once Cotton was done jumping on him, metaphorically and literally.

Dehydrated and dizzy, Sosa looked up the block. To his dismay, the Stratus was still parked. He would've preferred to drive the short distance instead of walking there and back. Yet he set out toward the trap in the steamy heat with his comrades close by. Despite feeling a bit woozy, he was on high alert because of the recent shootout his boys had with their rivals. He didn't think those H.O.L niggaz were loco enough to roll onto Ray Street because the street was a death trap. Nonetheless, he made sure his burner was ready to up and bust, just in case. And all of his dawgz toted firepower as well, with Pressure and Yak carrying so the world could see.

En route, Edson blurted out, "Did ya get that bitch info last nite?"

"What bitch?" Sosa replied, a bit confused and already sweating.

"Da kinda tall, older bitch ya was all boo'd up wit. I couldn't see her that good becuz of da lightin', but she looked like she coulda been Haitian."

Not in the slightest did Sosa know what bitch Edson was talking about. Trying to bring her to mind right now, however, wasn't worth hurting his head any further.

Sosa shrugged in response.

"You betta check ya phone, idiot," Pressure implied, "befo' ya go home an' Cotton go through it. Cuz if she finds it... No cap, I'm too lil' ta be luggin' ya casket, bro."

Sosa removed his phone from his pocket and began doing exactly what Pressure suggested.

As Sosa scrolled through his contacts, Huff said, "I ain't getta good look at da chick eitha, but what caught my eye fo' sho was da choker she had on wit a bust-down Jesus medallion. Da stones in that bitch was twerkin' harder than Megan Thee Stallion. I ain't cappin' when I say she slayed er'body chunk in da club, even ours. Fa real, fa real, I hope ya got her number so I can jack that bitch after you pipe her down."

Laughter erupted from one and all, including a slightly distracted Sosa.

Just as the laughter leveled off, Sosa made a face because he had just remembered something.

When Huff mentioned the Jesus piece, Sosa did recollect seeing the highly unusual piece of jewelry. But that was all he could conjure up. *Maybe I was on my shit and gave her my info instead*, he thought because he couldn't locate any unfamiliar names or numbers in his contacts. *Hopefully, she'll hit my line soon so I can see what this bitch hitting for while I'm sober.*

They finally made it to the trap.

Actually, "the trap" consisted of several traps.

The trap was nothing but a single level apartment complex. The property was square in shape, open on one side, with a half dozen fourth-rate efficiencies. The six apartments, which were duplexes, were ideal for the hustle due to their layout. Each unit was designed the same way, but it was how the bathroom was setup in those six that made it perfect for a go-getter. All the apartments were next to another apartment. As a result of them being back-to-back, every two units had a medicine cabinet in the bathroom that aligned with the cabinet in the adjacent unit. Removing both cabinets revealed an opening that allowed cash, guns, etc., to be passed between the apartments. That hole let trappers in the adjacent units to hustle jointly. One apartment would seem to be rented by an innocuous tenant, but it was, in fact, a stash and re-up site for the other apartment that dealt with all the walk-up traffic. The secretive operation kept the Jump Out Boyz from finding anything of significance to charge anybody with in the active apartment. And it also kept the Jack Boyz from coming up big if they were stupid enough to try their hand. So, overall, the trashy yet invaluable trap was the thing dope boyz dreamed of.

Years ago, the drop-outs Yak, Pressure, Cano, Edson and Huff had locked up one of the apartments. It took just about a year before they accidentally came upon the opportune hole behind the medicine cabinet. Subsequent to the discovery, they'd conspired to buy as many two-sided apartments as they could, as soon as they became available. As luck would have it, the property owner, a Nigerian slumlord, noticed their hustle and offered to sell the unprofitable complex to them for a measly fifty grand. They'd been twenty grand short, so they hustled, scammed and robbed in order to cop the complex. In less than three days they'd sealed the deal. They bought out all but two tenants in the suite of duplexes. Once they'd occupied four of the apartments, with the paperwork in various fiends' names for legal reasons, they put a little money into fixing the place up - just a little - and ran a felonious yet lucrative business out of the same structure.

Apartments One, Two, Five and Six were their moneymakers and vaults. They never operated the two duplexes at one time. They switched from one duplex to the other at irregular intervals, sometimes pulling a switcheroo every other day. But as a rule, they never used a duplex longer than three days.

Today, Apartments Five and Six were in play.

They approached Five. Pressure rapped on the door in a special cadence, then they waited. They heard the heavy-duty locks coming undone.

The reinforced door opened slightly .

"Aye Cano," Sosa began, "go see if Candie an' da old Haitian Fignole got that hundred-fifty weekly rent they owe. An' if they need anythang fixed, call Tukan. Then go empty da quarters outta da washers an' dryers in da laundry room."

"Why I gotta do that shit?" Cano complained. "Why ya ain't ask one of dem ta do that shit?"

"Cuz I asked you," Sosa shot back. "We ain't gonna be in here long anywayz. I'm just tryna see if Kentucky bought some of that backwater drank an' good clean work. I ain't tryna go ta jail fo' a junkie OD'ing on some fentanyl-laced shit becuz of that swamp donkey tryna make our shit mo' potent. Now go."

Cano sucked his teeth. Reluctantly, he went to put a handle on what Sosa said. Just before he got out of range, though, he said, "That's why da bitch ya were holla'n at last nite looked like a man."

Sosa heard Cano's cheap shot, but he shrugged it off. He pushed open the door instead. With one foot in the entrance, he suddenly heard…

"Yo', nephew, I been lookin' fo' you all day. I cut da grass 'round da building earlier an' I ain't get paid. You got'cha pa, rite? Do me rite now, nephew."

Damn, I should've ignored my phone and stayed in bed, Sosa said himself. "I got'cha, unc. I'll be out in a sec wit some ice fo' ya."

Gotcha Pa didn't want no meth. He only dabbled with that junk on occasion, and, needless to say, this wasn't that time. He would've liked nothing better than being given his fave, that good ole straight drop, for his unwanted labor. He would've politely asked for a nickel rock over a ten-dollar bag of meth right off, but decided to say nothing about it and take whatever his dirt poor ass could get his cruddy fingers on.

Before Sosa faded into the apartment, Gotcha Pa added, "I can use a few bucks fo' some gas, too, nephew. You got'cha pa, rite?"

You're going to get a handful of quarters, you slick beggin'muthafucka, Sosa ruminated.

BAM! An idea struck.

"Unc, I'll look out fo' ya if ya run... not walk… cross da tracks to Hallelujah's an' get me sumthin' fo' a headache." He went in his pocket and, luckily, found some cash. He handed Gotcha Pa a Jackson. "You got five minutes ta bring back my shit. You can get 'cha gas later. An' you can keep—"

Gotcha Pa took off for the store a few blocks away before Sosa could finish the sentence.

Phone rings

Shaking his head faintly, frustration masked Sosa's face. He entered the trap without thinking twice about answering the phone. *Fuck that. I 'm going back to my spot and crashing once I leave here*, he determined, *whatever happens happens while I'm on the bench recuperating.*

Chapter 5

January 26, 2020 - 9:07pm
Boynton Beach, FL

"It" was complicated.

And with his personality, there wasn't a chance in hell to clean it up or to make amends. If anything, he'd screw up the apology and make it more complicated than it already was, given his latest no-show.

But, of all people, she knew whenever duty called, he answered, which was the primary reason they were divorced now.

The inscrutable Harden had acquired his crabby, lone wolf character from growing up in the unrefined area of B-Town, identified as Cherry Hill. His sister, on the other hand, had attained a jolly demeanor. Though he'd been recognized in his hometown for being an outstanding football player for the popular Pop Warner Boynton Beach Bulldogs, he was notably disliked around his hood. In a short time, he'd perceived his high yellow skin, gender neutral name, and overprotective upbringing were the reasons behind the bullying and fistfights he endured all through elementary and middle school.

After talking his childish mother into switching him from Santaluces High to John I. Leonard High so he could enroll into the school's Reserve Officers Training Corps Program (ROTC), his school days became stimulating and refreshing.

Still, the psychological damage from his formative years being largely devoid of direction and peer friendship had been irreversible. The results were that he gradually withdrew from society and developed a repellant attitude.

Leaving out the fraternal connection he'd shared with his fellow ROTC members, if it hadn't been for a singular classmate's amiable persistency, he wouldn't have lightened up. That classmate, Adele, ended up becoming his high school sweetheart. After graduation his mother gave him the money his father left for him and he proceeded to work towards his dream of serving and protecting the unassuming and lawful citizens in his community, while Adele continued her education with the intention of working in the medical field.

But Adele's unplanned pregnancy not only cut her dreams short, it also compelled him to take on the *Traditional Family Man* role. Once they'd moved in together, he became the linchpin of the family, the sole provider of the household, and Adele became a stay-at-home mother. One kid turned into three in less than five years, which ultimately changed the family dynamics from something extraordinary into a daily fog of banality.

Adele knew in advance that the sob stories Harden told her about his tumultuous boyhood, in addition to his father never being present in his life, would strain their relationship one day. Nevertheless, she held out hope. But when Harden struggled balancing his professional life with his personal life, she'd blamed him wholly for their romance disintegrating. And it had been Harden's unwillingness to strike a balance that was the final straw, giving her the grounds for a trial separation.

Unfortunately, the trial wasn't successful. The divorce was contentious and the relationship with his children, two daughters and a son, fell apart. Through it all, it was his commitment to the *Rising Sun* case that became his motivation to rise every morning and soldier on.

Standing on the porch of the home in which he had once resided, he rang the doorbell. As he waited for someone to answer, he reflected on the final five years of his life in the home. Five years of unhappiness and becoming a stranger to his family. He tinkered with the rosary beads in his pocket as the door opened inwards.

The back of his oldest daughter was all he got a glimpse of. She trudged away from him without a word spoken. The unwelcoming reception was normal to him.

Unbothered by the rude treatment, he walked into the cozy home. He headed towards the sounds and smells that were foreign in his one-bedroom apartment. By the time Adele came into his view, she was moving about in the kitchen by herself.

As soon as Adele spotted Harden, she stopped prepping dinner in order to berate him, which was a frequent occurrence. "From doctor's appointments during my last two pregnancies to a dozen birthdays, to their sport's practices and games, to their recitals and other meaningful ceremonies, like the christening of your only son for Christ's sake! What's important to us has never been important to you. You've missed out on so many momentous milestones in our lives, Carol. Me, personally, I quit caring a long time ago whether you came to my special events, and I'm positive that the same goes for Madyson and Charlotte. But your son…" Adele, an overly passionate person, abruptly became emotional. "Instead of celebrating Ethan's once-in-a-lifetime achievement, you were elsewhere doing things *you* considered more important, I'm sure of it. I'm also sure that you've lost the last of us that cared about you. Let's see God help get you out of this one, Carol." She wiped the tears from her face and went back to getting dinner ready.

If there was one thing Harden hated these days about Adele, and everybody else, for that matter, was when she ridiculed him about his newborn faith. Although he 'd been to church quite a bit as a boy with his maternal grandmother, being in utter despair as a juvenile made him lose faith in everybody, even God himself. But after his sister vanished, he'd decided to delve into the Bible because, at that point in his life, he'd given up on life itself.

Though the Bible brought him out of the darkness, his relationship with God was... informal. Ideally, he didn't need to attend mass just to hear some guy barely teach him anything before passing the collection plate around. In his mind, all he needed was the intellect to pick apart the Bible and discern what was feasible and applicable to his life since being reborn.

Nobody could tell him his faith was assumed or questionable.

"Where's Ethan now?"

Going on with prepping dinner, she scoffed. "Because he was let down by you, William took him out to do a variety of fun things for the day to cheer him up. They called fifteen minutes ago and said they'll be back in a few." She stopped and faced him. "I'm not sure how he's going to react when he sees you.

"He was beyond hurt, Carol, before Willian treated him to a day of recreation. You really crushed him this time because you swore you'd celebrate his Defensive Player of The Year nomination at his favorite restaurant. Your heartbroken son and I ended up eating alone... in eerie silence. I believe there's nothing you can do to patch things up. I hope prioritizing your job was worth all of this." She returned to cooking, then uttered, "It's a good thing the kids have William as a role model. I don 't want them turning out to be like you... although I think it's too late for Maddy. She has your tendencies already."

Adele's last statement took Harden down more than a few notches. Her words steamrolled him, to be precise, for he knew it was true he'd neglected his family over his obsession to find one bad guy.

Speaking of "bad" guys, Harden couldn't catch on to what Adele found so appealing about her big-headed fiancé. He thought it was bad enough William had his late father's name. And if her new love was anything like his philandering father, then Adele was in for trouble and more heartache in the future.

But at least Willian handled their kids better than he ever had, so he had no rational reason to come down on the guy. True indeed, William was a good role model, particularly for his son.

"For everything I've put you and the kids through, I'm truly sorry, Adele," Harden said with genuine warmth. "Ever since Mackenzie vanished, I've been spoken for. I became dedicated to my work because nobody was taking the disappearances seriously." He sighed.

"After the fifth person disappeared without a trace in a short period, futility and despair set in amongst the investigators with the realization that the county was dealing with a probable serial abductor. The case was named *Rising Sun* because an actual rising sun is an enduring image of hope and encouragement meant to lift the spirit and to overcome obstacles. Plus, it represents that each new day will bring the break in the case.

"I've been working tirelessly, which you've clearly observed, every second of the day. My diligence has turned up things that has gotten us closer to revealing the true identity of the predator that has caused so much pain and despair. At last, I caught the biggest break yesterday, which was why I couldn't make it to dinner.

"I can't disclose too much but Bojanski discovered something by using a cutting-edge technology. I then spent the rest of the evening trying to talk the chief and other brass hats into letting me assemble several teams so we could descend on the likely suspects. Unfortunately, there was too much red tape to cut. So, I may have a list of possible suspects, but with one-point-five million people living in Palm Beach County, I must narrow down that list significantly before moving forward. The hunt is closing in on the bastard, though, and the monster will soon feel the full weight of the justice system and never see a speck of daylight again. And I'll finally able to put all this behind me."

Adele stared at Harden. What she'd just heard was great news. She was glad it was about to be over, for his wellbeing had deteriorated. He'd aged prematurely from loneliness and exhaustion over the years. "Your line of work has made you a woeful specimen, Carol, turning you into someone I wanted to leave behind... if it weren't for the kids. You became worse than you were before I met you and helped you mellow out. You changed back into a deplorable being." She took a break so he could reflect on her words.

"I didn't lose a sibling, Carol, so I can't truly understand how you feel. I understood, however, why you buried yourself in the case. I would've done the same if I were in your shoes. *But* still, I can't understand why you put us second to your work. You gave us up."

"That's where you're wrong, Adele. I never gave y'all up. Not in here, at least." He pointed to his head. "Or here." He then placed his hand on his heart.

She fought back tears. "Hopefully, when you catch the demon, you can move forward with your life and find happiness once more."

Harden opened his mouth to respond but...

"It smells good in here. Is that chicken cacciatore, my favorite?" William said as he barged into the kitchen. When he spotted Harden off to the side, he resumed, "Hey, Carol, what a pleasant surprise. Are you staying for dinner? Trying to make it up to Ethan, huh?"

Ethan then entered the kitchen. "Hey, mom, you wouldn't believe the amazing—" He noticed his father, changing his mood from jubilant to enraged in a snap.

Without delay, he did an one-eighty and plodded away.

"I guess that's my cue to get on out of here," Harden muttered with a sigh. "Enjoy dinner. I'll call soon. And for what it's worth, tell Ethan I'm sorry."

"Goodnight, Carol," said Adele as he headed out.

"Yeah, have a good night, bud," William inserted pretentiously. "And watch out for that kung-flu. That chink plague is in the states now, and it's going to be a doozie. Anyhow... drive safely."

Chapter 6

January 27, 2020 - 9:02pm
Palm Beach Gardens, FL

Severe acute respiratory syndrome coronavirus 2.

SARS-CoV-2, the abbreviation for the aforementioned, was highly contagious, and presently untreatable.

And it had made its way into American airspace.

Coronavirus 2019, or COVID-19, was originally detected in Wuhan, China, in December 2019. When the world's spotlight landed on the communist nation after witnessing the deadliness of the virus, Chinese health authorities attempted to whitewash the outbreak in their country. However, the doltish President of the United States and the far-right media convinced many shallow Americans that the disease was concocted in a Wuhan lab and purposely released into society. To date, the contagion had killed nearly 250 Chinese out of eleven thousand confirmed cases and spread to about one hundred people outside of China. The Chinese health authorities subsequently reported that the virus jumped from bats being sold at a wet market to the human population, turning aside the accusation that they created and leaked the virus by design.

The disease gained sweeping media coverage in the U.S. once the first case was confirmed last week in Washington state. A traveler that returned from China tested positive for the illness. Thereupon, epidemiologists from around the world, in coordination with the World Health Organization

(WHO), predicted a pandemic in the coming weeks if extreme measures weren't taken globally.

But little did Palm Beach County criminologists know that there was a worldwide apocalypse on the horizon. And once Baron Samedi possessed a new body and began to wreak havoc on earth with his chosen few, COVID-19 would become a thing of the past.

At the moment, ZooMan was at his Sabal Ridge condo trying to forget his unsuccessful seizure of the sixty-third victim yesterday. But forgetting was proving to be quite difficult. He couldn't forget about the setback because he sensed - and had sensed for a while now - that there was an opposing force making the final stretch problematic for him.

Now with COVID-19 in effect, facing another obstacle was inevitable, so he needed to wrap up his mission soon.

When ZooMan finished meeting with the *bokor* Francois last night, he promptly raced to hook up with Qa'Deejha. Though it was going to be their first face-to-face meeting, he knew just from the short time he'd been getting to know her that she had the life force he normally sought out. Her demeanor was sweet and decent whenever he texted or video chatted with her. However, during those FaceTime sessions, he witnessed the three-hundred-plus pound hood rat physically and verbally abusing her little ones when they crept up on her in the background. Those handful of abusive instances showed him her true colors. In his eyes, there wasn't a lower form of a human being than someone that brutalized the innocent, especially children and the elderly. And because of the relentless memory of his own old girl being victimized, he risked getting a speeding ticket in order to prey upon the unfit mother.

ZooMan's chance to haul Qa'Deejha away to the trap house was thwarted, though, by an unexpected development.

Just as he pulled up to Qa'Deejha's apartment building in Saddlebrook, he spotted her in the parking lot spazzing out on some white lady in plain clothes. Seconds after parking, he saw two police cruisers arrive at the scene. From the safety of his Jaguar, he watched a flustered Qa'Deejha continue to tear into the lady, who he eventually realized was an employee of the Department of Children and Family Services, while the police retrieved Qa'Deejha's three unkempt kids out of a second-floor apartment. Once he realized that the situation was ugly and his opportunity was ruined, he took his *L* and rode off into the twilight.

That was nothing but divine intervention, he thought, *but it's going to take a lot more than that to stop me.*

Incessantly thinking back to last night's bad break wasn't conducive with his game plan's execution, so ZooMan quit wasting his time reliving the past and got back to business. He got up off the cushiony long couch that hadn't accommodated anyone but himself since he bought the place three years ago. He went into the pristine kitchen and grabbed his phone that was charging near the unused blender. As he made his way back to the couch, he scrolled through his contacts. He quickly realized his contacts were depleted. *Instead of thinking I had this in the bag after I pulled Qa'Deejha, I should've anticipated future problems and kept reeling in potential victims,* he deduced before plopping down on the lounge and looking at a particular name in his contacts that should've been erased officially yesterday.

It was a longshot, but ZooMan called that person anyway. "Hello?"

ZooMan's ears weren't deceiving him when he heard sadness in their voice. Under normal circumstances he would've hung up. But he was dead set on acquiring a soul. By no means was he going to let emotions get the best of him now when he was so close to healing his mother and lavishing her with luxuries, such as the three-hundred-fifty-thousand dollar, twelve-hundred square foot condo.

"Wassup, Big Sexy? What'chu got goin' on?" he said upbeat, hoping his disposition would raise her spirits.

"Hmph. What else am I 'posed ta have goin' on? My babies... They took my babies. All becuz of a nosey, lyin'-ass neighbor all up in mine." Qa'Deejha snapped. "You saw most of what took place, so don't act like you dunno what's goin' on. I saw da car ya told me you were gonna be in pull up then leave from da front of my buildin'. So, ta answer ya dumb question, what I got goin' on... an' been up to all day ...is tryna get back custody of my babies."

"You ain't been ta sleep yet, huh?"

"What'chu think?"

"I'm sorry... Damn, I'm sorry ya have ta go through this bullshit. You're a wonderful mom," he lied before shooting his shot. "But is there anythang I can do ta help ya get 'cha mind off da situation fo' a while? I'll come through, pick ya up an' take ya anywhere ya wanna go."

Dead air.

"Qa'Deejha? You still there?"

"Not tonite. Maybe... Tomorrow. We'll see, okay? Just not tonite."

"I got 'cha. Well... I guess I'll let 'cha go now. Again, I'm sorry. I hope ya get 'cha lil' ones back soon." He sighed, not because he felt bad for her but because his shot was an air ball. "An' in case ya need anythang... I mean anythang... don't hesitate ta hit me up."

"Bye, Bilal," Qa'Deejha said curtly, ending the call with urgency.

Qa'Deejha's attitude didn't surprise ZooMan at all; he didn't expect a favorable outcome anyway. He simply called because the only thing that beat a failure was a try. And now that he took his shot and missed by a mile, it was on to the next one. Determination was his greatest trait.

Then an idea struck him.

ZooMan's sudden thought was to hop into his overlooked Ford Focus and cruise around a few hoods for a straggler. He was willing to act on his madcap thought but quickly passed on it. Because in retrospect, the plan of action that briefly crossed his mind wasn't worth him jeopardizing his almost finished mission, although he was in a desperate mode.

The complete reason behind ZooMan shooting the thought down was he'd run that tactic into the ground in the course of two months. He'd drove off with so many of his earliest victims, who were prostitutes or vagrants, that police departments countywide soon recognized a pattern and persistently appealed to the general public to not hitchhike or get in cars with strangers. And because police also recognized he only hunted at night like an owl, they swarmed the streets he was likely to prowl. Their determination to catch him in the act, as well as the continuous news coverage, caused him to stop kidnapping in that manner.

Although he'd had a great run with his very first scheme, it became tricky trying to cover his tracks after every kidnapping. Not only did he have to get rid of stolen vehicles without leaving behind DNA or prints, he had to learn, abduction by abduction, to be super-observant of wandering eyewitnesses and surveillance cameras on buildings, amongst other things. Overall, the things he learned during that stretch progressively gave him the backbone and awareness needed for the days that came and went.

He ultimately hatched multiple productive ways to entrap victims over the years, while also fine-tuning the supernatural ability that Francois offered to teach him. Many of his schemes lasted a short time, but they all were worth the time and effort spent. He had to take a break between schemes sometimes, though, because he either got too daring, which put the police awfully close to his trail, or he had a very close call that required him being bailed out and taking a long break. It was only after he mastered the skills that Francois taught him that he was able to carry out his most used scheme, which he frequently used to lure victims to the trap house.

Granted, it had been years since he drove around searching for a victim. So, he was certain he wouldn't be taking too much of a risk if he foraged for prey this one night. The only thing he'd have to be wary of was the location possibly being shared on the victim's phone. And that possibility just wasn't worth him falling just short of the finish line.

He highlighted the newest name in his contacts. He came across the person through his reliable, in-your-face tactic after he left Qa'Deejha's place. He was unable to run off with the jovial individual at that time. However, before daybreak endangered his life, he got the person's number and made it back to his vacant property with a few minutes to spare.

Even though it was a long shot trying to sweet-talk the person into linking up with him tonight, he still was going to shoot his jumper... with a lot of touch this time, though. And if he bricked, he'd just get to work establishing good vibes with the person in case he needed them in the future.

ZooMan pressed the call button. He cleared his throat, prepping his voice for the impersonation. When the person answered on the sixth ring, he said melodiously, "Heeyyy... Oh, my voice don't sound familiar? It wasn't that long ago we were all cozy and talkin' in each otha ear. You rememba that part, don't 'cha?... Well, you were pretty lit that nite, so it's understandable why you forgot about me." He then gave the person the same bogus name that he'd given them that night they met. Once the person said that they barely remembered him, he continued, "It's okay. Now my mission is to make sure you never forget ANYTHING about me again. And da sooner I can do that, da better for da both of us... Yep, that's on God. And you can most definitely find out tonite, if you wit it... That's what I'm sayin'. You can get to know me even better in person. I swear I'm harmless... Okay. I get it. Maybe some otha time when you not on go." He switched course. "Anywayz, let's pick up where we left off and see if we still click while you coherent. You good wit that?... Alright. So what'chu been up to, new boo?"

They carried on a decent conversation for a short while.

Once the person claimed they must go, ZooMan said, "Okay. I hope you call me soon becuz things might not be da same in da future... What I'm sayin' is, don't miss out on a good thing. So, are ya sure you don't wanna kick this friendship off rite tonite?... Well, have a good nite... Bye."

At wit's end, he negligently tossed the phone onto the elegant chalcedony coffee table in front of him. *Luck has been nowhere on my side this evening,* he concluded as he settled into the lounge, possibly for the rest of the night, *God be damned if He thinks His plan will deter me from my goal.*

The thought of the Almighty intervening in his affairs fired him up. Consequently, he rose up and went to the bedroom to change his appearance. As soon as he transformed, he grabbed his phone and headed out the condo in a hurry.

He was going to defy his better judgment just to put the being worshipped as the creator and ruler of the universe to shame. "Soon, mankind will bow down to me and the chosen hellhounds like me and you'll become a distant memory," he blasphemed God as he walked toward a disposable car he kept handy. "Tonight I'll show you I'm unstoppable and I don't need luck."

Chapter 7

January 27, 2020 - 10:53pm
Lake Worth Beach, FL
Doomed. Done for.

Zero hour had arrived.

And he could no longer avoid it... unless he cut and ran until karma finally caught up with him.

He'd bobbed and weaved around the situation long enough. By no means had he gone MIA out of fear because he feared nothing. He'd simply been snowed under with multiple issues the past few days. But now he just wanted to face the wrath then smooth things over like he'd always done before.

However, he knew that kissing and making up without suffering major consequences was wishful thinking.

About a dozen blocks away from the duck-off on Truman Street, Sosa pulled into the driveway of his main residence on 14th Court South. He parked his Maserati behind Cotton's undriven Lexus. He didn't kill the engine, and he also didn't budge. He just stared at his paid off home as Kevin Gates's *Big Gangsta* played at a low volume.

Sosa felt composed and ready for the expected tempestuous encounter with his *inamorata* after working things out between his crew and Da HOL Boyz during a private meeting with Wes an hour ago. But from past experience, he knew that no amount of preparation could brace him for the violent category five hurricane awaiting him inside his humble home. If the timeline of his whereabouts over the last two days wasn't accepted, he was very much a goner.

And in case his defense did not get him at least halfway out of the shit he was in, he had an ace up his Off-White cuff.

Before facing the music, he sparked up the half blunt that he had put out a few minutes prior to his homecoming. He might've been on a mellow cloud before now, but he wanted to get good and geeked when he confronted the storm, although his high was going to be blown almost immediately. Five pulls later, he cut off his whip, opened the door and flicked the roach into the freshly mowed grass. He then grabbed the fancy box from the passenger seat and climbed out of the car. He took a moment to draw a deep breath and exhale before walking towards his house.

"Hey, you."

Sosa instinctively upped his nine-millimeter, pivoted and pointed at the strange voice behind him in a single motion.

"Wait a sec, buddy! I'm... I 'm no threat!" the shaggy male cried out while holding his hands straight out in front of him.

"Who da fuck is you? An' what 'chu doin' at this house?" Sosa demanded, inching towards the unknown guy while holding the bulky box under one arm and the rod stretched out like an extension of his other arm.

"Look man, I'ma nobody. I'm... I'm not even from around these parts. I'ma drifter and... and I heard from some guys at that bar on Dixie down there that I could score some dope at a place called C Terrace. That's all. So, can ya help me out or point me in the right direction?"

"Get da fuck on, pussy-ass cracka," Sosa barked, playing past all that the middle-aged white man had said. "Or I'ma put a hot one in ya. Now, haul ass befo' you get done in rite here."

The man scooted off immediately.

Sosa kept an eye on the guy until he was flagged down by the roguish niggas hanging on the block several houses away. After that, he looked up and down the street suspiciously for a minute. Once he saw that things didn't look out of the ordinary, he returned his fire to his waist and strolled up to his house with his head on a swivel. He pulled his keys out of his pocket and unlocked the door.

"Help! Somebody help me!"

Like Sosa had expected the man he'd just ran off was getting ganged up on and robbed.

"Just take the money! Please! Don't stab me no more!"

Another presumption realized here in da 'hood, Sosa said to himself as he nonchalantly walked into his dark house and secured the door behind him.

"Yo' dawg ass was twelve hours away from findin' out that 'cha key no longer worked here," Cotton's voice emerged out of the darkness. She then switched on the lights. She was standing two or three yards from Sosa. Instead of having on one of his extra-large tee shirts that she normally slept in, she had on a casual top with jeans and sneakers. Her magenta-dyed hair was in a tacky ponytail. Her long nails were gone, and she was makeup-less. She was geared up for battle. "So, what fuckin' lame ass excuse you got this time for not answerin' my calls, callin' me back or comin' home da last two days, huh?"

Whether he told her the God's honest truth or invented a believable story, the way she had sized him up, whatever he said wasn't going to go over well with her. Nevertheless, he wasn't going to pussyfoot. He was just going to hope for the best outcome.

Before Sosa began, Cotton shifted from a battle-ready stance to a posture that Sosa knew very well. She had cocked her head to the left, furrowed her brow, contracted her lips, affixed her hands to her hips and tapped her foot steadily.

With Cotton focused and ready to find any cracks in his story, Sosa got straight to it. He recapped as much as he could remember about his birthday turn-up in the strip club. When she seemed unfazed by his account, he proceeded to run down all the chaos that transpired. He fully disclosed details from the time he woke up with an intense hangover to the powwow with Wes not very long ago.

"Lemme see ya phone an' da key ta ya car," Cotton insisted sternly as soon as he was done. She held out her hand.

Sosa suspected she'd want to go through his phone. But her shaking down his car caught him off-guard, since it was something she hardly ever did. He felt like she was acting more like a fed agent than a girlfriend at this moment. He readily coughed up both, though, because he had nothing to hide... this time.

After she left the house to invade his privacy, he put the box down on the couch and went to look upon his sleeping kids. Roughly five minutes passed before he heard Cotton reenter the house. He circled back to the living room. He laughed minimally when he saw the look of disappointment on her face. "Did ya find any receipts?" he taunted.

"Fuck you, nigga!" She threw his phone at him, then his key fob. "Yo' slick ass prolly erased all da incriminatin' evidence outta ya phone an' got rid of da hoe kit you had in ya trunk." She took off for the bedroom.

He went after her and grasped her from behind. In her ear, he said in his most convincing voice, "Baby, I just explained er'thang I did in da past couple days. I wasn't fuckin' around. I was handlin' bizness. I swear. I know you called my mom dukes an' she told you I was there."

She wriggled out of his warm embrace. She spun around until she was looking up at him, then fired back, "Just like you swore time an' time again you ain't do shit wit da hoez whose pictures an' messages I found in ya DMs in da past eitha. But I know ya fucked 'em. You're such a damn liar. Period. So, becuz you lied ta me once, all da truths you tell become highly questionable. Lyin' has become a force of habit ta you. It's like breathin' fo' ya."

"I keep tellin' ya that all those hoez slid in my DM an' sent me those thirst traps. I ain't fuck nan' one of them eaters." He thought for a few seconds. "Yes, I was at fault fo' entertainin' a few of 'em wit convo. But that's all I did was talk. I apologized fo' all that, tho'."

"Ha! Ya apologies meant nuttin'. Y'know why? Becuz an apology means you change ya behavior an' grow da fuck up. You neva fully changed. Altho' you seemed ta be well-behaved da past year, I still suspect that'chu are fuckin' behind my back. I let'cha turn up... all da way up... fo' one nite an' you try me by givin' yaself a *two-day* hall pass!" She laughed at his audacity.

"So, I... I'm done wit'chu this time. I've given you a million chances. You make me go against er'thang I said I wouldn't put up wit no mo' all da time. No mo' tho'. I'm so done. Period!"

"You trippin', cuz I aint do nuttin', bae!" He attempted to pull her to him again.

She blocked his advance. "Well... you shoulda becuz I'm done, nigga."

"You don't mean that."

"Yes da fuck I do, nigga. I'm goin' ta my people house in da mornin'. An' I'm takin' da kids an' Mondo wit me."

"Okay," he said passive aggressively. He was waving the white flag because defending his innocence was pointless right now.

"I ain't bullshittin', Julius." She reddened from anger. "I'm dead ass—"

"I said okay." He then proceeded with his plan B. He picked up the box and presented it to her. "Well, at least open this."

She sucked her teeth. "Nigga, I ain't fallin' fo' that bullshit no mo'."

"Just open it."

"No, I said."

He shrugged. "Fine. I'll open it." He began to pull the bowstring, undoing it.

Wrought-up, she watched him.

Before he removed the top and revealed the contents in the box, though, she snatched it out of his hand. "I hate you so much," she declared. "Now lemme see what da fuck ya got me ta try ta save ya ass. An' it betta not be keys ta anotha car I can't drive." She removed the top. She cleared away the gift wrap. What she saw inside caused her to gasp and her eyes to widen. "Don't play wit me, nigga. Is this shit real or nah?"

"One thing y'know 'bout me is I don't do fake shit."

With an overlarge smile on her blushing face, she lifted the gift out of the tissue paper as if it would disintegrate. She dropped the box and held the bag gingerly up in the air while examining it. Then, like a flip of a switch, her expression changed. She looked at him with a slightly crazy pout. "How'd you know ta get this exact one?"

"I saw ya lookin' at that specific one on ya phone a lot lately." He grinned like he'd hit a walk-off grand slam. "Besides, all women want at least one Birkin bag in their lifetime."

"Yeah, but most of 'em *eitha* getta phony one, a used one, or a cheap one. So, since you said this ain't fake, an' I definitely know this model costs thirty-three thousand dollas, this gotta be used, rite? Or maybe even stolen."

"Lil' white girl, you gon' stop tryna play me. That's straight from... That was made in... Hell, I dunno—"

"Paris, nigga. It's handmade in Paris, France."

"Regardless of where it's been made, that's brand spankin' new. *AND* if ya look in da bottom of that box you'll find sumthin' else."

Cotton delicately placed her bubblegum pink Hermes on the picture-laden bookcase nearby. She picked up the box from the floor and pulled out the remaining tissue paper. There was indeed something at the bottom, and she wasn't sure exactly what it was. "What's this?" she finally asked, taking the document out of the box

"That there says we're owners of a new home in Royal Palm Beach."

Cotton's long face clearly displayed her aversion.

Her reaction didn't surprise him one bit. He knew beforehand she wouldn't take to the plan of them moving. They would've relocated years ago if it weren't for her being so far gone on the hood life. He couldn't deny his love for his stomping grounds, either. But he felt it was way past due for them to resettle in a better community, with the intent of reversing their kids' hood mentality before it was too late. And because he had their kids' best interest at heart, he wasn't taking no for an answer tonight.

By now, the Birkin left her more than just a little vulnerable. This was the perfect time for him to play upon her openness. His dick game always bushwhacked her, no joke. However, tonight, he was going to pressure her into moving by applying extreme pressure to her pussy.

Sosa eagerly made his move by sweeping her off her tiny feet. He cradled her in his arms like they were newlyweds.

"Unh unh, nigga. I'm still ma—"

He cut her off by inserting his tongue in her mouth. He toted her to their dark bedroom and gently placed her on the pillow-top king-sized bed.

"Where are ya goin'?" Cotton immediately asked when he didn't get in bed.

"You don't want da brats all up in ours, do ya? So, I'm lockin' da door an' cuttin' on da lights."

"Noooo. Leave da lights off. I look a hot mess."

He locked the door and cut on the lights anyway. Next, he strolled through Spotify on his phone and said, "I'ma show ya what a hot mess really look like once I'm done wit'cha." He winked. He found a fitting song and, through Bluetooth, played it on the radio.

He got things going with *Exchange* off of Bryson Tiller's *TRAPSOUL* album.

He stepped to the edge of the elevated bed and pulled Cotton toward him until he stood between her legs. He began to unbutton his Off-White long sleeved shirt. He only got the top two buttons undone before she sat up and assisted him. She peeled the shirt off him. She proceeded to plant tender kisses all over his pecs while unfastening his belt. She wasn't fooling around, when her little hands latched onto his manhood she began stroking vigorously. He sucked on both sides of her neck like an empty leech while she primed him. He ripped off her thin shirt, removed her bra, then palmed and kneaded her firm B-cups.

He eventually laid her back and began to graze his tongue from her neck down to her chest. She snatched off his turban-like headdress and played in his dreads by the time he reached her abdomen. The aromatic essence emanating from her crotch set him off, causing him to pull down her jeans and panties together faster than a lightning strike. He inhaled sharply, getting high on the heavenly scent. He breathed out and took in a deep breath before he planted his head between her chunky thighs. His wicked mouth got to work. He went whole hog on her as if he were in a pie-eating contest. He took turns flicking his wet, large tongue up and down on her cherry-colored clit and slurping up her flavorful secretions like it was blessed Aquafina.

"Yes, Julius," Cotton cried out as she already neared climax. "You love this WAP, huh? Fill up on it then... Ooohhhh, find my spot. Y'know where... Yes, rite there, nigga... Faster... Mo' pressure... Yeah yeah yeah... I-I'm-I'm... Suck that shit, nigga... Yes, FUCK YEAH!" she yelled before she went boom.

Like a portable vacuum, Sosa took in every drop of her tangy fudge. Her cream slid down his throat smoothly. "Delicious," he managed to utter around her pussy that remained in his mouth.

Cotton was undergoing post-climatic tremors and panting heavily when she hissed, "My turn." She nudged him from her goodies and rolled over until she was able to get her phone from the nightstand. After about fifteen seconds her favorite song, *Hard To Do* by K. Michelle, began to play. Rejuvenated, she commanded, "Now hurry up an' take those damn pants off an' get'cha ass on this bed."

Sosa lost no time complying with her instructions.

To start things off, she aggressively pushed him onto his back. All at once she stood over him and began to dance sexily to the music. She knew she was regarded as a PAWG (Phat Ass White Girl), and that Sosa was insanely in love with her thickness, so her slow twerking was inciting a riot in his loins from the look she saw in his eyes. Teasing him delighted her, so much so that it made her wetter than the seven seas combined.

Before K. Michelle could sing the chorus, she had him harder than a granite countertop. She damn near nutted on herself due to her ability to still get him excited after all these years.

She continued swaying her hips while rubbing her titties and pinching her pink nipples and fingering her saturated vijayjay. Every now and then she'd drop her shapely ass low. As soon as she felt him at the entrance of her clutching depths, she rubbed her succulent cleft on his bulbous crown. When he tried to propel himself into her she stood up and resumed bouncing and wobbling her ass and caressing her body. She repeated the tantalizing act until her wetness glazed every inch of his pole, making it look like a jumbo iced chocolate donut stick.

"C'mon, bae, stop torturin' me," he begged, his face spelling out that he didn't want to be teased any more.

Ditto, she was torturing herself, too.

But she had an ulterior motive.

She was determined to exert maximum effort to put him under her spell again. She was giving him his belated birthday gift while making it clear to him what he'd be giving up if he strayed one more time. In order to reassure him that no other bitch could measure up to her, she decided to utilize two accessories he always objected to. She grabbed the never-used items out of her nightstand's drawer and took action.

"Hell no, CC! We ain't doin' that," he protested, sitting upright.

She pushed him back onto the bed again. She then hopped on his midsection. "Shut up, nigga. Like I said, it's my turn. So, yes, we are doin' whateva da fuck I want." She smiled mischievously. "Besides, who are you ta say no ta anythang I want after bein' gone fo' two days witout contactin' me?"

Sosa was speechless.

"That's what I thought, nigga. Now be still, shut up, an' enjoy what's ta come. Period!"

Cotton went ahead handcuffing him to the headboard and blindfolding him for the first time.

"I don't like this," Sosa confessed, now unable to see or move from his current position.

"You gon' be alrite. This gon' be fun fo' you an' me. Trust me."

"I trust ya but this gon' be mo' fun fo' you tho'. " He swallowed nervously. "So, what do I say or whateva when I want'chu ta stop?"

"You mean a safe word?"

"Yeah. What's da safe word?"

"Ain't none."

"What? Oh, hell naw." Her answer caused him to squirm. But with his hands and feet securely shackled to the solid bedframe, his struggling was for naught. Helpless as a kitten stuck in a tree, he said, "Don't fuck wit my ass, Anjelica. I'm serious."

Cotton ignored his warning as DaniLeigh's *Easy* came on. She positioned herself on top of him until they were sixty-nining. Simultaneously, she manipulated her pussy on his mouth and deep throated his dick. She slobbed and gagged, loving the feeling of the veins in his dick rubbing against her tongue. She eventually lowered her head to his balls and sucked and licked the ridges on them lustfully.

Once she showered more of her juices over his face, she moved into a different position. She squatted over him and slid down his slippery shaft until he took residence in her stomach. Like a vintage Tilt-a-Whirl toy, she rode him cowgirl style at various tempos. To inhibit him from nutting on his own accord, she mounted his face and fucked his mouth. When she felt his nuts had settled down, she switched to reverse cowgirl.

By the time she removed his dick from her ass after she rode him sideways and was about to clamber up on his face again, Sosa pitifully pled, "CC, my nuts 'bout ta blow up. They hurt like a muthafucka. Please baby... I surrender."

"Beg me, nigga, ta put'cha outta ya misery."

"I'm beggin' ya. Baby, please, lemme cum."

"First say that my fuck game betta than all those otha bitches."

"Yes yes. You da best, bae."

"Oh, so ya own up ta fuckin' otha hoez." She grabbed his swollen dick and squeezed it. "Was it recently tho'?"

"Aaahhhh... No... No, I swear. I ain't fuck around on ya since da last time ya caught me. No cap. Now, please, stop squeezin' my dick."

"Not yet, nigga. Now say you'll neva hurt me like that again." She tightened her grip. "An' you betta mean it, nigga."

"Aaahhh ... okay, okay, okay ... I-I-I'll neva cheat again. On GOD!"

"You betta not, nigga... or you'll get no mo' of this." Still holding his dick tight, she deposited his enlarged member back into the cavern of her warm mouth. She engorged herself on his meat. She crashed her mouth up and down dementedly until foam covered the base of his dick.

"Fuck, I'm 'bout ta explode. Work that mouth, bae... Shit. Suck that muthafucka. Here it come. Yeah... Uuuggghhhh."

Cotton kept her mouth latched onto his dick as he erupted like the Old Yellow geyser. He thrust into her mouth, pushing each jet of his seed down her throat. She gulped dutifully, savoring the taste like it was the most delightful substance ever.

Plop

That sound was Sosa's dick exiting Cotton's jaws.

Cotton, with lips glossy from his cum, proceeded to take off the blindfold and let him loose. Once she was done, she deflated onto his heaving, sweaty chest. "If I woulda let'chu shoot up da club wit all that, I know fo' a fact I woulda got pregnant." She licked her lips. "That was a lot, so I know you ain't fuck in a while."

Sosa pulled off the scrunchie in her hair and played in it. "I'm just glad ya ain't smoke befo' givin' me that neck."

"Why ya say that?" she asked, confused.

"I ain't want none of that cotton mouth. I like that wet, sloppy shit."

She punched him playfully. "Ass."

They both laughed.

Thereupon, they lowered the volume on the radio and got to pillow-talking. Great sex never fixed their problems, so they spent a good hour hashing over their rocky, complicated romance. They went over every dynamic of their relationship. Some issues were upsetting for them both. But overall, the discussion was sorely needed. In the end, they agreed to compromise and make sacrifices to revamp their union. They wanted to keep their family intact because they had already endured eighteen years of sharp disagreement, maturation and struggle.

And she also said yes to moving to Royal Palm Beach.

"Oh, befo' it slip my mind," Sosa began, "When I stayed da nite at my mom's, she told me my grandpa in Louisiana is sick."

"Do he got that new virus? I read on da internet that it's fuckin' wit older folks mainly."

"I dunno. But my mom wants me ta go wit her ta see him soon."

"How soon?"

"Like, real soon. We ain't seen him or my grandma in a while now. It's 'bout time we drop in on 'em."

"Okay. I hope all is good wit him an' he gets betta."

"I do, too." He paused. "Anywayz, while I'm gone, I need ya ta get er'thang ready fo' da move. All our important shit, get that packed up fo da movers. An' order some new furniture fo' da crib. No budget. Buy whateva. When I get back, I wanna walk into a laced out crib, okay?"

"Nigga, you must finna be gone fo' a month. Cuz that's da only way I'll have that bitch exactly how I want it." She laughed. "But I got'cha ." She kissed him. "I love you, Julius. Even tho' yo' Haitian ass get on my last nerve."

"I love you, too, lil' bit." He stroked her face before he began to climb out of bed.

"Where you goin' now?"

"Goddamn, P.O., I'm just goin' ta get sumthin' ta drink an' ta check on Dinky an' Mondo, that's all. I ain't seen 'em yet." He put on some boxers. "You got some weed ta roll up?"

"Yup."

"Twist us one up real quick while I'm gone."

"Bring me back some Kool-Aid, bae."

Sosa nodded and left the room.

Cotton lay there with a smile on her face for a moment. She replayed the last two hours in her head. She wished the remainder of her life with Sosa was passionate and upbeat like the past couple of hours.

Although marriage was not on either one of their agendas at the moment, she didn't want to come second to nobody in Sosa's life. She wanted him to love her unconditionally like she loved him. She wanted him also to not let temptation get the best of him ever again. Without question, she knew he loved her. But she was sick and tired of him fucking up and making up for it with gifts and great sex.

Speaking of gifts...

"Sosa!" she yelled as she scrambled out of bed. "Don't let Dinky outta da den! She gonna eat my Birkin!"

She bolted out of the room butt booty naked.

Chapter 8

February 12, 2013 - 10:13pm
Somewhere in Martin County, FL

"Mmmmmm," she moaned, coming to because she felt *unnaturally cold.*

She cracked open her eyes a splinter. Her range of view was limited. However, through the slit she only saw blackness. It took three or four seconds before it dawned on her that it was nightfall.

She shivered.

She tried to speak.

"Oooooo," she groaned due to the tremendous pain she *felt in her jaw.*

She moved to touch her aching mandible. But for some strange reason she didn't have the strength to do so. She tried to move any one of her other extremities. Similarly, she failed doing so. What's going on? *she wondered while straining to open her eyes fully.* Where am I? And why does it feel like I'm moving?

Once her eyes were partially opened, she initially saw nothing but fuzzy flickering white dots. Subsequently, she struggled to move her head. Before long she was able to crane her neck to one side. She flinched when she saw herself. She cringed because she couldn't grasp at that moment why she looked so gloomy and blurry. After staring at her unrecognizable self for several seconds, she craned her neck to the other side and...

"Good. You wake up, cherie."

Though the individual was ill defined as well, she heard a male's voice. And by their voice, she didn't know who the hell the heavily accented man was sitting next to her.

Panic suddenly overcame her.

Seconds later they came to a stop.

"We here."

Where's here? *she asked herself as tears gushed from her eyes, obscuring her vision completely now.*

He got out of the car. He walked around and opened the passenger door. He reached for her, and she went into survival mode. She tried to fend him off as best as she could, but he removed her from the car anyhow. For all the effort she put into fighting for her life, he threw her squirming one-hundred-two-pound body over his shoulder. He proceeded to lumber up to his newly designated house, which drew him to it without directions, for the first time with his first victim.

In a last-ditch effort, she screamed, disregarding the unbearable pain in her jaw.

A chilling echo was all that could be heard immediately afterward.

Nevertheless, determined to resist to the end, she resumed screaming at the top of her lungs while thrashing about with vehemence. Her turbulent resistance consequently caused him to drop her. She landed on the rugged concrete driveway. Yet that didn't hold her back from getting to her bare feet, ASAP, and making a run for it.

With no clue as to where she was, she ran erratically through the knee-high grass and down the lightless two-lane street without looking back. To her right she saw the silhouette of a structure and beelined for it. As soon as she reached the house's raggedy door, she banged and pounded on it while crying and hollering for help.

She was so focused on gaining the attention of somebody, anybody, in the house, or in the vicinity, that she was heedless to where her assailant was.

He eventually caught up to her. Furious about having had to pursue her, he shoved her head into the door with great force. His assault didn't knock her out. It did leave her on wobbly legs, though. Once more, he threw her over his shoulder and headed back toward the house with her limp body.

"Aaaaa... Ooooo," she moaned before babbling, "Heelllppp...heeellllpppp."

"No one hear you, cherie," he said just as he went up to the door. "It be over soon."

He was given no key to the house, so he intuitively grabbed the doorknob.

He recoiled instantly, almost dropping her again.

At first touch, he encountered an unusually heated doorknob. While it did shock him, he couldn't waste time. For that reason, with caution, he touched the knob lightly a few times. Upon realizing it wasn't hot enough to burn him, he grabbed and turned it. The door was unlocked, so he pushed in the sturdy door. Right away, scorching, stale air from inside the house bombarded him. He was already sweating from tussling and chasing after her, yet he eagerly opened the door fully and stepped inside of the blazing house.

Am I in hell already? she pondered once she felt the intense heat. What did I do to deserve this?

She unexpectedly lost consciousness seconds later.

***

February 1, 2020 - 10:39am
Lantana, FL

91

In the Homes of Lawrence subdivision...

"What was so important y'all bitches couldn't wait till later on ta talk about?" uttered Klutch as he walked into Wes's garage. "An' don't be tight wit da squeeze. Fire up. I know one of y'all got it."

Milk, Urnge, John-John, KD, DreBo and Wes, the one that assembled the gang, were already on the scene. 360 was due to pull up shortly. And Peezy was...

Well, the basis for Wes rounding up the clique was to inquire about Peezy's whereabouts.

"'You heard from Peezy lately?" Wes asked Klutch.

"Naw," Klutch replied. "That bitch ain't hit me up in a few days. Why?"

"He ain't hit nan' one of us up in a couple days now," Milk declared. "That's strange."

"Maybe Da Boogey Man got him," joked DreBo.

Klutch took a seat in the empty folding chair in between John-John and Wes. "Y'all know that bitch da real trick daddy. He get ghost wit a hoe fo' days at a time. So, I hope y'all bitches ain't bother me early this mornin' cuz y'all worried 'bout that nigga." He looked around with a quizzical expression, then said, "Bitch, why nobody sparked up yet?"

"On some real shit, Klutch," Urnge began, "all of us tried ta call Peezy this mornin' an' he ain't answerin'. Just like his ratchet, he keep his phone on him at all times an' he always pick up. Plus, y'know he love postin' shit on IG an' Snap an' sharin' his location. He ain't did none of that lately. That ain't like him ta go mo' than twenty-four hours witout postin' sumthin'. Y'know he a social media junkie."

"Man, on some *realer* shit, Klutch, these niggaz don't wanna believe me when I say those Haitian niggaz outta L-Dubb got sumthin' ta do wit Peezy missin'," KD, who was sitting across from Klutch, opined with irritation. "I been tryna tell these niggaz befo ya arrived what I *know* happened ta Peezy. But these niggaz think I'm trippin'."

"Yur trippin' hard, bro," John-John stated, "cuz I *know* them pie-ass niggaz ain't gettin' outta line like that. Unless they tweakin', they *know* betta than ta want smoke wit us."

KD's lip curled up. "I'm tellin' ya, Klutch, that Peezy got set up. Check out da last text he sent me." He showed Klutch the message in his phone that was time-stamped *1/27/2020 11:23pm.* "As you can see, I told him I was gucci, so he slid through L-Dubb solo ta holla at that bitch Shirley. She that nigga IronHead BM. So, I'm tellin' ya she lined my nigga up. An' if you can't see that then you blind as shit just like these muthafuckas."

"Klutch, I personally don't think they fucked wit da homie," insisted Wes, "becuz of da talk I had wit Sosa da otha day. I told y'all we came ta da agreement ta squash our differences an' let bygones be bygones. They don 't fuck wit us, we won' t fuck wit them, an' vice versa."

"I know you an' Three went ta school wit Sosa, but can you really trust that nigga? He ain't home team," DreBo said. "A mouth'll say anythang just ta double-cross a nigga, y'know what I'm sayin'?"

Before Sosa could reply to DreBo's valid point, 360 suddenly strolled up. "Where da weed at? An' why y'all niggaz look so... so emotional up in this bitch?"

"Did Peezy hit'chu up, Three?" Milk asked right off the bat.

"Y'all still ain't get no word on him?" 360 answered the question with a question.

"Naw," Wes said.

With no empty seats left, 360 stood between Urnge and Milk. "Well, I tried ta reach him last nite ta ask him ta bring me some work cuz I ran out. He neva got back at me, tho'. He prolly lost his phone, then got anotha one an' he ain't give us da new info yet."

KD, still agitated, then ran down to 360 what he *knew* happened to Peezy.

After 360 heard KD out, he looked at Wes , who sat opposite him. Since Wes had spoken with Sosa in the recent past, and he himself knew Sosa wasn't a snake, it was very hard for him to believe KD's suspicion.

But ultimately, he knew anything was possible.

"Did y'all call his people?" 360 asked.

"His ol' girl an' his brotha, T-Roy, ain't heard from him. They ain't worried cuz they go days witout hearin' from him," Wes said. "His otha brotha, Ike, an' sista Priscilla ain't pick up."

"Ai'ight, let's call around ta see if anybody seen him befo' we jump ta conclusions," 360 suggested. "'Sumbody we know in da county shoulda seen his yella Hellcat. He got da only Challenger wit that bright ass paint job."

They followed 360's recommendation and got on their phones. They spent the next twenty minutes calling and texting everybody they could. From the people they were able to talk to, they got responses saying, for the most part, that Peezy had not been seen.

Phone rings

"What's goodie, Ace?" John-John said into his phone. "Yeah, bro, I text ya ta see if ya seen my dawg Peezy around anywhere recently. He got da yella Hellcat... You did? Where at?... When was that? Do ya rememba?... Are ya sho'?... Gunshots? Who was bustin', do y'know? ...Ai'ight. That's cool. You gave me enuff useful info. I appreciate ya... Already. I'll hit'chu up soon, Ace. An' tell my sis I said wassup... Bet." He ended the call.

All eyes were on John-John, waiting impatiently for him to spill the beans.

John-John got straight to it. "Ai'ight, my bro-n-law said two or three nites ago he was hangin' out in front of da gym in L-Dubb at a party when he saw Peezy's Challenger roll by an' turn on Latona. Five ta ten minutes later he an' his pot'nahs heard gunshots close by. He dunno who was gettin' off, but he said seconds after da shots stopped he heard off in da distance da Hellcat haulin' ass from da area. That's all he rememba'd."

"See, I told y'all green ass niggaz them zoes got Peezy," KD blurted out, jumping up from his seat. "Latona is da street that bitch Shirley live on. I know this, an' so does Milk, becuz we been ova there wit Peezy. That hoe done tricked my nigga an' got him ambushed."

"Where her house sit at on da block is most definitely a perfect spot ta sneak up on a nigga," Milk stated. "'So, if what this nigga bro-n-law said is true, then we gotta go see 'bout them niggaz. Fuck all that truce, cease-fire bullshit."

Quiet.

"I see da uncertainty on y'all faces, Wes an' Three," Urnge said. "'But ya just heard our bro was last seen alive in Sosa territory. Becuz of that, it'sa must we give 'em a look."

Altogether, what was revealed by Ace and expressed by KD, Milk and Urnge caused 360 to backpedal. He was now ready to step on Sosa and his crew immediately.

Wes, however, was hot and cold about what to believe. He needed unarguable proof, not just a text or someone who heard shots, before he fingered Sosa for Peezy's unknown whereabouts.

DreBo said, "I say we getta couple quails an' bend a few of their corners ta see if we can catch 'em slippin."

"'Bitch, I'm wit that," Klutch agreed with DreBo. "Let's do that tonite."

Wes spoke up before anybody else went along with DreBo's idea. "I think y'all boyz movin' too fast. Lemme hit Sosa up first cuz y'all not even a hunnid percent sho'—"

"Fuck all that, is you ridin' or what?" KD tensely interrupted.

There it was: the pressure.

Wes never gave into pressure, and he wasn't going to now. His dawgz knew that, too. But, on occasion, their anxiousness caused them to space out - like they did just now. He couldn't stand when they pressured him because he felt his loyalty was being called into question. His allegiance to H.O.L. always overshadowed the friendships he had with outsiders, and they knew that - or at least they should have.

So, he might not have agreed one hundred percent with their plan, but he was going to ride.

No ifs, ands or buts.

Chapter 9

February 1, 2020 - 11:17am
Lake Clarke Shores, FL

After all the grueling man-hours spent dissecting and comparing scant crime scenes, checking out lukewarm witnesses, sifting through inadequate evidence, and poring over incomplete reports, who would've thought that an internet company would provide the crucial break in the *RISING SUN* case.

In 2018, Crime Scene Specialist Lou Bojanski learned of an innovative technology that California law enforcement were the first to utilize. Bojanski subsequently kept close tabs on California's progress with the unique tech over the last year. After observing the tech establish a suspect in a cold case, Bojanski implored the BBPD'S chief to approve of its use in PBC's enigmatic cold cases. Although the chief initially distrusted the practice that was incubated by progressive-minded California, Bojanski was given one chance to prove it worked.

In time, Bojanski hit pay dirt.

The technical term for the tech was *Geographical Fence.* Geofencing was its shortened name. It wasn't in demand right now because it wasn't proven reliable yet. Eventually, though, it was going to help police worldwide investigate otherwise unsolvable crimes.

But at the same time it was going to raise concerns about invasion of privacy and questions about how often it really solved crimes.

Geofencing essentially aided desperate investigators in California by requesting Google, via a filed warrant in court, to rake through its extensive data files for the mobile devices that crossed through a specific area at a specific time. The procedure created a virtual "fence" around potential suspects and witnesses, which allowed investigators to show their target's location down to ten feet.

Once a detailed request to the judge made it clear that Google's private data could jumpstart countless stymied investigations in Palm Beach County, Bojanski was granted a geofence warrant. Google received Bojanski's warrant and, bound by the Federal Stored Communications Act, began to exhaust their internal three-step process . First, the company relinquished to Bojanski a list of devices with time stamps indicating that those devices had been within an one-hundred-fifty-meter circle surrounding the abduction site at the specified time. Bojanski organized the vast nameless list, grouping devices by date of abduction, before analyzing it to see if any devices appeared relevant to the investigation based on elements such as how long the device was at the crime scene. Consequently, Bojanslki asked Google to provide additional geolocation coordinates for pertinent devices, and those coordinates were plotted on a map, revealing a virtual bread crumb trail of likely suspects. Thirdly, once Bojanski narrowed the staggering list down sufficiently, Google provided the names and emails associated with particular accounts and devices.

As soon as the list of names was in hand, Bojanski alerted Harden. While Harden began retracing the steps of those listed and questioning them,Bojanski submitted a "'piggy-back" warrant to get more information. The amended warrant was to get the location data for the devices of those listed ten days before and ten days after an abduction.

In addition to the graph of each individual's movement on the day of the abduction, the list that Bojanski gave Harden a week ago went back to the very beginning of the abductions. Newly inspirited yet overly cautious, he worked nearly twenty hours a day without anyone's knowledge but the chief's and Bojanski's. He started with the names in the first group of devices, which were tied to the first known case in 2013.

So far, he'd interviewed thirty-seven people. He ruled them all in the clear due to solid alibis. And, unfortunately, they were unable to give any useful information because they couldn't recall much that far back.

What was most unfortunate, however, was that there was nobody fenced with his sister's 2013 case.

Until the data from Bojanski's piggy-back warrant came back, he decided to skip over earlier abductions and tend to more recent cases.

Harden was now a few minutes away from having a *Q* and *A* with a person grouped with a late 2019 abduction. He had a good feeling about the middle-aged white woman he was about to meet. He'd already eliminated her as a suspect after scrutinizing her movements on the day of the abduction. He just hoped she could shell out some info he could work with.

He arrived at his destination, which was an apartment in a seedy complex. He fiddled with the rosary beads in the pocket of his blazer as he headed for the first-floor apartment. He promptly knocked on the door. *Please, Holy Father, smile on me this visit,* he prayed while waiting. *I know you've been leading me the right way this entire time. But no more stalling, please.*

The door opened.

Harden moaned. *Very funny, God,* he thought after he quickly looked over the bathrobed woman.

"Good morning, Miss Caan. I'm Detective Carol Harden. We spoke briefly yesterday evening."

With the dingy pink robe partly opened, the brittle, sickly woman, who was clearly an addict of some kind, said with a scratchy voice, "Yeah, I rememba talkin' to you."

He made a slight face at the sight of her blackened, decayed teeth, then said, "May I come in? I just have a few questions to ask. I won't take up too much of your time this morning."

She was hesitant to let him in because of her way of living.

Seeing her reluctance, he swore to her that he was only there for information, nothing else.

She eventually welcomed him inside. Of course, she had stuff tossed about high and low. She wasn't a hoarder; she was just plain nasty. And she didn't care what anybody thought about her living conditions.

The mixture of stale cigarette smoke, neglected cat litter, and only God knew what else, nearly caused him to noticeably gag. Besides the stench, he noticed a whole lot of drug paraphenalia everywhere.

"You can have a seat there," she said, gesturing at the couch that accommodated three mangy cats. "Want something to drink, detective?"

"No, thanks, Miss Caan, and I prefer to stand."

"You can call me Linda. Or Lin for short," she proposed before taking a seat in a worn recliner.

"Okay, Linda. Like I said, I just have a few questions." He removed a pen and small notepad from his blazer's inside pocket. He flipped through it until he found the right page. "As I explained yesterday, I'm investigating the September 2019 abduction of one Arthur Styne. He was last seen alive and well at Old Harry's bar in Palm Springs. You are familiar with the place, correct?"

"How'd I get entangled in all this?" she inquired first.

"Your phone's location placed you near Mr. Styne around the time he disappeared."

"Just me?"

"No, ma'am. There are quite a few others in line for me to interview from that night."

"Damn technology," she uttered. "Well, I do frequent Ol' Harry's. I've been hangin' around there for years."

"Did you know Mr. Styne?"

"Everybody knew Artie." She hacked impolitely. "He was like Dr. Jekyll and Mr. Hyde. He was real nice *before* he downed a few pints. Once he got drunk, though, he was a real jerk. We hardly ever spoke to each other because he was too volatile for me. But it's sad what happened to him. Harry's hasn't been the same since he went missin'."

"Is there anything you can recall that night that can help me?"

"Umm... Let's see." She grabbed a pack of Pall Malls off the little table next to her, lit one up and puffed it a few times. "I can't...I can't think of nothin' out of da ordinary."

"Are you sure, Linda? Anything can be of use, no matter how trivial you may think it is." He took a few steps toward her. "Did Mr. Styne get into an altercation with someone that night? Was there someone new in his company? Anything you can think of."

"Sheesh, detective, that was over five months ago. It's difficult for me to think that far back because... I don't dwell on the past for obvious reasons."

Harden scribbled something in his pad. Once done, he closed it and put the pen and pad back where he got them from. "That's all then, Linda. Thank you for your cooperation. I'm sorry for disturbing you this glorious morning. But if anything comes to mind later, please don't hesitate to call me. You have my number."

Linda snuffed the cigarette in a Chinese take-out container before she stood up. "I'm sorry I couldn't help you, detective." She ushered him to the door. "Can I ask you something, detective?"

Glad to be outside in the fresh air, he turned to her and said, "Sure."

"If you were able to track me down by my phone's location, how come you couldn't find Artie the same way?"

That was good question.

Without elaborating on it too much, Harden explained to her that Artie's phone, along with a number of others that went missing, mysteriously stopped sending its location not long after it crossed into Martin County.

"Would you happen to know if Mr. Styne had any family or friends in Martin County?" he asked for the hell of it.

"Ain't sure."

"Okay." He got ready to bid her farewell. But felt compelled to say: "It's never too late, Linda, to redeem yourself. All it takes is focus, commitment, sheer will, and God and you'll conquer all your demons."

"Yeah right! Only if you knew, detective. I've tried the Jesus thing and—" She stopped speaking suddenly. The look on her pockmarked face was ambiguous. Then she blurted out, "I don't know if this is worth mentionin', but the night Artie disappeared I saw him talkin' wit some young black guy wearin' a big flashy chain with an unusual Jesus medallion. Becuz Harry's is a place where drug deals go down regularly, I figured the black guy was a dealer. I approached them by the restrooms to see if I could buy some meth from the black guy. He said he had none on him, so I went back to where I was sitting. About five minutes later, I seen Artie walk outside with the black guy."

Harden had heard about a Jesus charm once or twice before. But he couldn't put a BOLO on a charm that most dealers and rappers wore.

"Do you know if Mr. Styne left with that gentleman?"

"Ain't sure. All I know is when I left with a date shortly after they went outside, they both were gone. But Artie's car was still in the lot."

Phone rings

"Okay, Miss Caan. Again, thank you. Have a blessed day. And may God bless you."

Harden walked off to answer his phone. "Hello?... This is he. How may I help you?... Really? Are you sure they're positive?... Tonight?... Okay, I'll be there as soon as possible." He closed his phone and jogged to his Lincoln Continental.

I knew I had a good feeling about this visit, he thought as he sped off. *God, you most definitely work in mysterious ways.*

***

Much later in Palm Beach Gardens ...

The city of Jupiter is reeling, began the front-page column in ***The Palm Beach Post.***

*Outrage over the abduction of real estate agent Robyn Perez three days ago escalated further after the Palm Beach County Sheriff's Office released a controversial statement. Yesterday, the PBCSO stated that Perez's abduction wasn't linked to the seven-years-long **RISING SUN** case. Perez, age 29, was out on her early morning jog when she was forced into a late model Ford Focus, surveillance footage showed.*

The sheriff disbelieves Perez's disappearance relates to the infamous case because of her reputable background and *the different circumstances of her abduction. Publicized documentation show that those seized in the **RISING SUN** cases were residents of impoverished areas and made off with in an ingenious and surreptitious manner. Those differences suggested to the sheriff that Perez's case isn't tied to the others.*

With the identity of the perpetrator obscured in the grainy video, investigators currently have no other leads. There is an urgent search underway for ...

ZooMan scowled and tossed the newspaper aside. He was highly displeased with himself. His displeasure derived from him implicitly letting his arrogance and his tenacity to prove to God that he couldn't be stopped blur his superior reasoning. Though he felt like what was worth doing was also worth overdoing, he should have called it a night after he bagged victim sixty-three.

Despite his irrational decision to hunt that night, trapping a soul without complications usually did the trick for him.

However, victim sixty-four was not only easy pickings, but she was also a wolf in sheep's clothing. He'd been on his way to ditch the Ford Focus when he came across her. Whereas the populace stereotyped one and all from disenfranchised neighborhoods as filthy swine, he knew that everybody sinned and that there was no difference between iniquities. Therefore, when his sixth sense detected her duplicitous spirit on that nearly empty thoroughfare, he jumped on the opportunity only because he deemed he had enough time to get her to the trap house and make it back home before daybreak. Not even once did he take his surroundings into consideration.

And because he used poor judgement and miscalculated the time it took to complete the journey, he couldn't ditch the car properly. His miscalculation forced him to abandon the car not very far from his condo because his survival depended on him getting home immediately.

For the past several days he'd been holed up in his condo letting his wounds heal. While he was on the mend, he spent most of his idle time browsing through different dating apps. He wanted to line up as many potentials as possible for when he was well enough to get back to work. With just a pair of souls left to trap in order to meet his quota, he wanted the last two to be a cinch.

CRASH!

"U.S. Marshalls! We have a warrant!"

ZooMan had been caught with his pants down. And he had nowhere to run or hide. The trapper had become trapped.

Yet what instantly shook him up the most was that he didn't sense it coming. And since he didn't, he wondered why his spells hadn't cloaked his location.

Caught unawares and undressed, he only had time to grab his necklace off the nightstand and put it around his neck. Shortly thereafter, his bedroom door shattered. About a dozen agents armed with AR-15s filed into his spacious room. He immediately threw his hands in the air and began speaking creole loudly. His shenanigans didn't stop more than several agents from pouncing on him, however. Half-naked and still wounded, they drug him off the cushy bed and threw him on the plush carpet before handcuffing him.

"Euclide Vilsaint," one of the masked agents barked in his face once they hauled him off the floor, "you're under arrest for the kidnapping of Robyn Perez."

Francois, I know you're not thrilled I didn't listen to you, he said telepathically to the omniscient *bokor* as the agent began reading him his rights, *but I just hope you'll have a change of heart and help your old friend once more.*

Chapter 10

February 2, 2020/ 1:46pm
Terrebonne Parish, LA

Gators, Cajun, king cakes, magnolias, crawfish, Mardi Gras, the Saints, and *voodoo*.

Louisiana's culture was indubitably like no other state.

Sosa and his mother, Garciella, were thoroughly enjoying the sights, sounds and smells as they drove through the Bayou State. He was glad his mother had a fear of flying, because they would've otherwise missed out on this convivial road trip. He initially thought the trip to his grandparent's place was going to be uneventful without Cotton and the kids, but he was having more fun than he envisioned with his deeply adored mother. He didn't get to spend much time with her because of his grind, which she turned a blind eye to, so the lengthy trip afforded him the opportunity to talk to her about the present and the future, among other topics.

Sosa didn't care to talk about the past that much with his mother because she almost always brought up his father, a man he'd never met.

Sosa wished his father, Lucson, was in the picture. A tragic series of events in Haiti robbed him of ever meeting his pops and his two older siblings.

From the collection of stories his mother told him, Lucson was a devoted family man that made a living as a market trader in the city of Delmas for many years. He slaved to save up enough money to smuggle him, Garciella, their two kids, and his parents out of anarchic Haiti. However, when he just about had the money for their passage to Florida his five-year-old daughter, Rosalynn, and six-year-old son, Edwin, suddenly ended up gravely ill. He promptly paid for the services of an *houngan (oon-Gun)*, a shaman/healer and priest of Vodou, to find out what was wrong with Rosalynn and Edwin.

The *houngan* discovered that a hateful couple next door besought a *bokor* to send numerous *gede (gay-Dee)* to attack the kids. The neighbors became jealous after learning that Lucson was resettling his family in a better country. The *houngan* recognized the black magick used was an *expedition mort,* and it prompted the restless gede (i.e., aimless spirits) to attach themselves to the kids and drain their energy at night. The *houngan*, with the help of the powerful *lwa* Madam Brigit, gave Lucson ingredients that, once mixed, smelled bad to the gede.

Lucson, as well as Garciella, bathed the kids seven times a day in the compounded ingredients, which consisted of vervain, thyme, elder flowers, sage, St. John's wort flowers, pine needles, raw rum, sea water, and some special magical items.

Sad to say, Edwin died in agony before the potion could take effect. And Rosalyn became excessively thin and angular before the bad magick was broken.

Lucson, low in spirit and hope, had no choice but to change his plans. With only enough to get three members of the family out of crisis-laden Haiti at that time, he made the ultimate sacrifice. He hurried Garciella, who was then pregnant with Sosa, and his parents off to Florida and sent an incapacitated Rosalynn to live with relatives in the city of Carrefour.

With no intentions of reuniting with his family, Lucson carried out his ulterior motive: he got revenge on his neighbors. He slaughtered the man, his wife, and their five kids with no remorse. As a consequence of the gruesome butchering, relatives of the slain family had another *bokor* steal his soul. In effect, the *bokor* turned him into a zombie, someone who was living but not truly alive. Thereafter, he roamed the streets of Delmas until his unknown death.

"Turn right in one hundred feet," the car's GPS directed.

Three seconds later, Sosa turned onto a dirt lane somewhere on the border of the city of Houma. At less than five miles per hour he drove down the extremely potholed lane that was lined by trees and vegetation. It seemed like forever before he came up to a cluster of dwellings surrounding a central courtyard. Once he stopped, he recognized in the middle of the courtyard the large sacred Mapou tree, which was considered to be the link between the spirit world and the earth.

"That one your grann house now," Garciella let Sosa know, pointing to a tin-roofed shanty up ahead on the right. "That one your granpe still live in." She then pointed to another tin-roofed shanty directly to their left.

Though this was the second time he'd visited his grandparents since they moved from Florida twenty-odd years ago, Sosa remembered them living together in the place to the left. The dwelling up ahead to the right used to be unoccupied. Two of the other three dwellings were lived in by unrelated Haitian families. And Jovenel, his grandfather's older brother, lived in the remaining dwelling.

"Why they livin' by themselves now?" Sosa asked curiously. "They get divorced?"

"Haitians no believe in divorce. But voodoo come between them."

Sosa was very familiar with voodoo because he grew up around it. He learned a lot about it from his mother and the parents of his homies. As he matured, he realized there were many different forms of the spiritual practice. But African Vodun, Haitian Vodou and New Orleans Voudou were the three primary forms he was up on.

Oral and written history declared that the word "voodoo" originated from the *Fons* people of southern Benin. It generally translated as "deep mystery," "invisible force," or "spiritual entity." The West African tribal beliefs that spawned voodoo held that a Supreme Being named *Bondye (bon-Dee)* created the earth.

By origin, voodoo was a religion rooted in healing and doing good to others. But once it was brought to New Orleans' French Quarter by West African and Caribbean slaves, it became a source of strength for all that were going through fierce conditions. As the enslaved were transplanted throughout the South, the use of the religion varied. It eventually became tied with black magick and witchcraft because it was not just being used to heal but to torment one's foes also, particularly the ruthless slave masters. The practice of making and wearing charms and amulets for protection, healing, and harming others became important aspects of New Orleans Voudou.

In time, the Louisiana *Black Code* was enacted to ban the religion of "uncivilized savages, dark arts, and black magick." Slave masters had to convert their slaves to Christianity and baptize them within eight days of their arrival to the colony. However, the religion didn't die. It simply merged with the newly adopted Catholicism to give the impression of conversion, thus the hens in the henhouse outfoxed the fox.

Nevertheless, the mixing of the two religions formed different beliefs and practices in Voodoo, and that created the rift between the followers of Vodun, Vodou, Voudou, and the other forms of the religion.

Sosa didn't practice a specific form. He did believe in it all, though: the good and bad root doctors, the djabs (evil spirits), the zombies, and the *lougarous* (loo-Gar-roos), aka shapeshifters.

"Who ya wanna see first, Ma? Granpé Neus or Grann Marie Sophia?"

"Neus, since he sick."

Sosa pulled the rental in front of the rustic dwelling. He climbed out of the car and his first thought was how exceptionally muggy it was for it to be winter. His second thought as he walked up to the place with his mother beside him was how could anybody stand the pungent and swampy stench in the air.

Standing cautiously on the weather-beaten porch, Sosa rapped lightly on the clapboard door.

Cough, cough

"Come!"

Hack, hack

They stepped into the antiquated dwelling.

It had been a while since Sosa was last in the place. But right away he could see, even with the sunshine barely lighting the inside, a major difference from way back then to now. He quickly presumed the dramatic change had something to do with his grandmother moving out. While the exterior was more or less in the same condition, he observed the interior hadn't been cleaned in forever.

Besides the uncleanliness, he detected the smell of rotten meat. His nose directed his eyes to something in a corner he couldn't clearly make out. He curiously went toward that corner until he saw...

"Don't touch!"

Cough, hack

"Get back!"

Sosa spun around like the cylinder of a revolver. He had to step back a bit because his grandpa was nearly nose-to-nose with him. He stepped around his grandpa with weak knees instead of embracing the venerable old man. "Who them is?" he mumbled.

Evading the question, Neus went up to the decrepit table that barely supported his altar. Dust and cobwebs covered the three-tiered altar. On the first tier there were four bone-colored candles, decomposed flowers, a lusterless white plate, an indistinguishable food offering, and, front and center, was an old small black and white photo of the Voodoo Queen Marie Laveau, a pivotal figure in the history of Louisiana Voodoo. Queen Marie Laveua was feared and respected by white men and was the protector and healer of colored people during the 1800s. The second tier had a portrayal of the *lwa* Papa Legba on one side and a depiction of the *lwa* Ellegua on the other, three more off-white candles, a glass of polluted water, and a stick-and-twine crucifix, which represented the union of spirit and matter and the crossroads where the living and dead meet. The topmost tier had a larger sepia photo of Marie Laveau, a cruddy snake figurine at the photo's base, and a smudged blue candle next to the display.

The setup on the table didn't complete Neus' altar.

What perfected the altar was what Sosa inquired about.

Situated on both sides of the table were two mummified nude corpses. One was a man, the other was a woman. They appeared to be African American. Above them hung two handmade wooden crosses.

Neus walked lightly over to the putrid corpse of the young man. A giant cockroach suddenly crawled out of the carcass' mouth and perched on its head. He calmly brushed the bug away. He then explained to Sosa in creole, the language he preferred to speak at length, that the bodies served as the souls of every ancestor. Their presence signified that the sacred dead were never forgotten but remained an ever-present part of society.

If this is what caused Grann Sophia to move out, I don't blame her, Sosa thought before posing the apparent dreaded question. *Who in their right mind wants to live with TWO dead bodies?*

"Did you kill them, Neus?" Garciella beat Sosa to the punch.

Neus smiled, exposing his pearly white teeth and pink gums. He was sixty-six-years old and in better physical shape than men half his age, so he was surely capable of taking someone's life, no matter their age. But "No," he said.

"Where they come from then?" asked Sosa.

"Harvey hurricane come and I go out and find them." He smiled again. "It's okay."

Sosa and Garciella were both relieved - to a degree - that Neus didn't actually kill the pair. Knowing the truth didn't stop them from tingling all over though. It was just unfathomable to them that he explicitly went looking for casualties of the 2017 hurricane and brought them home to be a part of his altar.

They eventually settled in Neus' messy bedroom, a part of the house that wasn't as odorous and unsettling as the living room.

Sosa carefully copped a squat in a well-used chair. "So, what's wrong wit'chu, granpe? We came unannounced becuz Jovenel called an' said you been sick fo' a while."

Once seated on the creaky bed, Neus said, "It's okay. I—" He stopped momentarily to clear a hacking cough from his throat. "I not sick. My brotha know nutting."

Garciella sat next to him. "Neus, you sure?" She touched his forehead with the back of her hand, and he wasn't noticeably hot. "How long you have cough?"

"Uhhh... *pou yon mwa.*"

Cough, cough

"If you been coughin' like that fo' a month, then you definitely sick wit sumthin' granpe," Sosa insisted. "I see you still don't have no tv, but do y'know 'bout that new contagious virus? You prolly got that when ya went ta town a month ago. It's killin' alotta old folks, so we gotta—"

"It's okay," Neus cut him off. "I have this." He lifted the small worn leather bag that hung around his neck from a cord. "This protection from *djabs*. And this, too." He grabbed the dried-up hollowed out pineapple that was beside him on the end table. "Magick lamp. More protection from demon. Nutting harm me. It's okay."

Hack, hack

Neus was a devout practitioner of New Orleans Voudou, better known as Laveau Voudou. In Laveau Voudou, magickal traditions were commonly known as *gris gris* or Hoodoo (i.e., conjure and root work). Hoodoo relied on spiritual powers harnessed through ritual actions to affect change. Popular notion was that Hoodoo was a magickal practice and Voudou was a religion, owing to the fact that Hoodoo worked with roots, powders and fetishes and Voudou revolved around spirits, intermediaries between people and *Bondye*.

Other than the dry cough, Sosa didn't see anything visibly wrong with Neus. He wasn't plugged all the way in with all of the coronavirus' symptoms, but he did know for sure that it affected the lungs. It crossed his mind that those rotten carcasses may have something to do with Neus' hacking. The only way to truly assess what was afflicting his grandpa, though, was to get him to a doctor as soon as possible. He'd pay whatever to get Neus the best care.

However, he knew Haitians, especially older ones, were extremely stubborn. It would be easier beating a murder one rap with a smoking chopper than it would be getting Neus to agree to go to the nearest hospital.

They spent the next two hours or so catching up.

Why Marie Sophia was no longer living there wasn't mentioned at all.

"We're gonna go see grann now, gramps," Sosa said. "We'll be right back, okay?"

Neus sucked his teeth just before another short bout of coughing and hacking. "It's okay. Go."

Sosa and Garciella got up and headed out.

"Wait," Neus yelled before they could exit.

Cough, hack, hack

"What is it, grandpé?"

Neus approached Sosa with something clenched in his veiny hand. "You need this." He opened his hand. In his palm was a gris gris bag like the one he wore.

Sosa took the bag. His instincts made him squish it. His best guess was the innards contained "special" sand. "Thanks, granpé. But why you say I need this?"

"*Lwa* Ogoun tell me to give you." Neus proceeded to explain to Sosa that everybody was born the child of a specific *lwa*. And Sosa's was the Great Warrior Ogoun. He activated Sosa's *lwa* before moving to Louisiana. He was giving Sosa the talisman now because he felt that Sosa had lost Ogoun's protection. He said that Sosa did something that the *lwa* forbade him, so the gris gris bag was protection Sosa could wear until he made amends for doing what wasn't allowed.

What Sosa just heard was new to him. He never knew he had a "guardian angel," let alone one that he had angered and ran off.

Sosa looked at his mother, and she nodded in confirmation.

Is that why I never got into major trouble or had any major injuries? Sosa pondered while adding the stringed bag to the two gold chains already around his neck. *I wonder what I did, though, to make the spirit mad.*

"Nutting harm us now." Neus smiled. Then, he continued with a stern face, "Don't take off."

"*Mèsi*," Sosa thanked his grandfather before hugging him. "We'll be back."

Sosa and Garciella walked the short distance to Marie Sophia's place. The exterior was almost a carbon copy of Neus' place. On her rugged timber door, however, was the sacred ritual symbol of a specific *lwa* drawn in white chalk.

Fearing the symbol, Sosa avoided knocking directly on it.

In less than thirty seconds, the door cracked open.

Refreshing air infused with incense welcomed Sosa and Garciella on the spot.

"Neus, I told you—" Marie Sophia started until she realized it wasn't her nagging husband. Once she recognized the faces, her radiant eyes lit up and a movie-star smile enveloped her beautiful face. "Hey! Long time no see." She took a quick glimpse behind them and frowned. "'I see you didn't bring my great grandbabies to see me. When am I going to finally meet them? When I'm dead?"

"Grann, it ain't like that," Sosa said, feeling bad that he'd yet to formally introduce his kids and Cotton to his grandparents. "I swear I'll bring them ta visit ya soon."

Marie Sophia simply stepped aside to let them enter.

The home's aura didn't necessarily surprise Sosa because Marie Sophia had always been obsessed with cleanliness. He was in disbelief, however, with his sixty-four-year-old grandmother's appearance. While he noticed she'd added a few pounds to her heavyset frame, her copper skin was as smooth and unmarred as a newborn's. She still kept her hair wrapped in a headcloth and she wore an elegant hand-sewn muumuu. To him, she hadn't aged a day since he last saw her.

After they hugged and kissed cheeks, Marie Sophia led them to the family room at the back. The core of the house was bright from natural sunlight and spotless. There was various flora, African-themed paintings, and wood-carved figurines of *lwas* and ancestral artifacts all around.

What Sosa saw was all once in the house Neus lived in now.

Stepping into the family room, Sosa noticed a corner area that Marie Sophia used to contact her ancestors and worshipped her *lwas*. Unlike Neus' altar, hers was tidy and simple. The altar's table was draped with a snow-white cloth. White and blue candles, money, feathers, fresh flowers, water-filled goblets and heirlooms were strategically placed There were also pictures of family and the *lwas* Oya, the Goddess of the Underworld and Storms, and Shango, the God of War and Lightning.

Above all, though, Sosa didn't see anything dead or defiled on, above, beneath, or near the altar.

"How are you, grann?" Sosa asked once he and Garciella parked themselves on a loveseat. "You still as lovely as ever."

"I know, baby. My homemade cosmetics keep me looking fabulous," Marie Sophia humbly bragged. Her English was exceptional due to her desire to be looked at as an American and not an immigrant as soon her feet touched U.S. soil. She tried to get Neus to follow suit, but he was content with his illiteracy. "So what brings you two here?"

"Jovenel called and said Neus was very sick," Garciella answered. "We came to look over him."

Marie Sophia giggled girlishly. "Jovenel is mistaken. That old fool isn't sick. I just called upon the ancestors to irritate his throat because I got tired of telling him that Haitian Vodou is stronger than Louisiana Voudou."

Sosa and Garciella couldn't believe it. They were truly stunned by the confession.

"Is that why you moved out, grann? Becuz y'all beliefs ain't da same?" inquired Sosa.

"Are you kidding me? I know you stopped by there first, so I know you seen... not one but TWO... dead people. That's why I moved," she sneered. "Hurricane Harvey just missed us so I sent that man to get some groceries. After being gone for hours, he returns with... who knows who those people are.

"Before he brought those poor people in our home, we were bickering a lot about voodoo. We were practitioners of Haitian Vodou until we moved here to Louisiana. Not long after we got settled here, Neus decided to follow Marie Laveau Voudou."

"Why he do that?" Garciella sought.

"Because of Jovenel. We moved here so Neus could be close to Jovenel. Jovenel was already following what the locals around here follow. It was monkey see, monkey do." She shook her head in disappointment "We were good after he switched. But once I became a *mambo* and started healing others nearby with the help of the ancestors, he began trying to heal people with magick.

"Word quickly spread about my healing powers and my ability to extract people's evil spirits, so I turned the place next door into a peristyle once Pierre and his family moved out. And Neus didn't like that at all. He became jealous because his magick wasn't healing people, so he started using it to do harm to others. He was using death and coffin spells and voodoo dolls, which are not used that much because its considered weak magick in both Haiti and New Orleans. Him jabbing pins into dolls caused us to argue a lot.

"As you may know, Garciella, people like Neus that use voodoo in a bad way cause others to demonize the religion. It's already bad enough that tv shows, movies and tourism always portray the religion as evil. I absolutely hate that. Voodoo - as well as *Ifa*, *Orisha* and *Santeria* - is an extremely misunderstood spiritual practice." She sighed. "The bodies of those dead folks was the breaking point, though. I had to get out of that place, so I moved over here."

After digesting what was just disclosed, Garciella said, "Marie Sophia, you must heal Neus. He sound terrible."

"I know he sounds terrible because he walks over here, day and night, coughing all up in my face. I love him dearly, and I'll never leave him, so I'll never do significant harm to him. I just wanted to watch him struggle trying to cure himself with his contemptible magick." She giggled. "But because you asked, Garcie, I'll ask the ancestors to heal him tonight."

"*Mési*," Garciella said.

"So, where are you two staying?"

"We plan ta getta hotel in Houma, grann."

"You don't have to do such a thing. I have clean rooms in my Vodou church next door."

"We stay here," accepted Garciella.

"Good." Then, Marie Sophia saw it. "I see your granpé gave you a gris gris, Julius. So, what silliness did he tell you you needed it for?"

Sosa touched the bag. "Granpé said da *lwa* I was born to no longer protects me so I need this."

"Really? Hmph. You don't need that for protection. Besides your appointed *lwa*, I used to bathe you every chance I got in a special mixture when you were a baby so no one could ever curse or do evil magick on you... Like they did to my son and your siblings." She paused momentarily as Lucson, Rosalynn and Edwin crossed her mind. "But if Neus sensed your *lwa* no longer protects you, you need to make offerings to that *lwa* and your ancestors and ask for forgiveness.

"On top of that, you must start depositing goodness into the Bank of Karma. Put others needs before your own in order to reap the benefits, because, at the end of the day, you create your own 'heaven and hell.' You manifest your own reality. This—" She waved her arms around. "—is just a place to learn. And if you don't learn, you'll come back and repeat until you transcend. Do you understand?"

"I... I think so, grann."

"You'll get it sooner or later." She grinned. "'Now, keep that gris gris because your grandpé gave it to you. It has sentimental value now. Wear it proudly. But I'm going to go out in my garden and pick some flowers and leaves to boil for you both to drink. It'll make the blood bitter, so it'll taste and smell bad to *djabs* and keep them away from you."

Phone rings

Sosa removed the phone from his pocket.

It was Cotton calling.

Shit, I forgot to call to let her know we made it safely, Sosa said to himself as he answered her call.

"I'm sorry, bae, fo' not... Whoa whoa whoa, slow down. You ain't makin' no sense cuz you talkin' too fast... Say what?... I can't just up an' leave! I just got here. Y'know I was gonna be here fo' a—"

Boop boop

Sosa looked at his phone to see who was on the other line. It was Yak.

Fuck, all hell is about to break loose, he thought before continuing to get the fucked-up news from Cotton. *Man, I wonder if my grann or granpe can ask the ancestors to do something to delay the massacre that's in the cards.*

Chapter 11

February 2, 2020 - 5:07pm
West Palm Beach, FL

It was hate at first sight.

Harden wanted nothing more than to wake the vile piece of shit up and stomp his head in until it was puree. He preferred to exact his own justice right then and there because he vowed to give the devil his due. He knew the law of man was too good for the beast, so taking matters into his own hands would not only save taxpayers' money, but it would also be cathartic. He liked his chances of getting away with the unlawful killing, even in a federal building, since law enforcement openly expressed his current sentiment.

Instead of yielding to his hidden desire, though, a deadpan Harden entered the interrogation room in the Paul G. Rogers federal building. He stepped lightly to the table where the monster sat with his head resting on folded arms. He placed the briefcase he carried on the table indelicately. His deliberate action caused the guilty-until-proven-guilty evildoer to stir and raise his head.

Harden was immediately taken aback by what he saw.

Still, collectedly, he unbuttoned his blazer, pulled out the chair and sat, all the while marveling at the hideous, withering individual.

"Mr. Vilsaint, I'm Detective Carol Harden from the Boynton Beach Police Department," he introduced himself in a professional manner. "I've been granted special jurisdiction on the *RISING SUN* case. I'm here to question you about that case. Do you understand?" He paused to see if any of what he said registered. When the noxious old man seemed to look right through him with bloodshot red eyes, he continued, "Before I start, do you need medical assistance?"

An afflicted ZooMan smirked faintly.

Harden overlooked the gesture and proceeded to unlock his briefcase. "I've been told you don't want counsel. So, are you willing to talk to me?"

"None of this will soon matter," ZooMan said weakly.

Rather than have ZooMan explain that statement, Harden removed a file, set it down on the metal table and opened it. "First things first, and I'm pretty sure others have asked you this already, is Robyn Perez still alive?"

"Define alive?" ZooMan replied before cackling dryly.

Trying not to lose his cool and jump across the table, Harden articulated, "Is... Missus... Robyn Perez... still alive?"

ZooMan, in excruciating pain, sat as vertical as he could in the hard iron chair. "Soon, all the sinners of the world will be condemned and the few that remain will become subjects of the Great Baron Samedi."

"Baron Samedi? Who is he?"

"He's the Father of the Dead, Controller of Spirits, and soon-to-be ruler of this pathetic world."

Is he serious? wondered Harden. *He must have suffered a major concussion during his arrest because he's delusional.* "And let me guess, you're a chosen one."

ZooMan cackled some more.

Harden sat quietly staring into demonic eyes for a few seconds before he removed another file from the briefcase. He pushed the other away, laid the current one down, and opened it. He briefly scanned over the file he received not twenty-four hours ago. "According to this, your legal name is Euclide Josef Vilsaint. Your alias is listed as ZooMan. Your current age is fifty-eight. You're a Haitian immigrant that has been in this country illegally since at least 2001. You have no family or occupation listed. You have no prior history of arrests, either. But it's reported in this file that you were associated with a now deceased member of the defunct RockBottom Family crime organization."

Every third or fourth word that Harden said was all that ZooMan heard. The indirect mention of Virgil caught his ear, though, and that caused him to reminisce about the time he did business with his Jamaican buddy.

ZooMan, aptly nicknamed for the large amassment of reptiles and farm animals he'd kept at his Lake Worth Beach residence years ago, encountered Virgil at a local West Indian restaurant in 2004. At first glance he saw that Virgil, with his ostentatious persona, was his means to make good on his promises. Since he knew a tad bit of black magick, he quickly put a hex on the unsuspecting Virgil via a handshake. After exchanging their contact information, they went their separate ways for a brief time until Virgil advanced him a few ounces of coke. He quit the labor force once he got his first bird from Virgil. In time, Virgil had reliably supplied him with eight bricks a week.

At no point did ZooMan feel bad for using voodoo on Virgil. Because of his spontaneous decision he was able to put other fresh-off-the-boat Haitians on their feet that were willing to sell cocaine. All of that was in addition to fulfilling his promises to finance his family and close friends' voyage from his homeland to the U.S.A.

Following years of doing good business, he did establish a solid rapport with Virgil. Despite never rubbing elbows in public, he knew it was their no-nonsense camaraderie that led Virgil to ask him to take part in a sweet and fruitful scheme. Once he agreed to join, Virgil told him the scheme required him to move to New Orleans, and he readily did so the first week of January 2009.

Virgil's brainchild had been doing exceedingly well... or at least he thought so .

When Virgil called and informed him to return to Florida with urgency one day, he felt something wasn't right. Yet he still took the trip back to PBC. The day before he was supposed to meet up with Virgil, he called him and let his bad feelings be known. He listened to his gut and skipped out on the rendezvous. The very next day he learned that Virgil's mutilated body had been found in the Everglades. For fear that his safety was imperiled, he fled to Little Haiti in Miami, and his life thereafter went into a tailspin.

He had roughly three-hundred-grand stashed, but he knew the money wasn't enough to maintain him and his dependent loved ones for long. After several months of deliberation, he'd invested in ventures, both legit and illegal. Nevertheless, over the stretch of three years he ran through more money than he brought in. He also made more enemies than friends during that span. And it had been one of those green-eyed haters that led to his life's drastic change.

On the evening of Decemeber 12, 2012, he was driving around Little Haiti, simply checking up on his investments. Not long after he walked away from an establishment he acquired on Sixty-Fifth, a random young zoe closed in on him as he was entering his vehicle on the side of the building and shot him five times at close range. The assailant, who clocked him for months, flipped his pockets then drove off in his car. He then called upon Baron Samedi to not dig his grave as he lay dying in a puddle of blood. That was when he was saved by the insidious Francois.

Cutting a desperate deal with Francois that forced him to forsake the people he took care of until he captured a set number of souls should've been the worst part of his ordeal - but it wasn't.

Two months into his obligated mission, his mentally infirmed mother, who hadn't heard from him in months, thought he had abandoned her, so she went back to Haiti. She'd been there only a week when she became sick. Her condition worsened as the days passed. She successively lost her faculties: Her vision went first, followed by her voice and hearing, before she wound up bedridden.

Fulfilling his end of the bargain as quick and safe as possible had been his ultimate objective from the start. But once his mother fell ill, the sicker she got, the sooner he wanted to be by her side. And because of his urgent need to be there for her, he went about his mission with determined focus.

If you only listened to me that day, Virgil, you'd be alive still and I wouldn't be in this predicament, he said to himself for the thousandth time.

"Mr. Vilsaint, this is your chance to clear your conscience…" *That's if you have one,* Harden thought. "…because you 're going to be put in a hole and that hole will trap and torment you until you die, which will be soon from the looks of it. You can try all you want to convince a jury that you're insane with your 'chosen one' claim but it won't work. There's clear-cut evidence of your abduction of Mrs. Perez. And now that we have your prints and DNA at last, I'm sure we'll be able to tie you to many other abductions, some of which probably involved sexual assault before you murdered them and disposed of their bodies. Were any of them children, Vilsaint?"

"I preyed upon no one under eighteen, nor did I rape or kill anyone," ZooMan proclaimed in an uncompromising, unapologetic tone.

"So, you admit to kidnapping others besides Mrs. Perez? And if you didn't murder your victims, where are they?"

"That's neither here nor there."

Harden was making progress and he didn't want to lose the momentum, so he switched tactics. "I was informed that you were healthy as a horse... disregarding the minor burn scars over your body... until a few hours after you were booked. The doctor that evaluated you said he can't explain your extreme decline or how you were burnt. He believes your diminishing health, however, may be a combination of stress and the old gunshot wounds you didn't get patched up at a hospital. Why didn't—"

ZooMan cackled again. "Is the peanut gallery enjoying the show?" He nodded at the camera mounted in the corner. "What sense does it make telling you imbeciles something you're not going to believe until it's too late? Biased people like you don't understand that what you consider fiction has a foundation in reality."

"Try me," Harden said before leaning back and folding his arms across his midsection.

Despite him knowing there was hell to pay for crashing and burning so close to the end, ZooMan's current "fuck it" mentality incited him to unveil what was soon to come.

"My instincts tell me you're a religious man," ZooMan began, "so you're aware that almost every religion has a celestial being that's worshipped as the creator and ruler of the universe. This deity has many names. God, Jehovah, Allah, and Dios are the most noted of them. Likewise, you know if there's a divine being there's also a supreme spirit of evil. This loathed entity is known as Satan, Lucifer, Devil, Diablo, or Beelzebub.

"Well, my African ancestors believe in *Bondye*, an unknowable and uninvolved creator god. Unlike mainstrem religions, there isn't a cardinal archfiend in the religion I swear by. Instead, my religion has the very powerful spirit Baron Samedi, the Ruler of the Dead. He isn't a sinister spirit. He's a powerful healer and a gentle protector of the children that've just come into this world. But after he saw how mankind incrementally wreaked havoc on itself for millennia, he felt the wickedness of this century presented an opportunity for him. So, he planned to put that sinfulness to use and reign over this planet once he eradicated the black sheep." He smiled slightly. "If there's one thing you can say about mankind these days, there's nothing kind about man.

Unstirred, Harden asked, "Exactly how will this spirit that has made himself the judge, jury, and executioner of the human race go about ruling the earth?"

"He'll gather the power needed for reincarnation from the spirits of sinners. Once the required number of souls have been obtained, a grand ritual will take place and Baron Samedi will take physical form and rule with severe justice."

This scum just might be the one that flew over the cuckoo's nest, Harden deduced before responding snidely. "Since you're a so-called chosen one, I take it you 're one of the gatherers of souls for this Baron Samedi, who must be a Republican from the sound of it. And if what you say is true, where are these souls stored until this grand ritual?"

ZooMan smiled. "In a safe place until it's time."

"Is this place in Palm Beach County?" probed Harden. "Or maybe it's in Martin County?"

The bright smile on ZooMan's ugly mug dimmed a bit.

Harden noticed and said, "You've taken the victims to a place in Martin County, I see. That explains why some of the victim's last phone location showed them entering Martin County. But can you explain why their location STOPPED pinging shortly after crossing into Martin County?"

"Detective, I can see in your eyes and from you posture that you find what I'm saying hard to believe. But believe this if you don't believe nothing else: The soul of your sinful loved one will help give life to Baron Samedi."

Harden expected that beforehand. He was sure he'd be able to contain himself when the moment arrived. But…

As if the iron chair was suddenly charged with electricity, Harden jumped up. He then reached across the table, grabbed ZooMan by his neck and jacked him up. "You killed my sister, you demented bastard! Where is she? What have you done with her body?" He was foaming at the mouth. "I'm going to kill you!"

Seconds later, three agents burst into the room. It took all three of them to restrain a hog-wild Harden. They forcibly towed him out of the room as he continued to make a scene.

In the hallway, a gray-haired agent that knew Harden well said, "What was that? You crossed the line in there. I should've known better. I should've known that once he mentioned your sister you weren't going to keep your emotions in check."

Breathing erratically, Harden retorted, "I thought I could …" He stopped so he could catch his breath. He wiped his mouth, then resumed, "If you knew the hell that evil bastard put me and my family through, you'd understand, Fisher. I lost my wife and kids because of me working tirelessly to nab him. But since he didn't abduct somebody you care about and discard of their body, never to be found, I don't expect you to fully understand."

"Look, we're sorry you experienced that," a tall agent professed, "Each one of us in this building wants to tear that motherfucker to pieces. But we can't because we 're not inhumane like he is. We're just here to extract as much info as possible from him so we can find out what happened to the victims. Then due process will take care of him."

Harden began fingering the rosary beads in the pocket of his slacks. He started calming down in no time. "I apologize for overreacting in there. I let the devil win that round."

"How'd he know you were related to one of the victims anyway?" asked an athletic-built agent. "It's like he purposely hit below the belt to get a reaction out of you."

Almost back to normal, Harden said, "Serial kidnappers and murderers like him have memories like elephants and they usually keep trophies of their victims, like wallets, purses, clothing, or other personal items. So, I suspect my sister, whose last name is Harden as well, had something on her person that links her to me. Or he got her last name from the news."

"Quick question," the tall agent chimed in. "Did anyone of you by chance buy his apocalypse bullshit? Like, seriously, I 've heard a lot of crazy shit over the years but none as crazy as that."

"Harden said it best. He can try all he wants to convince a jury that he's insane but it won't work," Fisher, the gray-haired agent, insisted. "Now, come on, Harden. Let's get you some fresh air and water."

"Will I be able to finish questioning him?" Harden asked. "I truly apologize for my outburst. I promise it won't happen again. But I feel like he was being a showoff, deliberately exposing himself to me. Did he say anything to anybody before me?"

"No," answered the athletic-built agent.

"See, he'll spill his guts to me. I know he will. He wants to grandstand because he believes his fantasy will happen."

Fisher sighed. "*After* you get air and water, I'll think about letting you continue… with one condition however."

"Name it."

"One of us will be present in the room with you this time."

"That's fine with me," Harden replied. "Now, I don't need water. What I need to do is call the sheriff in Martin County, though."

Fisher turned to the tall one and said, "Go check on Vilsaint while we 're gone, okay? If he needs medical attention, get it for him."

The tall agent nodded. He promptly returned to the interrogation room. He stood by the door and watched Zooman, who had his head back down on his folded arms. "Fucking Haitian. You're so full of shit. Let's see that witchcraft bullshit get you out of the lethal injection."

The lights then flicked off and on.

ZooMan hadn't budged.

The agent, however, walked to the table and sat down. He cocked his head while staring at Zooman. "Look at you. You're a disgrace."

ZooMan lifted his head upon hearing the distinctive and familiar voice. He looked into the agent's eyes and smirked. "I knew you'd come to save me again, buddy."

In possession of the agent's body, Francois said, "You look half dead. And it's because your egotistical ass didn't listen." He pitifully looked down on him. "First time you needed saving was because of your bright idea to pose as an Uber driver at the airport. That went south for you when a suspicious passenger called the cops and gave up your car's description and tag number. Then your well-thought-out plan to use BackPage to lure victims to your hotel room backfired when you solicited a police officer, and they swarmed your room. Now this."

"You don't have to remind me. Just get me out of here, please."

"Get you out of here? Ha-ha, ha! How do you expect me to do that? The first time it was just one police officer. I was able to let you off with a 'warning' after you got pulled over. The second was a little tricky, and took some ingenuity, but I pulled it off without revealing your identity. I've done more than I was willing to do for you. Now you want me to break you out of a federal building that's teeming with police."

"What are you doing here then? You come to poke fun at me before snatching my soul, is that it? Well, go ahead and put me out of my misery. I'm in a lot of pain right now anyway. Death isn't far away how I'm feeling."

Francois groaned. "'You excelled at much over the years. For one, your English is such that you sound like you could oversee a Fortune 500 company. You also mastered the shape-shifting ability I taught you a while back, although you let the sunrise almost kill you several times, even recently. You're one of the best to do it, by far." He paused. "But the one thing you perfected that gets on my nerve is your ability to make me feel sorry for you. No more though."

Francois stood up and left the room.

You should've left me for dead in 2012 instead of now, thought ZooMan before laying his head back down. *I take accountability, mother, for failing you.*

About ten minutes later, ZooMan heard the door open again. He didn't move a muscle because he was no longer in the mood to put up with the grilling agents. He'd said enough already, so he was just going to keep quiet and await his fate.

He didn't care about the fate of the world either.

Clunk

The loud noise of something metallic falling upon the table caused ZooMan to lift his head. What he saw in front of him on the table instantly perked him up. He sat up and saw the tall agent.

"That should help you get yourself out of here. I'll be your diversion," Francois said prior to pulling the service pistol from the waist holster he just retrieved. "If you don't make it, I'll be back for what's rightfully mine." He walked to the door, then looked over his shoulder. "'No more. And you owe me." He went into the hallway.

ZooMan quickly put his chain and charm around his neck. He felt the surge of power and strength at once.

Boc Boc Boc Boc

"Aaaahhh!" someone yelled.

"Carlson, what are you—"

Boc Boc Boc

If it had been after dark, ZooMan would've changed his appearance so he could get out of there undetected. But since nighttime was a couple hours away, he got up and dashed to the door. He peeked into the hallway and saw two people dead on the floor.

Boc Boc Boc Boc Boc Boc Boc

"No, Carlson!"

ZooMan slipped into the hallway and bolted away from the screams and gunshots.

Chapter 12

May 26, 2020 - 1:27pm
Royal Palm Beach, FL
Lockdown. Mask up.

Those terms had totally different meanings now. They normally connoted something criminal, but the Covid-19 pandemic changed that, likely forever.

It wasn't that long ago when the explosion of coronavirus deaths in the U.S.A. pressed the MAGA-loving Florida governor to finally adhere to the Covid-19 guidelines set by the CDC. Unlike China's "zero covid policy" and blue states' prudence, lockdown and quarantining weren't strictly enforced in the land of sunshine, although social distancing did cause many small businesses, mainly restaurants and bars, to shutter their doors. Wearing masks wasn't mandated either. They were worn at one's own discretion.

Some Floridians took advantage of masking up, nevertheless, by wearing hoodies with gloves and N95s to commit robberies, car-jackings, and even murders, in broad daylight.

Sosa sure as hell had his black hooded pullover, surgical gloves and mask on standby to use criminally because niggas had violated in the worst way.

The grim news he received in that phone call less than twenty-four hours after he left L-Dubb not only spoiled his little getaway, it fucked him all the way up. What made the crisis even more upsetting was that nobody he called in the hood could tell him much about the unfortunate event at that time. When he finally touched home base four days later, he knew what deserved his immediate attention, and it wasn't orienting himself in his new home with Cotton and the kids. He stopped by the crib just to gear up before he dropped in on Pressure to get a firsthand play-by-play of what went down at the trap.

Pressure's detailed story opened with him and Huff at the trap running the bag up as usual. He was in the stash spot and Huff was next door in the apartment that was accessible to fiends. He was counting money and scrolling through SnapChat when he heard a loud bang and crash. In nothing flat, he grabbed his modified Glock and ran to check out what the suspicious sounds were.

Just as he opened the door, he heard multiple gunshots coming from next door. The rapid fire only lasted four or five seconds, then he saw three masked niggas breaking out of the trap. With balls of steel, he hit the button on his big-nuts glizzy and took on the trio by himself in the small courtyard. His barrage of slugs struck one of them in the upper body. He got hit in the lower leg though. Once all the clips emptied, he limped next door to see about Huff. When he caught sight on him, Huff was slumped on the floor, perforated with bullets. As soon as it hit him that Huff was a lost cause, he cleared the scene and hobbled down Ray Street to Cano's mom's place to elude troll.

Unfortunately, Pressure's account in no way served to definitively pin down who had the balls to run up in their trap. And because no money or dope had been taken, a question of motive wasn't readily established either. However, once the fat mouths and loose lips began flapping in the streets, the who and why had become clear.

A couple days after Huff's death, word had spread that HOL Boy Peezy was missing and had been last seen near IronHead's BM's crib.

Sosa and his clique were aware of the shooting that occurred around the time Peezy was on Latona, but they weren't to blame. Even so, he put two and two together and concluded that Da HOL Boyz ended the cease-fire because they pinned Peezy's disappearance on him and his bros. The situation couldn't be redressed, but he still attempted to contact Wes several times to confirm what he already knew. He'd been unsuccessful, so, at that point, locking horns with Da HOL Boyz was locked in.

The second Huff's funeral was over Sosa and his squad, as one, pressed pause on the hustle. They made a quick transition to Ghetto SEALs and got active ASAP. The convenience stores, gas stations and fast-food spots around H.O.L. were staked out. They were hoping to catch any recognizable niggas from Da HOL slipping. They resisted taking any action inside of the no-outlet H.O.L. subdivision since it mainly put their lives on the line. Their end-all, be-all had been to body bag as many HOL Boyz as possible, including Wes and 360, without being crash dummies.

The first turbulent encounter ultimately happened when Edson and Cano spotted KD in the Checker's drive-thru down the street from the entrance into H.O.L. Though it was midday, they unsubtly sent over fifty shots KD's way. Luck was on KD's side that day, but there were no lucky breaks during the next confrontation. At the 7-11, also close by Da HOL, Sosa, IronHead, T.P. and Edson were backed in next to the air pump when 360 pulled up with a female passenger. Sosa didn't want to greenlight the play, but the murderous look in his homies' eyes led to 360 and the female being cancelled.

Soon after that, absolute anarchy erupted in the streets of L-Dubb and around H.O.L. So many niggas ended up getting caught up in the vendetta that it eventually sparked conflicts everywhere in the county. Hospitals were at capacity with gunshot victims and ventilated covid-stricken patients. And funeral homes were packed with the casualties of both calamities.

Two epidemics were playing out in PBC at the same damn time.

During a lull in the action, Sosa was enjoying his in-ground pool. His four-hundred-twenty-thousand-dollar two story home in La Mancha, a non-gated community on Royal Palm Beach Blvd., was set far away from the unrest. Once 360 had been stepped on he personally felt they'd got back at Da HOL Boyz for Huff's death, so he retreated to appreciate his new four bedroom, three bath residence with his family.

"DaDa, look at me," Kia demanded. She then jumped into the shallow end of the pool feet first. A second later she popped up to the surface. With the flotation devices on her arms, she proceeded to kick her little legs wildly until she reached the pool stairs. She stood up, wiped the water from her chubby face, and gleefully said, "See that, DaDa? I dive and swim."

Basking on a gator-shaped pool floatie with a blunt fixed in his mouth and a Heineken in his palm, Sosa smiled richly. "I see ya, Fat Fat. Now you can teach ya mama how ta doggie paddle, then all of us can finally go on a cruise."

"Whateva nigga. I can swim too. I just choose not to. Period," Cotton declared from the safety of her chaise lounge chair that was by the pool. "An' I told ya, unless da boat plans ta stay in sight of land, I ain't gettin' on it." She went back to looking at her phone while getting a natural tan.

Sosa pulled hard on the blunt. He took a swig of the beer next, then exhaled and said, "I know why ya don't get in da pool? You afraid ta get that wig wet. I'ma give ya some money ta buy a waterproof one if that's da case."

"Ugh! You so damn aggy, nigga, I swear." She chuckled. "This is *real* human hair, FYI. Besides, I'm 'bout that jacuzzi life."

"Yeah, that hot tub strictly fo' doin' da yucky."

"Sosa, really? You say that in front of da kids?"

"Why not? Them lil' demons know what goes on."

"CANNON—"

"—BALL"

Splash, splosh

The two choppy waves created caused Sosa's floatie to flip over. He went under water briefly. When he emerged, he spit water out of his mouth like a fountain. As he began to tread water, he heard hysterical giggling. "Oh, y'all think that was funny?" he said after he laid eyes on the culprits. "Y'all done ruined a perfectly good blunt and wasted my cold beer. Now y'all gotta pay… wit y'all lives!" He then swam towards the agitators like a mako shark.

J-Mill and Jerri screamed together. They then split and desperately tried to swim to the pool's edge and exit before Sosa got one of them.

Sosa was having a blast tossing and chasing the kids all around the pool when a familiar face walked into the backyard.

"Wassup, fam? Da kid here."

Sosa and the kids quickly acknowledged the drop-in and returned to horse playing.

"Hey, Slater," Cotton replied, moving the oversized sunglasses she wore onto her head. "You're late."

"I know, right?" Slater countered, taking a seat alongside Cotton. "But I was tied up soakin' up the latest scam from my mom."

Kevin Slater was Cotton's cousin that lived six houses up the block. Although Cotton wasn't fired up about moving at first, she was beyond thrilled when she found out Sosa wittingly moved to this suburban neighborhood so she wouldn't feel isolated. And what made the situation even better was she and Slater were thick as thieves because they both were taught the game of fraud by Slater's mom, who was the manager of a local bank.

"What'chu an' Aunt Ruby cookin' up now? I know y'all done made a fortune so far rippin' off da IRS outta them twelve hundred dolla stimulus checks."

"Yeah, up to now we made a little over a hundred thou. What about you? How much you hit for?"

Cotton put the shades back over her eyes, then she inconspicuously looked Sosa's way.

"Ooohhh, you didn't tell him, did ya?" Slater asked after noticing her reaction.

"Y'know I didn't becuz y'know like I know he don't want me doin' that shit no mo'. We made promises to each otha."

"I don't get it. He hustle in the streets, right? So why can't you hustle the government?"

"Becuz he makes good money doin' what he do. Just look at this place an' da cars we got. He bought all this wit nuttin' but dope money. An' altho he ain't hussle in 'bout two months cuz of all da stupid killin' goin' on, he got plenty money put away."

Barring weed peddlers, Slater wasn't too fond of drug dealers since his mother struggled with a meth addiction for years. Even though his mother was a functioning addict, he knew her drug habit was what fueled her scamming obsession, which supported her vice as well as compromised her job.

"Scammin' for those stimulus checks will come in handy if he's currently not makin' any money," Slater asserted. "You can use the money you come up on for a rainy day. Or for your kids' college fund."

"Yeah, but… I just don't want him ta find out I'm still at it. I don't wanna piss him off cuz he changed alot an' checked all da boxes I asked him to. So, da lil' twenty grand I took in is good fo' now."

"Twenty grand? That's it?" He sighed. "Well, that's too bad because me and my mom... So, what you got planned later on?"

Cotton fumed. "Don't do that. Don't up an' change da subject like that becuz now I gots ta know."

Slater grinned boyishly. "You heard about PPP loans, right?"

"Yeah. That's da Paycheck Protection Program."

He nodded. "So, you know what it's about?"

"Somewhat. From what I read on Google its Covid aid relief fo' strugglin' biznesses, just like da stimulus checks are helpin' U.S. citizens from goin' deep in debt."

"You on point. So, my mom said the businesses, mainly small ones, that've applied for PPP loans already at her bank have been approved for sixty-five grand, on average."

The figure gained her full attention. She looked to see if Sosa was paying attention to them. He was fully involved in the rough and rowdy play with the kids, so she refocused intently in the conversation. "What we gotta do?"

"It's we now, right?" He cracked up a little. "Anyways, we have to setup some realistic looking businesses that can survive da fast-track approval process. We can't use personal ones unless you want to go to prison. We fill out the loan applications online. My mom will process a couple loans at her bank. We'll give her a percentage if the money comes through. Then, we will go to other banks."

"That's it?"

"Shit sounds too easy, right? Well, it is," Slater responded. "Now, I'll come up with two bogus businesses to start with and then you'll make those accounts and fill out the loan forms online."

"I got'chu. Just don't tell—"

"I won't. But it'll be hard for you to hide all that money we're about to rake in. We're going to be rich, Lil' Jelly Bean."

"I told ya 'bout callin' me that, Kevin. We ain't kids no mo'."

"Lil' Jelly Bean is a better nickname than Cotton, Anjelica." He stood up, then said to Sosa and the kids, "I'm gone, y'all. I swing by later."

"Nooo, come swim, Slater," Kia cried out while dog paddling.

"I would, baby girl, but I don't have on the right clothes for swimmin'."

"That's a lie," Sosa yelled. "Wit'cha lil' hoochie-daddy shorts and tank top on, you look like a Old Navy model."

"Bullshit! This here is Dior, kid, not that cheap flea market shit you be wearin'."

"That's anotha lie."

The grown-ups broke out laughing.

"Ai'ight, Slate," Sosa said as he grabbed J-Mill, hoisted the flailing boy over his head and threw him. "Don't fo'get ta get at me wit those gas cards."

"I'll have them for you when I double back, kid."

"Bet. I'ma have Cotton CashApp you that bread now."

Slater nodded and bounced.

Cotton was just about to do what Sosa said when something disturbing popped up on her Twitter newsfeed. "OH MY FUCKIN' GOD! Not again!"

Cotton's sudden outburst caused Sosa's heart to skip a beat then palpitate. *Please, don't let it be someone I know that got killed*, he prayed.

"What happened, mama?" Jerri asked while clinging to Sosa's back.

"First, it was that black boy joggin' in Georgia, then that girl in Louisville that got killed in her own apartment. Now da damn police in Minneapolis done killed a black man yesterday." Cotton sucked her teeth hard. "Just like da joggin' boy killed by those hillbillies, sumbody recorded da murder an' da video shows a punk-ass white police kneelin' on this po' black man's neck while his hands were cuffed behind his back. That muthafuckin' cracka didn't budge as da black man said ova an' ova he couldn't breathe an' cried out fo' his mama. Mm Mm Mmm. That's past fucked up. Now this man, whose name is …" She looked for his name. "… George Floyd will be anotha black man that's killed by da racist crackas an' nuttin' happens. This shit gotta stop."

Sosa was relieved… somewhat. *This shit has to stop but it won't, unfortunately, because them crackas, especially ones with badges, have a license to kill niggas*, he thought as he grabbed J-Mill and Jerri and hugged them tightly. *Damn, 2020 is turning out to be the worst year of my life and there's still seven months left.*

***

May 26, 2020 - 2:17pm
Lantana, FL
For there to be betrayal, there would have to have been trust first.

After cohering in grade school, Sosa gained Wes' trust. Then once they began buying weight together, he grew to trust Sosa nearly as much as he trusted his closest homeboys. And he genuinely felt that Sosa trusted him similarly.

That trust became questionable to Wes, however, shortly after KD hastily concluded that Sosa was responsible for Peezy's disappearance. While his hotheaded homeboys bought KD's selling points, it wasn't enough for him to find Sosa undeniably guilty of betraying their friendship and

140

reneging on the cease-fire they'd agreed upon. Still, the allegation had planted seeds of doubt in his head, and they grew until he conjectured that Sosa could've betrayed his trust and double crossed him.

Then the truth came out.

Rather than being set free by the truth, it pissed Wes off. So many lives had been destroyed in a four-month span because he and his dawgs had jumped to a hasty conclusion. He knew he should've taken the initiative to look deeper into Peezy's puzzling disappearance. But his loyalty moved him to act in haste. And because he didn't investigate, he ended up being the actual betrayer of trust, as well as the spark that brought about the widespread bloodshed in PBC.

Other than the person who told him, Wes was the only one in the H.O.L. that knew the real story so far. He decided to unveil the truth to John-John first because John-John was rational like he was. And for that reason, he wanted to pick John-John's brain and see if the bad blood between Sosa and him could be set right.

He arrived at the house that John-John inherited after his single mother passed from breast cancer three years ago. He honked the horn twice. Seconds later, John-John, gangly and coal-black with vitiligo, stepped out of the house and hopped into the passenger seat of Wes's Genesis G80.

"What's good, bro? Er'thang gucci?"

"Naw, not really, Jay. We threw shit at da fan an' now its rainin' down on us."

"What'chu mean, bro?" John-John asked, perplexed.

Wes went into the center console and retrieved the Dutch Master. He removed the sandwich bag of ZaZa from his pocket next, then handed the two to John-John. "Roll that while I put this bug in ya ear."

Prior to pulling up on John-John, Wes looked in on Peezy's kinfolks. He stopped by to see how they were holding up and to drop off Peezy's monthly percentage of the profit they made hustling. Peezy's people always kept him posted with the latest update in Peezy's case every time he dropped in, and today was no different.

Peezy's pops had fresh news today that left Wes of two minds.

The day before, the detective that was working Peezy's missing persons case had called the family. The detective let them know that the location data from Peezy's phone had come back, and it revealed two significant discoveries. The first was several devices had been in the vicinity at the time of Peezy's last known location. The detective immediately interviewed those persons of interest. After piecing together their versions of that night, the detective learned that an unknown man had popped up out of nowhere and carjacked Peezy as he was about to drive off from Latona. Peezy tried to prevent the snatch by opening fire on the mugger but his effort was ineffective because he was taken along with the car.

The second, and most helpful, finding was that Peezy's location last pinged in Martin County. The detective said that discovery strongly suggested Peezy was a victim of the notorious serial kidnapper terrorizing PBC. The detective closed out the call with the assertion that local police and multiple federal agencies knew the suspect's identity and were out in force looking for him.

"Damn, bro, Peezy dead then," John-John said while putting the finished blunt between his pink lips. He lit it, hit it twice and passed it. "So, ya mean ta tell me that becuz we jumped da gun, 360 an' his sista dead, da homies Woody an' NaNa fightin' M-Ones, our hussle game fell off enormously, an' da whole county at war?"

"Yeah, that's da size of it," Wes responded before handing over the jay.

"Fuck." John-John sighed heavily. He took a big pull on the blunt and held the smoke in until it tickled his lungs. He blew the smoke out, then said, "Bro, I dunno what ta say becuz we can't cut off da shit we powered up." He hit the blunt again and handed it off.

"I know that." Wes pulled on the jay and exhaled. "What's done is done. But I wanna try ta clear things up wit Sosa."

John-John coughed, and couldn't stop, and it wasn't because the interior was now foggier than the foggiest day in PBC. He was coughing frantically because what Wes proposed caused his breath to get caught in his throat. Once he was done hacking, he said, "'How you plan on doin' that, bro? You musta fo'got we dirted his pot'nah, shot da otha one, an' leveled they streets after what happened ta Three."

"I ain't fo'get." He hit the blunt and passed it. "But I know Sosa. He a reasonable nigga. If I can get da chance ta explain what caused us ta get active then he'd undastand… I think. Now, I ain't sayin' he'll forgive an' fo'get, but he'll realize it was a misunderstandin' that set this shit off." *Pause.* "I knew I shoulda answered da phone when he called me after we merked Huff. Maybe we coulda deaded this befo' it got to this point."

"Shoulda, woulda, coulda, but'chu didn't." John-John shrugged. "Anywayz, becuz I'ma sensible nigga myself, if I was in Sosa's shoes, I wouldn't wanna hear nuttin' ya gotta say. Especially after all that went down."

"You rite. But I gotta idea that might work. If ya tell ya bro-n-law Ace what really happened ta Peezy, then word will get ta Sosa. An' if I know Sosa like I think I do, he'll be wantin' ta know if what he heard is true or not. He knows that rumors are carried by haters, spread by fools an' accepted by idiots. So, he'll get in touch, hopefully, an' we'll be able ta have a one-on-one again an' figga out where ta go from there. What'chu think 'bout that?"

John-John rubbed his mainly ebony face with his mostly pink hand. "Well, bro, you have a betta chance of hittin' da lotto. *But* I'll hit Ace up fo' ya."

"I appreciate it." Then, "Hit da gas, nigga. You lettin' it smoke itself, bug-ass nigga."

High as fuck, John-John smiled before hitting the blunt.

"By da way, when was da last time ya heard from Woody an' NaNa Man?" Wes suddenly asked.

"'Bout a week ago da lil' nigga NaNa hit me up."

"He Gucci?"

"Yeah. Lil' bro built tuffer than ten F-150s."

Wes went back into the center console and pulled out five hundred dollars. "Put two-fifty on his books an' da otha half on Woody's." He handed the bread to John-John. "An' get me they info so I can send them boyz a sheet wit K2 sprayed on it. They can make some money in Gun Club wit that."

Chapter 13

June 2, 2020 - 8:35pm
Boynton Beach, FL
"Is that'chu, Christmas Carol?"

"Yeah, that's da girlie man."

"Hashtag HIGH YELLOW LIVES MATTER!"

The group of four laughed boisterously.

"Seriously, tho', what's good wit'cha, officer? It's been a while since we seen ya on patrol around here."

Like always, Harden refused to feed into the hoodlums' nonsense. Reacting or responding to his oppressors since childhood wasn't worth it then, and it damn sure wasn't worth it now, because they turned out to be zeros, people worthy to become one of the downtrodden victims in the *RISING SUN* case. All he ever saw most of the peers he grew up with do when he came back around the hood was hang out at the hotspots and smoke, drink, hustle, and bullshit. He always figured they'd become pathetic individuals stuck in Cherry Hill like so many before them, so he ignored the doomed devils, then and now.

Harden only travelled to the dreaded hood to see one person.

He knocked once on the door and entered.

"Who's there?"

"It's me ma."

"Oh, Carol sweetie, I'm glad it's you," his mother said as she joined him in the living room. "I thought you were that aggravating busybody, Diane. That heifer always comes over here around this time running her mouth and freeloading. She act like I'm her psychiatrist and lesbian lover."

Born in St. George, Bermuda, but bred in B-Town, Ursulanda Jefferson, was in her late fifties yet still full of life. She was always the "cool" mom, behaving more like a friend than a mother, because she always acted frivolously. Her carefree behavior could be attributed to her riding the gravy train since her teenage years.

Ursulanda was nineteen years old when she fell in the lap of luxury. She was working as a maid at the Breakers Hotel when she encountered forty-one-year-old William, a white Briton and the CEO of a global law firm, during a corporate convention. What was supposed to be a one-night stand evolved into a love affair.

During the decade after their meeting, William worked four to six months out of a year in the U.S. He doted on Ursulanda up to the day he had to return to the U.K. He fully supported her to spoil her and keep her under his thumb until he came back stateside. Two months after his return, she became pregnant with Mackenzie. Three years after that she gave birth to Carol.

In 1992, William, who wasn't a hands-on father, revealed to Ursulanda that he sold his stake in his company and was going back to London and never returning. Before departing though, he gave her three-hundred-fifty-thousand dollars. He called her every now and then to send more money and to ask how Mackenzie and Carol were doing.

Then, in early 2005, William called and dropped two bombshells on Ursulanda. The first revelation was he had a wife of thirty years and four fully grown children. The second was that he had terminal pancreatic cancer. He ultimately transferred her two million dollars and told her to use it wisely because no more money would be sent.

When William died later that year, Ursulanda decided to secure a good life for her and her kids by blackmailing William's wife. His wife knew William was a lascivious philanderer. So, to avoid having mud thrown on the family's prestigious name in England, she wired Ursulanda three million dollars hush money and got her a secretary job at a prestigious law firm in West Palm Beach. From 2006 to 2013, she worked for the blue bloods. She walked out on the job without notice, though, once Mackenzie vanished.

Harden sat down on the couch that was covered in plastic. "How have you been, ma?"

"I'm good. You know me, no major complaints," she replied, taking a seat in a plastic covered recliner. "How about you? You look frail, son. When was the last time you had a home-cooked meal?"

"I'm up all day and most of the night working so I don't have time to cook. I simply tough it out with fast food and grab-n-go items at convenience stores."

"I told you, Carol, you better leave that processed food alone. Consuming too much of those preservatives is going to alter your DNA and make you sterile. You keep on eating that junk and you'll wake up one day and be a spermless Klingon."

Harden couldn't hold it in. He chuckled at what his facetious mother said. He knew it was only a matter of time before she said something outlandish.

Besides having no filter on her mouth, she constantly popped off some of the craziest conspiracy theories. She wholeheartedly believed that aliens were walking amongst mankind, climate change was a hoax, the planet was flat, and Satanic world leaders dined on the blood of kids. Her beliefs not only made her sound thrown off her rocker, it caused her to lose a fortune to con artists and other quacks peddling gimmicks that would "safeguard" her.

But it was her belief in the supernatural that prompted his visit.

"Ma, do you believe in voodoo?"

"Of course, I do. Why do you ask?"

"Out of curiosity." He paused for a millisecond. "So, uh… What about it do you believe?"

"All of it. The voodoo dolls, zombies, animal sacrifices, mutators, mermaid-like creatures, it's all real. Yes, I'm a Christian - and not in name only - but that doesn't mean I don't believe other religions are real. Ask your God-fearing grandma, she'll tell you voodoo is real, too."

Harden would've simply laughed off her outlandish answer if he hadn't witnessed the inconceivable a week ago. He didn't know what or what not to believe anymore when it related to voodoo after what he saw that shocking day. All conspiracy theories could suddenly hold some truth in them, including the existence of Big Foot, he considered.

"Well, I was convinced that I knew better than to believe black magick was real. Because I attended church with Grandma Cleo regularly when I was a child, my eventual conception was that voodoo was a fictitious dark art similar to Satanism that was meant to terrify people, and it only affected the believers of it. To me, it's a laughable practice undertaken by crazed, ungodly savages and those in America stupid enough to follow such bullcrap."

"Sweetie, you must understand that some things just aren't for everybody to accept. Everybody that knows me know that I believe there's an Area 51, that the Illuminati governs the world, and Tupac is still alive. Do I belong in a loony bin for believing these things? NO! You just have to respect that people believe what they want, and they have their own opinions, and that shouldn't concern you. Like the saying goes, what people eat doesn't make you… go to the restroom."

Harden smiled at the watered-down analogy.

But the expression swiftly disappeared.

"Ma, I stopped by really to tell you something unbelievable that I know will unhinge you because it unhinged me. It's a moment in my lifetime I'll never let go and might need counseling for."

From the look on his face, she broke out in a cold sweat. She knew what he had to say was no joke and distressing. "What is it, son?" she asked, almost afraid to do so.

He swallowed the recently formed lump in his throat. "A week ago, the elusive person responsible for the mysterious disappearances the past seven years was in federal custody and—" He choked up a bit. Clearing his throat before resuming, "And he, a Haitian immigrant up in years, boastfully confessed to abducting Mackenzie when I interrogated him."

The hairs on her body stood straight up and her flesh crawled.

The unexplained disappearance of her first born left her in a state of uncertainty for months. That had been the only major period of instability in her life. Her faith restored her in time, though. But she thought about her daughter and prayed for her daily while slowly bouncing back to her old ways.

Tears began welling up in her eyes. "Where is she? Where is her—"

"I hit the roof, ma, before I could get that answer," he interrupted. "I had to be drug out of the room before I killed him."

She stared at her son blankly for a brief spell, then said, "You said he was in custody. What happened? Was he let go because you assaulted him?"

149

"No, he wasn't set free because of my actions. The bastard escaped."

"What!? Escaped? How? How did he manage to escape federal detention?"

He remembered, against his will, all the details of that surreal day. "After reviewing the surveillance footage, it seemed that... This is the unbelievable part... But it seemed that one of the agents standing guard over him suddenly became... possessed." He paused to check out her reaction. She remained motionless, so he continued. "Once the agent was possessed by who knows what, he went on a shooting rampage in the building, which caused a distraction for the monster to somehow slip out of the building."

To say she was mad was an understatement. She was livid. "You find him, Carol. You find that... that... animal, then you weld spiked chains around his neck, wrists and ankles and cement him in the darkest dungeon there is. You hear me, Carol? You find him for your sister. She's counting on you."

He didn't need to be urged on. Besides, he planned to punish the beast much worse than what his mother recommended. He'd made up his mind immediately after the smoke cleared in the federal building about what he was going to do to the escaped advocate of the devil.

Speaking of the devil ...

"Ma, there's something I failed to mention about the interrogation. It's the most ridiculous thing I've ever heard, and I don't believe it one bit, but I feel I must tell you."

"Go ahead. I'm listening," she said, flamed up.

"Before he owned up to the abductions, he claimed a spirit that's the ruler of the dead named Baron Samedi has condemned the sinners of humanity because of their wickedness. He alleged to be one of the chosen ones that serves this spirit. Essentially, those who serve this dominate spirit are tasked to abduct sinners, which might account for the spate of abductions in Palm Beach County in the late nineties. He claimed the souls of those abducted would be used to give life to this Baron Samedi. Then once Baron Samedi is brought into existence, he'll eradicate sinners and rule over a new world. This is supposed to be happening real soon.

"On my own behalf, I Googled Baron Samedi. To my amazement, there was quite a bit of info on him listed. From what I've read, he's connected with the end of life, and no one can be killed if he refuses to dig their grave. He's also noted for being a powerful sorcerer that's disruptive, obscene and corrupt. There were several depictions of him, too. He's... a skeleton wearing a black suit and top hat with a skull and crossbones on his chest, a scythe in one hand and a wooden coffin in the other. He looks very evil. I never read anything about him being capable of using souls to come to life and take over the world, though."

His first two sentences brought to Ursulanda's mind the Judgment Day in the Book of Revelation. She visualized this spirit Baron Samedi being Jesus Christ rising from the dead and becoming the ruler of all the kings of the world and the chosen ones being the horsemen. She envisioned Baron Samedi and his disciples striking down all those who didn't have the seal of God on their foreheads.

By the time he finished speaking, however, she realized Baron Samedi was actually the Red Dragon in Revelation and the chosen ones were the fallen angels that bore the mark of the beast. *I pray Michael and his army of angels come down from heaven and defeat the dragon and his demons again and throw them into the fiery lake of burning sulfur when the time comes*, she silently invoked before speaking.

"People nowadays may not love God as much as our ancestors did, and they seem to turn toward evil instead of away from it. But we're all God's children. We all fall short, but God never forsakes us. Jesus disagreed with loved ones, but he didn't disown them.

"Take Mackenzie for example, she wasn't a wicked person. She just strayed because the devil tempted her with drugs once I gave her the money y'all father left for you two. Money is the root of all evil, but I believe all things happen for a reason, and if she was given a little time she would've repented and got back in God's grace. So, that demon that took my baby and the others is an inhuman hypocrite. And whoever the hell Baron Sam Eddy is, he's not going to rule nothing. Him and his followers are going to burn in flames forever.

"Now, Carol sweetie, let's remain faithful and pray because our God is an awesome God and no weapon—"

"Formed against me shall prosper," he finished the proverb.

"That's right. You'll catch him again with God's help, for you are God's weapon. Now, bow your head and close your eyes."

She then led them in prayer.

As soon as *Amen* was said, his phone rang and someone knocked on the door.

"Hello?" he said, as Diane walked into the house, running off at the mouth.

On the line was the Sheriff of Martin County. And he had an unexpected development to tell Harden.

Chapter 14

June 10, 2020 - 9:52pm
Royal Palm Beach, FL

It was another night of Netflix and chilling.

And as long as there were Black Lives Matter protests going on in PBC that could get out of hand, lying around the crib and watching movies would be the routine.

"Fo' him ta come up wit these crazy ass movies, Jordan Peele gots ta be smokin' tunechi," Sosa declared. *Get Out* was a mind fucker, but it was like that. It made a nigga go deep into thought. But this *Us* movie was weak. Shit like that ain't likely ta happen. *Get Out*, tho', that can happen. Hell, it's prolly really happenin' now. Who knows what those rich crackas doin' on da sly."

"I dunno what'chu talkin' 'bout nigga. This movie was good as fuck," Cotton contended, curled up against Sosa on the deluxe sectional. "That endin' fucked me all da way up. It makes me wonda if Washington got replicas of us sumwhere undaground."

Phone buzzes

"Damn, nigga, who bombin' ya phone like it's a hotline? That's why ya ain't like da movie, cuz yo' ass was lookin' at 'cha fuckin' phone every five minutes."

Sosa tuned her out and looked to see if who was calling this time was worth answering.

He would've cut the phone off instead of putting it on vibrate, that way he wouldn't have had to deal with Cotton's insecurities every time he checked the phone during the movie. But he kept it on and glimpsed to see if it was money on the line.

Seeing that it was one of his big-time regulars that bought weight, he took the call. "What's good, *baz*?"

"I'm coolin', Sosa. I was just hittin' ya line ta see if ya were bizzy tonite. I'm tryna get out da house."

"I'm at home. I just finished streamin' a flick wit my ol' lady. I'm free now, tho'."

"Who that?" Cotton grumbled, lightly elbowing Sosa in his side. "An' who said you were free? Not me."

"This big money, kill that noise," he told Cotton after he muted the call. He unmuted the caller and said, "What'chu tryna get into tonite, *baz*?"

"I'm tryna hit da club. Hopefully, there's some bad bitches out tonite that ain't worried 'bout social distancin'."

"Which one? Ain't that many open nowadays."

"We can hit da same spot as last time."

"Bet. But what da streets lookin' like out there? Is niggaz lootin' an' wreckin' shit?"

"So far, it's all peaceful."

"Ai'ight. I'ma stop by da RaceTrac near Military Trail an' Community Drive first, baz, ta fill up. I'll call ya when I'm at da spot."

"Already."

"I'm in da wind." Sosa hung up. He then tossed the blanket that covered Cotton and him out of the way and stood.

"You gotta hour ta handle ya bizness," Cotton said at once.

"CC, you trippin'. It's gonna take about thirty minutes ta pick up da work in L-Dubb, anotha fifteen minutes or so ta get ta da RaceTrac ta do da swap, then anotha twenty ta thirty minutes to get back here. An' ain't no tellin' if I run into protestors in da streets an' get held up. So, ta be on da safe side, I need at least two hours ta do all that."

She gave him the evil eye. "You got that. Ya curfew is midnite then."

"Curfew? Ha! You still on that curfew shit, I see. But I'ma grown ass man, not a jit."

"Well, yo' grown ass gonna be sleepin' in ya car in da driveway if ya ain't in this house at twelve on da dot. Period. All jokin' aside, Julius."

"Okay." Sosa bent down and kissed Cotton on her neck. "Try not ta fall asleep cuz I'm tryna go deep an' score in da Cotton Bowl befo' bed."

She heehee'd like Michael Jackson. "If ya make it back here befo' ya deadline, we can make our own version of da movie Da Cotton Club. We'll make it rated triple X. An' you can be da director." She reached out and stroked his captive snake.

He looked at the time on his phone. "Bet," he said before taking off like a bat out of hell.

"Take Dinky wit'cha fo' extra protection in case ya run into protestors. An' wear a mask. Me an' da kids ain't tryna catch that 'rona," she called out.

***

June 10, 2020 - 11:21pm
West Palm Beach, FL

He couldn't fault nobody but himself for the extension. He didn't even try to contest it because he was in the wrong. After all, he knew he'd be penalized for needing help beyond what was necessary.

And the price for the extra favor was trapping an additional two souls, with one of those victims having an ideal body for Baron Samedi to inhabit.

Immediately after being rescued, ZooMan dropped off the grid as well as forwent using any communication devices. He did so because he had no doubt that Francois was NOT going to get him out of another tight spot. He hated shutting down his mission due to snags. Doing nothing just slowed him up from reuniting with his weakening mother. Be that as it may, he used the down time to recuperate and ponder how to move forward with both caution and urgency.

Counting the past four months, he'd spent a total of eleven months inactive because of his slip-ups. But today he was finally breaking cover. Thanks to the nationwide police brutality and racial injustice protests fueled by the unjust killings of Ahmaud Arbery, Breonna Taylor and George Floyd, he could hunt once more.

Of course, the heat was still on him. In fact, the heat was turned up to the max. The day after he became a federal fugitive, he was placed on America's Most Wanted list, ranked number eight. As a result, his picture was aired on the news countrywide and social media newsfeeds daily. While trying to fulfill his obligation, he had to blend in like a chameleon and finesse the last seven victims like a crooked preacher fleecing his congregation.

Right now, ZooMan was gassing up his storage-kept late eighties Buick Regal. Since the best members of the force in the county were tied up keeping the protests under control, he felt somewhat at ease in the open. Yes, he was in disguise, but he could only alter his features so much. Whether he masqueraded as a man or woman, he couldn't lighten his dark skin tone to match a Caucasian or make himself look younger than thirty-eight. After morphing, he virtually looked like a close relative of the publicized picture of him.

"Excuse me, bro."

The jarring voice behind ZooMan jolted him, causing him to wheel around, step back and square up with the masked stranger in designer getup.

"I don't want no smoke, bro," the stranger assured before pulling the N95 mask down and revealing his face.

"What's good then?" asked ZooMan, standoffish.

"I seen this clean ass old school an' wanted ta know if ya were tryna come up off it."

ZooMan didn't reply. He simply sized the man up until the man started to look familiar.

Then ZooMan had an *aha* moment.

"Naw, I ain't gettin' rid of my baby, big dawg. She a valuable antique."

Dog barking

The guy peeped over his shoulder, then said, "Okay. But if you ever change ya mind, give— "The fellow stopped mid-sentence because his eye caught a striking object. "That chain an' chunk ya got on flexin' harder than Arnold," he went on. "I seen a chick wit one just like it a while ago. An' ta be honest, you an' da chick favor each otha."

The eye-catching chunky necklace around ZooMan's neck was a twenty-four-karat gold Cuban-link that was clustered with VVS's, including the clasp. Although a few rappers had the same one, it still was something to write home about. The twenty-four-karat gold charm, however, was one of one. It was a three-dimensional face of Jesus covered with brown gemstones, and it was about the size of an average man's palm. What truly made the charm stand out were the red blood diamond eyes, the sinister grin on black Jesus' face, and the devil horns atop Jesus' head instead of a crown of thorns.

ZooMan stroked his fancy Jesus piece, which by itself weighed close to three pounds. "You prolly seen my sista wit it on. She be stealin' my shit from time ta time so she be snatched in da club." He scratched the right side of his neck.

"Demonica ya sista?"

"Yeah. Y'know my lil' sista?"

"Yeah. We talked a few times. It's been a hot minute since I heard from her, tho'. She good?"

"She doin' okay. She a lil' stressed these days cuz of da pandemic. She workin' overtime as a nurse at St. Mary's Hospital." His stomach itched, so he gave it a scratch. "What they call ya, big dawg?"

"Sosa."

Dog barking increased

Sosa turned and yelled, "Dinky, *femen bek ou!*"

Dinky, in the driver seat of Sosa's ride at at a gas pump, was trying to squeeze out of the halfway open window. She stopped barking on Sosa's command. But she began growling and slobbering all over the window, though, for she sensed danger.

ZooMan was glad the hulking dog was secured in the car because he would've been forced to take it out otherwise. Dogs' insight always detected his true essence, provoking them to go after him, which was why he killed them every chance he got.

"You zoe?"

"Yeah," Sosa replied, turning back around.

Excellent, ZooMan thought with a genuine smile. "That's wassup. I'm half Dominican, half Haitian, like my sista, if she ain't tell ya."

"She told me what she was."

"Cool. So, what'chu said ya name was again, big dawg? I fo'got that quick."

"Sosa."

"Hmmm… I think… I think I rememba Demonica talkin' 'bout ya not that long ago."

"Really?"

ZooMan clawed at the tingling sensation on his left hand. "If I can recall rite, I think I rememba her mention a dope boy from Lake Worth that had a birthday party in a strip club."

Sosa flashed his immaculate porcelain teeth. "That was me. But I can't rememba too much 'bout that nite cuz I was lit... Well, I rememba'd that chain ya sista had on. I barely rememba'd her, tho'."

"Maybe you should hit her up one of these days. She'd love ta hear from ya, fa'sho."

Sosa faltered because Cotton instantly crossed his mind. They were in a great space, and he didn't want to fuck up their renewed harmony. He knew he was wrong for entertaining Demonica with conversation some months ago, which was why he ignored her calls afterwards. "Uh... I—"

"Look, its no pressure. But take my number cuz I know you a D-Boy so y'know Covid travel restrictions got dope in short supply now. Me, tho', I got that A-one work fo' da low-low still. Whateva ya need too." He winked, then pulled out the pre-paid cellphone he bought at Walmart earlier. "An' if ya fuck wit me an' buy in bulk, I'll part wit my baby fo' a good number."

Sosa had already bit the hook.

But now, he was being reeled in.

Fuck his sister, I'm trying to see exactly how low his ticket is, because paying damn near forty per brick and making two grand off it is ridiculous, thought Sosa as he withdrew his phone from his pocket, *I'm also trying to take this Regal off his hands, get it wet, drop a 'Vette engine in it, and squat it on thirty-two-inch Forgies.*

"What's ya name, bro?"

"Around my way I'm known as none otha than ..." ZooMan rubbed his eyes because they began to sting "... Lucifer."

Chapter 15

June 23, 2020 - 12:03pm
Lake Worth Beach, FL

Let's change the narrative in our culture by putting an end to every argument or disagreement resulting in violence. We need to learn how to settle our differences with words and not guns. Instead of turning to violence on the spot over minor altercations and pettiness, put your pride to the side and air out your beef face-to-face and, hopefully, the parties can come to a peaceful resolution.

Sosa couldn't remember what media platform he recently heard that soundbite on, or who the black man was that said it. It was on point and thought-provoking, nevertheless. It took him an hour or two of stirring the marrow of the statement around in his head before he caught onto its relevancy. He grasped how it was pertinent to the predicament he was caught up in.

His inner voice then proceeded to harass him nonstop about the restless issue he had no real intentions of ironing out. His conscience plagued him so much that he eventually gave in. Notwithstanding his aversion to hash things out, he only reached out for the sake of addressing the hearsay he'd got wind of.

It was too much of a delightful, gusty summer afternoon to be cooped up indoors. Although Covid infections and deaths in Florida were the highest in America, that didn't hinder a significant number of Floridians from enjoying summer days like this one, maskless and in groups. Besides, there was no better place to "social distance" than in the great outdoors. And if what was circulating on social media was no lie, the heat from the fireball in the sky was enough to kill the infectious virus, so there was no harm in having fun in the sun.

Sosa might've agreed to the powwow in John Prince Park, but he wasn't taking any chances of being ambushed by the enemy, whether visible or invisible. He was masked up and seated on a bench by the lake with something holding fifty blue tips to keep him company. He was optimistic he wouldn't be meeting with a present-day Judas, but he wasn't quite as positive about making it home coronavirus free.

He got to the scene early so he could pick a position that gave him a tactical advantage. With his eyes scanning the terrain like a raptor and his finger on the trigger, he clocked his surroundings. As the time rolled on, he observed the boats and jet skis whizzing back and forth on the water, the people walking the asphalt track that went around the lake, and the sparse traffic that tootled by.

He was becoming lost in thought when…

Bing

where u at, the text read on his phone.

He typed his response and prepared himself for the unpredictable.

A couple of minutes later, a vehicle pulled up. The person got out of the car by themselves and looked over the landscape. They then typed on their phone and waited. Once they got a quick response, they scanned the area once more until they spotted Sosa and headed towards him.

"Lemme guess, you way down here cuz ya thought I was on some bullshit."

"Are ya on some bullshit?" Sosa replied with his rod visible.

"Betta safe than sorry, huh?" Wes said, seeing the fire with an extension on it. He took a seat on the vacant bench beside Sosa's. "Well, I thought we'd neva be able ta cross paths again witout it bein' bust on sight."

Sosa remained alert, head on a swivel. "We here now so let's get straight to it. Is what I heard 'bout Peezy true?"

"Yeah."

"How y'know it is?"

"Becuz I been keepin' in touch wit Peezy's folks eva since he went missin'. Peezy's pops told me a few weeks ago that da cop workin' his case found out two important things. Da first was that some nigga carjacked Peezy an' drove off wit him in da car."

"My dawg IronHead's hot-in-da-ass BM an' a few othas told us what went down that nite. That wasn't us, tho'." Sosa took a second to study Wes's eyes. "Look, it ain't a secret that Peezy an' ya homies been in da hood fuckin' Shirley, her sista Eunice an' da hoes that be wit 'em. I didn't care, an' neitha did da rest of my bros. IronHead, howeva, ain't like da fact niggaz was fuckin' da air outta his BM. He ain't blame nobody but her, tho'. He just beat her ass like he was Ike an' she was Tina, but she still be givin' that box up freely.

"So, whoeva that was that took Peezy wasn't us or a nigga we know, or sumone that anybody 'round da hood knows. On some real nigga shit, I'm still tryna find out who that nigga was that stirred up shit on our turf."

Wes sighed. "I knew from da jump y'all boyz ain't have shit ta do wit Peezy disappearin'. I tried ta tell my dawgz you wouldn't violate da cease-fire we shook on becuz you ain't two-faced. But my dawgz were so determined ta accuse y'all fo' killin' Peezy becuz he was last seen on y'all block."

"If ya knew I ain't that type of nigga, Wes, why ya ain't stop ya bros from hittin' my spot then?"

"Loyalty," Wes answered brusquely. "Once my dawgz got it in their heads that they were gonna run down on y'all, my loyalty was what made me go along. I know ya undastand that. Trust me, tho', I wanted ta hit 'cha up first ta see what'chu knew 'bout da situation. But my dawgz were gonna spin on y'all no matter what. Their minds were made up, an' I couldn't go against da grain, so callin' ya was pointless."

Indeed, Sosa understood. If the shoe was on the other foot, he wouldn't have let his bros down either. Plus, he knew it was better to kill a friend in error than to let an enemy live to smile in your face. "Why you ain't pick up when I called ya after da fact?"

"I ain't answer becuz... becuz... I dunno why I didn't answer." Wes shrugged. "I mean, what was I 'posed ta say, anyway. We'd just merked ya homie. Wasn't nuttin' ta say after repayin' y'all back fo' supposedly takin' one of ours. I just knew it was on like Donkey Kong at that point."

"Were you there that nite?" Sosa asked, eagle-eyeing Wes for any indication of dishonesty.

Wes swallowed. "Yeah. I was da getaway driver."

Sosa's trigger finger twitched. "How'd y'know that was our trap?"

"We found out on some fluke shit. We were bendin' y'all corners in a splack four deep when we saw a random junkie type muthafucka wit a lawn mower. We pulled up on him an' asked where we could score. He was hesitant ta tell us at first, but quickly changed his mind when we offered ta cop him whateva he wanted. He told us where ya spot was an' we met him there. Once we confirmed it was y'all spot, we left an' doubled back later that nite."

Goddamn Gotcha Pa, Sosa said to himself, *you'll sell your soul for some dope.*

Then, Sosa asked, "What was da second thing da cop found out 'bout Peezy?"

"He said that Peezy's phone location showed him bein' in Martin County befo' his phone stopped workin'. That there led da cop ta believe that Peezy was snatched up by da same muthafucka niggaz in da street been callin' Da BoogeyMan. I woulda neva thought in a million years sumone I knew would be kidnapped, let alone by da creep that took so many othas ova da years. But da cop said wit certainty that Peezy was abducted. Befo' Peezy's pops told me what da cop said, tho', it neva seriously crossed my mind that Da BoogeyMan might'a got my nigga."

Prior to now, it also never occurred to Sosa that Peezy could've been a victim of Da BoogeyMan, the farcical name given to the mysterious kidnapper by people in the hood and on social media. He was well aware of the big-name niggas that had just up and disappeared off the face of the earth. He knew some of them personally. Moreover, he heard that the homies of the missing hood superstars had picked off niggas they suspected of foul play... just like Wes did.

The BoogeyMan had caused a ton of blood to spill in the streets, and niggas were either too oblivious or too green to know, or want to know, who was actually behind it all.

Once it all made sense to Sosa, he took his finger off the trigger. "Didn't that muthafucka escape da Fed buildin' in downtown West Palm a day after dem folks locked him up?"

"Yeah. Da old zoe cleared it when a Fed agent went ape shit up in there. Da news said da agent prolly went off suddenly becuz of da tumor in his brain he ain't know he had. So, that muthafucka was at da rite place an' rite time. Lucky bitch." Wes grimaced. "Now da FBI, DEA, ATF, US Marshalls, sheriffs, local police... Hell, er'body!... lookin' fo' that nigga. Even me an' my dawgz keepin' a eye out fo' that nigga. That old muthafucka didn't just cause us ta lose good niggaz over misreadin' da lick an' da streets gettin' outta control. Me an' my dawgz lost... an' still losin'... alotta bread becuz we can't fully focus on gettin' ta da bag."

"l feel ya on that tip. My numbers ain't been up since this shit kicked off. An' this shortage ain't makin' it no betta. I'm tryin' get back ta where I was befo' all these homicides an' chaos.

"I need a betta plug ta recoup losses. These Puerto Ricans I fuck wit ain't sellin' me nuttin' ova a bird nowadays. An' they chargin' me forty-two bandz fo' it." He sighed exasperatedly. "I wish my dawg JuneBug was still in da game so we could cop sumthin' togetha like we did back in da day."

With that being said, Sosa began thinking about whether or not things could be forgiven and forgotten so easily. Sure, Wes had forgiven and started to forget when his bros overreacted and rolled through H.O.L. and blew on whosoever for Peezy's disrespectful post on InstaGram. But his bros didn't kill or critically wound nobody then. Wes and his dawgs, however, falsely accused him and his squad and killed Huff and left Pressure with four slugs in him. It wasn't too much of a difference between the two situations, but what Wes did was out of line in his eyes.

After a minute had passed, Sosa said, "Me an' you can be cool again. *But,* it's gonna take sumtime fo' me ta get my boyz ta let this shit go."

"Your dawgz an' mine gotta play past what can't be undone, Sosa. Life too short. We got families ta feed. Peezy an' 360 gone ova bullshit, so I gotta take care of their peeps. An' my immuno-compromised nigga John-John up in JFK Hospital on a ventilator fightin' off that punk-ass virus, so I gotta take care of his brothas an' sistas an' his bills till he get outta that bitch. I gotta get my bread up fo' all that."

"Damn. My bro Cano just went ta JFK last nite cuz he havin' trouble breathin'. He most likely got Covid, too."

"See, we got mo' important shit on our plate ta see 'bout than ta be at each otha's throats. Da truth is out there now, an'

I apologize fo' me an' my crew actions. I just hope we can move forward an' run da bag up cuz it's too many junkies an' square-ass niggaz out here wit stimulus checks an' bogus PPP loans ta blow that wanna jump in da game. Them lames see there's a drought, so they see a opportunity ta come up. I'm tryna chew on 'em all ASAP. Like how they got essential workers, I'm tryna be a essential trapper, a Trap God in Palm Beach. An' I will be once I find a betta plug wit dope on deck an' lower prices."

Since Sosa extended the olive branch to Wes, and they both had near identical ambitions, he decided to lend a hand and share his plug with him this time around. "I got this new connect, Wes, an' he got whateva fo' a reasonable tag. So, if we put our cheese togetha again, we can getta pack fo' da low-low."

"Ya plug on that level?" Wes asked with a raised brow.

"I mean... I only fucked wit him once so far. I gave him a trial run, an' he came through like he said."

"Was whateva you copped stepped on heavy?"

"His coke was a major upgrade from what I been gettin'. I'ma try him out one mo' time, tho', just ta make sho' he ain't no fraud. If he come through again wit some good shit, I'ma put my otha plug on da bench an' holla at'cha fo' da third order."

"Bet." Wes smiled and held out his hand.

"Naw, we ain't doin' that," Sosa said, looking at Wes' hand as if it was smeared with shit.

"What?" asked Wes, searching for the problem.

"You ain't gon' have me in ICU wit a tube shoved down my throat. We can bump elbows or salute each otha."

Wes laughed before sticking out his elbow.

"Now, peep game," Sosa began once they touched elbows, "if we gonna do this, you gotta keep ya niggaz in line, an' I'ma do da same. Ain't no sense in us deadin' shit an' our homies still at war. I'ma take advantage of this plug so we all can eat. It's time ta put da guns down an' get our bags up.

"An' last but not least, we ain't leavin' each otha in da dark no mo'. If you hear some bullshit 'bout me that affects you, you hit me up ASAP ta make sho' it is what it is. I'ma keep it a buck wit'cha."

"As long as you do da same, we on da same page then."

"Say less."

They said a few more words and, now reconciled, parted ways.

***

June 23, 2020 - 4:17pm
Boynton Beach, FL

"Can he be caught again?"

"That remains to be seen," Harden answered Chief Brewster's question, which happened to be a question everybody seemed to be asking a lot lately. "Despite many saying he made off back to Haiti, I say he's still in this county."

The overweight chief reclined in his ergonomic office chair, causing it to creak menacingly from his heftiness. "How can you be so sure, Harden? The bastard has been on the loose for nearly five months now and nobody has seen him. Five months is ample time for him to find his way back to that shithole country. So, why do you think the destined-to-die asshole would stick around?"

It had been quite a while since the last time Chief Brewster requested to see Harden in his office. The old warhorse usually let him be, and Harden returned the favor. However, once in a blue moon, he looked for Harden to give him an update on the *RISING SUN* case. He wanted to send for Harden right after the cataclysm in downtown WPB, but he gave Harden time to reflect over the incident.

"Vilsaint remains in Palm Beach County, hiding out until he feels it's safe to resume kidnapping, because, according to him, he's on a satanical mission for an evil spirit. He's going to see his mission through at any cost, Brewster... just like whoever it was in this county kidnapping in the nineties."

"But those kidnappings back then came to a halt."

"And you never wondered why they stopped? Nobody was ever arrested for the reported forty-eight people that mysteriously disappeared and were never found. Not very long ago I used to believe the same person was behind the nineties rampage and the recent one. But I now surmise that whoever it was doing those kidnappings back then shared the exact same beliefs as Vilsaint and they completed their mission by meeting their quota. Then others with the same beliefs also kidnapped people they viewed as evil and met their goals in Jackson, Mississippi, Washington, DC, and Dayton, Ohio, before Vilsaint went on his tear."

Chief Brewster sat upright. "Harden, it's hard to believe that those cities are linked by people that bought the same pipe dream. I, for one, had a firm conviction that the latter-day kidnappings were the work of a group of sex-traffickers. But I... I—" He took a moment to gather his thoughts.

"I've seen a lot in my thirty-two years on the force, Harden, so I know anything is possible. Saying that, that repugnant prick is more than capable of jumping from city to city and kidnapping... miscreants like he's Batman. And I suspect that he simply got reckless with age, which resulted in him being collared at long last."

"After seeing with my own two eyes what took place that day, Brewster, I now know myself that supernatural things can happen. When I reflect on the absurd things I heard Vilsaint say during that interrogation prior to him taking flight, I just don't cavalierly discount voodoo now. I no longer consider Vilsaint to be a brainwashed crackpot. I etched the intense look in his eyes in my mind, and I ultimately concluded that he wholeheartedly believes his malicious acts will bring about a cleansing of the earth. So, Vilsaint is right up under our noses and isn't going anywhere until he fulfills his mission. Trust me, Brewster."

"Alright, Harden. You've been working this case longer than anybody in this entire county, so nobody knows better than you. I know you know what you're doing, and I value your opinions. However, since time is of the essence now, you need someone that can give you a new perspective, someone with a fresh point of view. So, I'm assigning the newbie Noah Schw—"

"Negative, Brewster," Harden broke in. "I will not. I work best by myself, and you know—"

"Yes, yes, I know it," Chief Brewster broke back in. "But the situation at hand calls for it. The time has come for you to work with a partner. Two heads are better than one, haven't you heard?" Chief Brewster observed the frown that formed on Harden's face deepen, so he added, "You've always been a good cop, Harden. And because of that, there's no one better in the department I'd choose for Noah to partner with. Admittedly, though, you're not a cop I'd want Noah to model himself after because he's still impressionable and you're mean as a bulldog."

"Yes, I am, Brewster. And to recapture this piece of crap, I'll have the perseverance of a bulldog, too.

Harden made a quick exit and retreated to his messy workspace. He put his blazer on the coat tree and sat down to turn over Chief Brewster's directive in his head for a moment. He marveled at the piles of folders while factoring how he was going to get out of working with…

Knock at door

"Heavens to Betsy, Harden! I didn't think it was possible for your desk to be more unkempt than the last time I saw it."

I must change the unwritten policy of people barging into my office without my verbal permission, Harden thought, *I've reached my breaking point.*

"How has your day been so far?" Noah asked, approaching the desk. Still, there was no chair, so he stood.

"On a good day, I'm okay," Harden replied temperately, trying not to come down hard on his newly assigned partner. "And on a bad day, I'm okay. Now, what do you want?"

"Well, I seen you just leave out of Chief Brewster's office with a face as if you'd sucked on a lemon, so that tells me the chief told you the new arrangement."

"Yes. And?"

"And I'm wondering what can I do to help."

Harden blindly picked a file off a stack, opened it, and acted like he was reading it. "You're old enough to have heard the cliché… You can help by staying out of my way."

Noah walked over to the enlarged map of Palm Beach County that was placed on the wall beside Harden's desk. "If I'm going to be of use, could you please share with me what the red, blue, green and yellow pins signify. I'm very quick to learn so you won't have to repeat yourself."

On a whim, Harden decided to use Noah's willingness to pitch in. He put down the folder, got to his feet and joined Noah. "The pins on this represent the last known locations of all the people that've been reported missing. The red ones are for those that have absolutely nothing, no helpful leads or witnesses, that can point me in any direction. The blues ones are for those that have leads and witnesses. They helped me to piece together a possible motive and a profile of the suspect. Yellow is for John and Jane Does. They're people from out of town with no jobs or places to stay. As you see, it's only a handful of them."

Silence.

"And the green ones, who are they? Why are they grouped like that at the Palm Beach, Martin County line?"

The green pins were recent additions. They took the place of other colored pins once Harden got up-to-date locations from the geofencing data. And they were Harden's ground zero.

"Those... They are... They're not in use," Harden misled Noah. "Anyhow, there is something I need you to follow up on for me... I mean, for *us*, partner."

Noah's gullibility caused him to say, "Shoot."

Harden smiled. "I need you to go to the stations... DO NOT CALL... in Riviera, West Palm, Lake Worth, and Delray and see if there have been any people reported missing lately. If there are new missing persons, get those files and bring them back to me at once, okay?"

"No sweat. I'll do that right away." Noah left.

"That was easy," Harden said to himself as he sat back down. He then checked his phone to see if any of the stations he'd mentioned, and more, had sent him a text with any new missing persons. There were no new texts. "I'll just have to continue to find meaningless tasks for him to do to keep him out of my way, because I feel that this will all be over shortly."

Chapter 16

February 12, 2013 - 10:37pm
Somewhere in Martin County, FL

The sensation of being on fire caused her to regain consciousness.

She slowly opened her inflamed eyes. She was lying face-up on a hard surface. In her limited view was a ceiling. On the ceiling's facade was a dynamic glow, and it gave her the impression she was floating above a giant glass of orange soda. The hallucinatory effect left her briefly mesmerized until...

"I call upon Papa Legba, the Gatekeeper. Open the gate ..."

She was brought back to reality by that dreadful voice. She got goosebumps. As her abductor murmured in a low monotonous tone, she attempted to talk, but the pain in her fractured jaw was too much to bear. She tried to get up but couldn't. She strained to lift her aching head so she could figure out what was restricting her movement.

She became paralyzed right away at what she saw.

No, the lined-up black and purple candles she spotted just beyond her feet weren't the reason for her acute paralysis. It was seeing her naked body encircled with rope from her chest down to her ankles that left her frozen.

She frantically looked to the left and saw a row of candles. She observed more candles when she turned her head to the right. What's going on here? Why am I in the middle of a ring of fire? Am I being sacrificed or something? *she asked herself as she started to tilt her head back.* Please, God, if you hear me, forgive me because I don't want to die.

Standing just outside of the circle's perimeter she saw him, and he held a clay pot in his hands. The ghoulish pitch in his voice and his heinous expression prompted her to try to break loose in a last-ditch effort.

"I now call upon the Great Spirit Baron Samedi. By exercising the power vested in me by you, oh, Exalted One, I hereby seize the soul of this unclean life form and entrap it for safekeeping. My Master I vow to safeguard this soul until the day you draw on its energy to come into existence. Please, Honorable Baron Samedi, accept this sacrifice so your will may be done on this immoral planet soon."

As he launched into a repetitive chant in Creole, an unexplainable feeling suddenly hit her chest. She began having trouble getting air. Her lungs seemed to be constricting. She stopped moving in case her struggling was causing her to hyperventilate or the ropes to tighten. After a while of lying motionless and focusing on her breathing, she realized she wasn't taking in as much air as she was letting out. It was as if her chest cavity was in a vise.

On the verge of passing out from the invisible force weighing down on her chest, she watched, in confusion and horror, a radiant vapor gradually discharge out of her mouth. Her heavy eyes followed the emission as it wafted directly into the clay pot he held. Nearing unconsciousness, she observed the vapor thinning out. Mama, I'm sorry for being disobedient and for using most of the money you gave me on drugs, *she said to herself as tears trickled down the side of her once angelic face.* And I'm sorry Carol for never protecting you like a big sister should have.

Mackenzie gasped for air twice before taking her final breath.

ZooMan, meanwhile, waited for the last of her life force to drift into the clay pot. He placed the cork on it once the extraction was over. "That was… exciting."

As instructed, he walked to the master bedroom's closet and opened it. To the right in the closet, he set down the govi *(go-Vee), which was an earthen receptacle the souls of the dead may be housed in. He looked to the other side where the vacant clay pots were stored and said, "I don't know why Francois do this, but I fill these sixty-five fast." He shut the closet door.*

Thereafter, ZooMan strode back over to the lifeless body. He wasn't told what to do with the corpses. It took him roughly ten minutes of thinking while staring at the dead woman before he devised two plans.

He set out tackling the plan he was going to use this one time. The first step was undoing the rope and putting her clothes back on. The following step was hauling her back to the car. He then drove approximately an hour before he located the perfect spot, which happened to be a secluded area along the shore of Lake Okeechobee. The final steps were grabbing her body out of the car, fastening rocks to her, wading into the dark, cold water and releasing her.

"Your body have good resting place, cherie," he said aloud, sloshing out of the water. "The others will be food for my snakes and pigs that I take to the house soon."

ZooMan got into his car and drove off. His next destination was Miami to report his inaugural abduction to Francois. After that, he was heading back to PBC to look for his second victim.

***

July 1, 2020 - 10:44pm
Miami, FL

ZooMan hung a left on Sixty-Third Street and parked seconds later. He got out of the pre-owned white F-150 bearing goodies in a plastic grocery bag. With the streets bustling around him, he sauntered up to the residence he was sure would be the last time he visited.

Apart from his must-have coruscating necklace, he was not dressy tonight. Because the full power of the federal government had come down on him, and the quarter-million-dollar reward on his head, he wore a casual black v-neck shirt, blue jeans and work boots. He was purposely driving the most popular truck in America with construction and American flag decals. He sought to blend in with the commoners. He confidently felt at home and invisible in Little Haiti, having no fear at all being around his stock. But he was taking no chances.

Without announcing himself, he opened the rickety door. The foul odor and ever-present heat greeted him. His feline optics enhanced as he moved through the darkness toward the altar. Once in front of it, he put the bag he held down on the floor and plucked the sooty black candle from its chipped glass holder. He smeared the unrefined oil over the candle, put it back in the holder and set fire to it.

In the twinkling of ZooMan's eyes, as expected, the infernal priest broke out of the shadows. He then sidled in ZooMan's direction.

"*Kisa'k nouvo la, zanmi'm?* I know you haven't finished your mission, so what have I done to deserve this unsolicited visit?"

"What HAVEN'T you done?" replied ZooMan.

"Sheesh, you said that as if I made your life more miserable than it was before I saved you from the damnation that's coming soon. You should be thankful."

ZooMan wasn't there to play games and make small talk. He was there for a specific reason. "Look, I didn't come to hear you say for the hundredth time how thankful I should be. I came to talk to Baron Samedi."

The demand surprised Francois. As a rule, it was HE that determined when ZooMan could see Baron Samedi.

"For what reason? I thought all of your concerns had been cleared up during the last time you two conversed."

"You're the one with the gift of ESP, so you should know why I want to see him."

"Don't patronize me. You've become too crafty and farsighted for your own good. Over time you've learned how to effectively shield your thoughts, allowing me to only see what you want me to see nowadays."

"That's how I like it. Now, please stop wasting time and invoke Baron Samedi."

Francois grunted at ZooMan with displeasure. He didn't know what ZooMan was up to, but he complied. "I'll do it. But remember, don't mention anything we agreed to, including the extra people you're required to obtain. You know the penalty for insubordination."

Francois then approached the altar. He lit a red candle and proceeded to call upon the Gatekeeper Papa Legba first to open the portal between the worlds. Once the doorway was opened for Baron Samedi, and he began slipping into a trance, he latched onto the machete and struck the floor three times. Lastly, he formed three x's on the floor with graveyard soil.

Moments later, the soon-to-be Ruler of Earth seized Francois' body.

Baron Samedi began laughing loudly and dancing in a sexually suggestive manner all around the empty living room. When he was finished, he crept up on ZooMan.

Avoiding direct eye contact, ZooMan grabbed the bag he'd brought and presented it to Baron Samedi.

Baron Samedi took the bag without hesitation. He looked in it, and the contents made him smile from ear to ear. There were all of his preferences: a bottle of Barbancourt rum with twenty-one red chili peppers within, a ten-piece box of Popeye's chicken, and a cedar case of Cuban cigars. With joy, he pulled out the rum, put the bag down, uncapped the bottle and knocked back a couple of huge swigs. He then offered the bottle to ZooMan.

ZooMan, who didn't indulge in alcohol or drugs, eagerly grasped the bottle. Saying no to the extremely generous and best loved *lwa* in Haiti was considered insulting, so he arrived prepared to imbibe the spicy rum. He had learned from prior experience that drinking rum laced with hot chilies set his mouth and throat on fire, as well as aggravated his stomach so much that he vomited not long after drinking. All of which made Baron Samedi crack up.

ZooMan tossed back a few sips and passed the bottle back to Baron Samedi. Having drunk some milk before getting out of the truck, his mouth and throat didn't burn as much. And the liquid fire filling his stomach didn't instantly disturb it like it had the last two times he'd drunk with Samedi.

Again, Baron Samedi hoisted the bottle to his lips for two or three gulps. Half the bottle was gone when he put it down on the altar. Next, he removed the fried chicken from the bag and said while opening the box, "What is the essence of this sudden engagement?" He fisted a breast, bit off a mouthful and chewed it bearishly.

Straightaway, ZooMan opened up. "Master, your arrival has been put off to a later time. Because of *bokor* Francois Gedeon's aid after my recklessness led me to be detained in federal custody, he requested that I pay him back by abducting two additional people. Thus, instead of having two to capture before the ritual to bring you to life can commence, I'm back to four. And now that my identity is known nationally, it may take a while to—"

"The additional souls serve what purpose?" Baron Samedi jumped in, talking with his mouth full.

"My Master, Francois is only interested in the bodies, not the souls. You'll be settling permanently into the body of my last victim, according to Francois. He didn't say what the other was for."

Baron Samedi crushed the lukewarm juicy white meat, bones and all, and grabbed a thigh. "Disregard Francois' foolish injunction. Obtain your last two souls posthaste. My displeasure with mankind has peaked. I'm ready to lay waste to the ungrateful habitants of this oppressive world before that man-made pathogen that's ravishing the planet steals my glory." He tore a chunk out of the dark meat.

"What about the body you'll take possession of?"

Baron Samedi finished wolfing down on the savory meat before responding. "I can occupy the corpse of the final pariah. Just guarantee the corpse is a male that's in quintessential condition."

"Don't worry, Master."

"Now, is there—" *Burp!* "—another matter you need addressed?"

"Yes."

"Speak, devoted one," Baron Samedi said, retrieving the wood box of cigars from the bag.

Prior to showing up there, ZooMan had decided, if given the chance, he'd face up to Baron Samedi like he was an ordinary mortal being. He'd planned to look him in the eyes and give him the rundown on everything he never had the opportunity to do before.

No more secrets, he concluded. *To hell with Francois and his threats.*

"Master, bear with what I have to say, for this will be wordy," ZooMan proclaimed, bravely gazing into the spectral eyes of Baron Samedi.

Baron Samedi, normally commanding the spotlight during his cameo, lit the cigar, puffed on it, and tuned in.

"Before I started this mission, I was torn about what I had to do to repay Francois for saving my life. Although I hated the requirement of keeping away from the people that depended on me, I came to appreciate my second chance at life, and I gladly took on my obligation. I had absolutely no idea whatsoever why Francois tasked me with kidnapping the unlawful and trapping their souls. But quite frankly, I didn't want to know why. I just wanted to satisfy my debt and get on with life.

"However, the first time Francois bailed me out for not being careful was when he explained that I was a small part of a bigger machine. I was completely in the dark about your plan to purge the earth before our introductory meeting. Once I was in the know, I became torn once again because I thought about the fate of the loved ones I took care of. Still, I handled my business, cleaning up my act and educating myself as I moved on at a leisurely pace. All the while I was trying to figure out how to save my loved ones from your wrath.

"Then my mother became ill. At that point, I told Francois about my mother's illness and how I needed to be there for her. Francois wouldn't give an inch of ground on the terms we agreed upon, though, which pissed me the fuck off. But he taught me how to transform my appearance so I could achieve my mission expeditiously. Moreover, he transferred a portion of his power into an amulet and gave it to me. I customized it so I could stand out and fit in with my targets." He displayed the charm.

"Next, I wanted to speak to you about restoring my mother and sparing her from what's to come. Francois was against that. Instead, he promised he'd talk you into giving me unlimited powers once I was finished so I could heal my

179

mother myself and give her refuge from your divine punishment. The catch, though, was if I discussed with you anything he promised me, he'd add an additional thirty souls to my assignment. That's why I never had much to say during our occasional meetings until today. Francois' shady behavior and actions in the past have finally made me approach you with this."

Baron Samedi puffed on the aromatic cigar and blew out a cloud of smoke. "I welcome your candor. I lacked all knowledge of the affairs between you and Francois Gedeon. I have more important matters to mind than being interested in the trivial.

"Now, I will inform YOU about all of Francois' misleading utterances and actions. To start, the evening you were shot and subsequently rescued by Francois Gedeon, sorry to say, you were not going to succumb to your injuries. I was not digging your grave that day." He revelled in the shocked look on ZooMan's mug.

"Secondly, your obligation to reserve souls for my reincarnation was originally Francois' burden to bear. The cunning Francois exploited your tragedy and put a *wanga* (one-Gar) spell on you. You were cursed the moment you accepted his terms. As for the amulet, the longer you wield it, the worse the *wanga* gets. Thus, you have become the living embodiment of Francois' will, doing what he was commissioned to do. Once your task has been fulfilled, Francois Gedeon more than likely will zombify you, and you'd have no will left to undo what was done to you. So, essentially, you are Francois' slave, and will forever be... even after I purge this world." While soaking in the mean mug look on ZooMan's face, he luxuriously puffed on his cigar.

"The next issue is Francois' pledge to coax me to grant you unlimited powers. To level with you, that's laughable." He roared in laughter. "No way will I bestow you, or

Francois, or any of my adherents, for that matter, absolute power. My only gifts to you and the others that have took part in my grand scheme are immortality and ambassadorship with select powers. I will be the only one wielding limitless capability on this worthless planet." With a curled lip, he gave ZooMan an evil look to make sure his point was made.

"And lastly, your mother's gradual decline in health is due to a powerful *expedition mort* being placed on her. Unfortunately, I will not undo the hex. But I will give immunity to your mother - and only your mother - from condemnation and bring her into our fold once you conclude your duty."

"But once I conclude my duty, I will be Francois' slave. That's what you said a minute ago."

"No worries, devoted one. You will be no one's slave once done."

Through gritted teeth, ZooMan grunted, "My Master, since you had to agree to the spiritual attack on my mother after the proper appeals and offerings were made to you, please tell me who was the person, or persons, that placed the spell on her so I can personally pay them back in time."

Baron Samedi puffed on the cigar twice before flicking the inch-long ash on the floor. "Francois Gedeon hexed your mother."

The admission immediately left ZooMan lightheaded.

"Anything else you have need of, devoted one?"

Out of all people, why my mother, Francois? was what ZooMan craved to know. He couldn't wait to confront Francois with this new request.

In order to get down to the nitty-gritty without further delay, his reply to Baron Samedi was, "No, my Master."

"Albeit you were used as a pawn by Francois Gedeon, I must say before I bid you adieu that I'll be pleased to have you as an envoy. In the few sessions we have convened, I can sincerely say you are more commendable than Francois will ever be. My apologies for never giving you the liberty to explain who you were and how you got involved in this plot. Obviously, I was too busy babbling during the previous encounters. But I'm looking forward to us deliberating together again soon. And as long as you remain allegiant, and you don't become duplicitous and envious like Francois Gedeon... " He winked at ZooMan. " ...you'll become my trusted advisor."

And with that, Baron Samedi puffed on the cigar once more, took a gulp of the rum, chomped into a chicken leg, then faded back to govern over the dead in his realm.

The flames on the red and black candles went out.

Drained, Francois swallowed the remaining food in his mouth and put the cigar on the altar. "Have you finally—" He stopped short. "Why are you looking at me like that?"

"Pitit bouzen," ZooMan yelled as he charged Francois. He plowed into Francois and drove him into the altar, knocking it over. "You intentionally put a hex on my mother." With his left hand clutching Francois' throat, he drilled him in the face several times. "I want to know why, you son of a bitch." He drew back to wallop Francois again.

Francois, though unhealthy in appearance, broke free and shoved ZooMan with great force. His maneuver caused him to soar across the room. A millisecond after ZooMan crashed into the wall and crumpled to the floor, Francois was upon him. He effortlessly lifted ZooMan up by the solid necklace and thrust him into the rotten wall, literally. He extracted a nearly unconscious ZooMan from the wall and pulled him to within an inch of his own bloodied face. "I knew one of these days you'd defy me. I guess today is that day. It was only a matter of time before you gave in to your curiosity." Bloody spittle spattered ZooMan's face with every syllable he spoke. "I'd destroy you, you weakling. But I know after your little talk with Baron Samedi, he'll refuse to take you." Then, like a ferocious canine, he snapped at ZooMan's face three times.

"Wh-why… why my mother?" ZooMan stammered faintly. "I-I've done every… everything you asked."

"That, you certainly have done. But, if you must know, after I helped get you out of your first screw up, you moved forward being too cautious. That close call had you second-guessing your every move, so I chose to act. You needed motivating. I knew your mother, who you love dearly, would be the energizer you required. I knew your desire to save her would make you pick up the pace." He released a feeble ZooMan after his confession and took a step back, then continued.

"This undertaking that I agreed to do twenty years ago when I was a young visionary has overburdened me. I didn't know at the time that acquiring and stowing souls would be so… exhausting, to say the least. I just wanted to prove to Baron Samedi that he appointed the right one for the job. I was simply naive to think I could gather one thousand souls all by myself. After I captured over a hundred souls in two cities in four years, I knew I needed help. I became frustrated, though, when none of the faithful voodooists I contacted wanted to fall in with the cleansing of the world, so I decided to use spells on gullible and vulnerable West Indians and make them carry the rest of my load. Just like I've done to you, I secretly put hexes on their loved ones to propel them forward when they lollygagged." He got back in close to ZooMan's face.

"Now that you know it all, it doesn't change anything. Your life still belongs to me, and Baron Samedi can't save your neck. Him and I have an agreement just like you and I have. So, you'll finish your contract and get those two extra people or it's the inside of a *govi* where you'll dwell for eternity. You understand?"

Silence.

"Do you understand?" Francois yelled in a ghastly voice, showering ZooMan's face with viscous blood.

ZooMan nodded in agreement as Francois' thickened blood mixed with spit dripped down his face.

"*Bon. Sa bon anpil,*" he said before backing away from ZooMan. "Now, if you need drugs, you get it, then leave." Just before he receded into the darkness, he added, "Oh, and because you dared to go against me, you have three days to finish this up. Also, I insist that you don't harm the last two. I want them in immaculate condition the night of the ritual."

Then Francois vanished from sight.

And ZooMan, who didn't need to reup, shuffled off irate and feeling like a jackass. *Why did you have to die, Virgil?* he thought after entering the truck. *Fate is kicking my ass.*

Chapter 17

July 4, 2020 - 4:29am
Royal Palm Beach, FL

The odd tombstone was in the middle of the street in front of the church. Except for the lone streetlight that illuminated the marker in a paranormal yellowish light, the street was quiet and deserted. Shadows of creatures stood out on the sidewalk surrounding the streetlight. It seemed as if there were more shadows of the creatures than there were shadows of other things.

Snaillike and spooked, he sidestepped up to the tombstone on legs that trembled like a newborn calf. As he got closer to the unmarked tombstone, his thumping pulse grew louder and clearer in his ears. Once he got right up to it, he looked down and noticed he was standing on a rectangular patch of dirt instead of a paved surface.

An indistinct buzzing sound was the next thing he heard. It took him a while before he realized the droning was coming from under his feet. Spontaneously, he knelt and put a hand on the soft dirt. The vibrations he felt reverberated within his body.

"Help me."

Though muffled, there was no mistaking that he heard the voice. He lowered his head until his ear came in contact with the ground.

"Julius, help."

Hearing his birth name being called from the grave was petrifying. Yet he immediately got to digging with his bare hands. The more dirt he scooped out the more the voice pled for help. By the time he hit something solid, most of his fingernails had been ripped off. Still, with bleeding fingertips, he excavated dirt until he uncovered an old-fashioned plywood box coffin.

Pounding

"Help me! Get me out of here! Please, hurry!"

He wanted to let the person know he was there but, strangely, he couldn't speak.

At last, he cleared out enough dirt to allow him to open the coffin. Lacking a crowbar or a tool he could use to pry open the box, he employed the little strength he had left to force the coffin open.

When he was able to glance into the coffin, he couldn't believe his eyes. Looking up at him was his own putrefying body. Flies and maggots covered his face, feasting on the remaining flesh. A colossal python emerged from his hollow abdomen and hissed at him. He stood up in a hurry. He swiftly reached skyward for the edge of the grave while keeping an eye on the snake. His raw fingertips just barely got a hold of the ledge. He pulled himself up.

He thought he was safe once his head popped out of the hole. But glowing red eyes and fangs like a sabretooth tiger met him head on. It was a menacing black panther, and the big cat swiped at him with a large paw with nine-inch nails. He let go of the ledge in the nick of time. He fell back into the hole and landed hard on his back, knocking the wind out of him. The big cat looked down at him and roared. He sat up. Something caused him to touch his throat. The python had coiled around his neck and body and began constricting. He tried to uncoil the powerful snake but was pulled backwards. He was in the coffin, lying next to himself, when the lid slammed shut. Hysteria overcame him. He screamed but nothing came out. He heard dirt hitting the lid, which indicated he was being buried alive. He fought in the darkness to get free of the python before it asphyxiated him. Then...

"You're not going anywhere, Julius, so stop fighting," the corpse yelled in his ear. "You're going to rot in hell where you belong. So, welcome home. Ha Ha Haaaa!"

The laughter persisted until...

Sosa woke up flailing and kicking and punching the sheets and blanket. He was also wailing like a banshee and sweating like he'd just finished a marathon.

"Julius."

"No," he bellowed as a chill ran down his spine.

"Baby, open your eyes," Cotton squealed, shielding herself from Sosa's blows. "Sosa, please, open your eyes!"

Sosa eyes abruptly shot open. Wide eyed with fear and wheezing abnormally, he scanned his surroundings first. He frantically swatted at his neck next. "Wh... where is it?"

"Where is what, Julius? Baby, you scarin' me."

"Da snake. An'... An' my dead body."

"Your what?" Cotton asked, shaken. She got her phone off the nightstand and used it to cut on the lights. "Look, there's no snake or... or dead body, baby. You... you had a bad dream, that's all. You're safe at home in da bed wit me."

Fuck, what the hell was that about? Sosa wondered as he came to grips with where he was and began to relax. *I never had a dream that felt as real as that one.*

"What time is it?"

"It's 4:33 in da mornin'." She wiped the big beads of sweat from his forehead with her hand. "Are you okay now, bae?"

Sosa tossed the covers off and got out of bed, totally ignoring Cotton. Head down in his hand, he walked blindly to the bathroom to wash and compose himself. Fifteen

187

minutes or so later, he exited the bathroom and began to get dressed to leave the house.

"Where you goin' so early, nigga?" she asked, switching from concerned girlfriend back to her ratchet, controlling ways. "I know ya ain't fo' get that we settin' off fireworks wit da kids since they cancelled da show at da beach this year."

"I ain't fo'get. I ain't gonna be gone that long. I'm just gonna stop by Ray Street ta make sho er'thang is gucci ova there."

"Well," she said while climbing out of bed, "do ya need me ta do anythang?"

"Naw, just chill. I'll be back real soon."

He shuffled into the walk-in closet. Though a lot calmer, he was still discombobulated by his strange dream. His mind was elsewhere as he browsed through clothes erratically. His careless rummaging on a top shelf caused several of Cotton's designer handbags to fall on his head.

The oversized bags snapped him out of his inattentiveness. He groaned. He then bent down and picked up the purple Chanel bag he'd bought Cotton some years ago. Right away he determined the heaviness of the bag was unusual. His nose itched, a telltale sign he utilized when something suspicious was afoot. He unfastened the bag and looked inside.

"What's takin' you so long ta find a fit?" Cotton said, walking into the closet. "An' what was that—"

"You hidin' money from me now, huh?" Sosa exclaimed with stacks of rubberbanded money in one hand.

Looking like a kid caught acting like an ass in public, Cotton stuttered, "I-I wasn't… It ain't what it look… See, I was gonna tell …" She sighed, then flipped the script. "Nigga, what da hell you doin' goin' up in my shit?"

"Unh unh, CC, don't deflect. We had a agreement, an' yo' ass agreed ta do no mo' scammin'. I told ya ain't no use fo' both us bein' in da streets, throwin' rocks at da chain gang.

Who 'posed ta look after my jits if we get jammed up? I guess one of our people." He shook his head disappointedly. "I make enuff bread ta take care of us an' maintain our lifestyle. So, this lil' fifteen, twenty bandz you got here ain't worth you getting' locked up fo'. I got damn near *fifty* times this put up fo' da worst-case scenario. We good, so stop. Last warnin'. EXCLAMATION POINT!"

Once he had finished scolding her, she mumbled, "I'll stop. An' I'm sorry, bae." She advanced toward him. She hugged him and leaned her head against his bare chest. "You fo'give me?"

"You straight. Just don't let it happen again... or I'ma fuck ya up, lil' Oompa-Loompa."

She bit his nipple and latched onto it.

"What da fuck?" he yelped, dropping the bag and money and trying to back up.

"Now you apologize, nigga," she said with his nipple between her teeth.

"I'm sorry! I'm sorry! Lemme go!"

"Okay." She let go of his nipple. She then proceeded to suck on it. She moaned while mouthing it. She kissed across his chest and sucked on his other nipple. She did that for a minute or two before she became hot and bothered. She kissed and licked down his torso until she was on her knees with stacks of money around her. He was hard as a sledgehammer when she pulled his dick through the slit in his boxer briefs and put it in her mouth and slobbed on his knob.

Damn, should I tell him now about the eight-hundred-thousand dollars in PPP loans Slater and I got coming? she wondered as she mouth-fucked him with gusto. *Because I won't be able to hide that much money in my bags, for damn sure.*

***

July 4, 2020 - 11:51am
Lake Worth Beach, FL

The place in Sosa's nightmare was easily recognizable. It was Ray Street, without a doubt.

If Cano wasn't still hospitalized, Sosa would've called him before he left the house to see whether or not all was together around the trap. But since Cano was out of play for the time being, he went to check out the scene to see if his vision was just a dream and not a premonition. With high-quality, low-cost work, the operation at the trap was humming again after almost four months of being shut down, so keeping the area secured was a top priority.

In the last seven plus hours, Sosa had navigated through several issues. He first verified that his active bros had the trap on Ray Street in order. Thereafter, he handled his tenants' complaints before stopping by Cano's crib to be brought up to date on his bro's health. He then drove to the man cave he held on to and kicked back.

Being in his duck-off, a place where nobody disturbed him, used to be gratifying. It no longer was, though. He remembered when he first got the place, and how he thought it was the best investment he ever made. There was nothing like having a place where he could get away from all his troubles for a few hours. And strangely, he found the noise nearby therapeutic.

Now, however, the noise was bothersome. And being in the place made him feel... empty? Paranoid? Lost?

Sosa contemplated how he acquired his new perspective on life. From the bungled response to the coronavirus pandemic, to the persistent brutality that unarmed blacks and peaceful protestors bore at the hands of the police, the grievous events of 2020 weighed heavy on his mind. It pained him to reflect on his role in the beef, started in error, that caused so much death and destruction in the streets that he called home. Of late, he considered himself blessed to be alive and healthy with a family of his own that was intact and healthy, too. He had come to fully appreciate his life, the good, the bad and the ugly, and to not take it for granted.

He glanced at his watch. *It's time to head on home so I can get the fireworks ready,* he said to himself. *But first, I got to pull up on Huff's people and drop them off some bread.*

Phone rings

He pulled the phone from his pocket. The person hitting his line was someone that was saved in his contacts.

The name displayed on the screen read Lucifer.

"What's good, *baz?*" Sosa said, acknowledging the caller with the chummy Creole term that meant "dawg."

"All is good, big dawg," ZooMan returned in his concocted form of speech. "But peep game real quick cuz I'm short on time. I gotta once-in-a-lifetime play on candy fo' ya ice cream truck biz ya wanna start. I need a answer now, tho'. Believe me, you gonna feel real stupid later on down da line if you don't jump on this."

"What's da tag?" Sosa asked, nibbling on the baited hook.

"Fifty cent fo' a bag of M&Ms."

Sosa's nerves were instantly shot after hearing the million-dollar ticket for fifty birds. Jumping on the storybook deal wasn't a problem since he had the bread. He was a bundle of nerves because he'd never made a purchase with that much money. The most he ever conducted business with was four-hundred-fifty-grand for twenty-five bricks, and that money was pooled by him and his bros.

"Uhhh ..."

"Big dawg," ZooMan resumed his work on Sosa once he detected hesitation, "you'll neva top that now or after Covid. If you can, split it wit one of ya homies." *Pause.* "An' ta take some pressure off ya, I'll take half now, half later. I know we only had two small tit-fo'-tats, but I might as well test out ya trustworthiness now."

This nigga like The Godfather, making me an offer I can't refuse, Sosa thought with a smile. *I guess I'll sell the last two of the five I copped from him a few days ago for thirty-two a wop then off these fifty I'm going to get for the low price of twenty-eight per.*

"You gonna come off that Regal now?" Sosa asked.

ZooMan laughed. "You still on me 'bout my baby, huh? Well, next play, big dawg. That's my word."

"I'ma hold ya ta ya word now." He chuckled. "Okay, when you tryna rendezvous?"

"Tonite."

"Ummm… Damn… I dunno if can do it tonite, *baz.* I'ma be settin' off fireworks wit my fam."

"It can be late late, big dawg. I just wanna get off 'em tonite befo' they soften. I got no cool place ta store 'em."

Sosa took a few more seconds to chew over the phenomenal deal. True, he'd only bought work from Lucifer twice. Both times he got superb coke. Kentucky had better meth, though. He also felt good vibes during the public-area exchanges with Lucifer.

Sosa eventually said, "'I gotta big enuff fridge fo' 'em. So, where we huddlin' up?"

"Becuz of da situation, my place. You cool wit that?"

"Eerrrr… I'ma brang my pot'nah wit me. I'ma need help movin' those goods. You straight wit that?"

"Yeah, big dawg, brang ya homie wit'cha," ZooMan said, trying to keep his excitement out of his voice.

"We gucci then."

"Ai'ight. I'll text ya da directions after I hang up. An' you text me at least thirty minutes in advance so I can be ready."

"Bet."

"Okay, big dawg, I'm gone."

The call ended.

Sosa immediately scrolled through his contacts, found Wes' number and called him. He was keeping his word to holla at Wes for his third order. *Wes, tonight is your big break and mine*, he thought as the phone rang, *that's if you got every dollar of a quarter million on deck now.*

Chapter 18

July 4, 2020 - 8:27pm.
Boynton Beach, FL

If you don't have an effect, you don't care what happens to yourself.

That was Adele's opinion.

In his dissent, he had an effect. Just not the one he intended.

Despite his tireless work on the dreaded case destroying his household, and realizing it was destroying him also, he still didn't care.

"Fudge, Harden, when will you take a break?" Noah inquired as he and Harden exited the station together. "It's Independence Day. Be independent tonight. You're too one-track minded. You've let this case control your life all these years." He sighed. "I personally understand your anguish. I swear I do. I *need* justice, too. But I also know I sometimes need peace of mind, or I'll lose my mind."

"Listen here, bucko, I'll take a break when this case is closed. Hell, I'll do you one better and retire once this devil is underground in Colorado's Supermax or dying in front of my eyes from capital punishment. Until then, I'm vengeance personified. I'm relentless. And I'm sticking to my guns like Dirty Harry."

"So, if you want to be independent tonight and pop your little firecrackers with your loving family, be my guest. Me, however, I have no family to enjoy the explosions in the night sky with. Instead, I'm going to cruise around the most popular clubs and bars that're flouting Covid restrictions to see if my objective sticks with his latest blueprint."

"All work, no play… ever," Noah breathed humorlessly before they got ready to go different ways for the night. "You're on Beeline Highway, going nowhere fast while watching your life pass by in the window."

Harden's body locked up without warning. A force of some sort had him boxed in to where he couldn't move.

His immobilization didn't alarm him at all, though. The occurrence wasn't new to him. After he turned his life over to God and developed a special connection with Him, he experienced sensory quirks that couldn't be scientifically explained.

Nevertheless, he knew exactly what caused him to stop dead in his tracks and stand stock still: It was God giving him a helpful hint.

"Why'd you stop so suddenly? And why are you standing so awkwardly?" Noah asked, stopping a few feet ahead of Harden.

"Repeat what you just said."

"Huh?"

"Repeat everything that you just said… please.'

"I didn't say anything discerning. But I said, as you already know, you're all work, no—"

"Nope. After that."

Noah scratched his head. "Aahh… I believe… I think I said something along the lines that you're on a highway, going nowhere and you're watching your life pass by."

"Your exact words were *Beeline Highway.*" At that instance, he regained function of his limbs and took off for his car.

"Where are you rushing off to?" Noah sought before walking behind Harden rather than towards his own car.

Looking over his shoulder, Harden replied, "Does it matter?"

"Did I say something wrong?"

"No, actually, I believe you said something right for once." He made it to his vehicle and opened the door. He was just about to hop in when he looked over the roof and saw Noah standing at his passenger door. "Where do you think you're going?"

"With you. Duh."

"I thought you were heading home to gather and celebrate your independence?"

"Well… to be frank, I just got a weird feeling that I'll be celebrating Independence Day differently in the future if I go with you tonight."

Harden bore into his partner's eyes, and he didn't see any lack of conviction. "That was God."

"Come again?"

"That weird feeling you claimed you just got, that was God."

"Uhhh… That's… Well, with all due respect, Harden, I don't believe in God or the devil. You don't need the devil because people are evil enough without him. So, since I believe the devil is made up, then God must be, too."

"Kid, you believe in God. You just don't know it yet. And I have a funny feeling that after tonight you'll retract your words. Now, get in or get lost."

Noah slapped the roof and jumped into the car.

And together they drove off into the dark.

***

July 4, 2020 - 10:03pm
Royal Palm Beach, FL

"Okay, it's bedtime. Now get y'all narrow behinds upstairs an' get ready fo' bed," Cotton instructed as the family entered the house.

"Oh nooooo," Kia shrieked. "I want to pop new fireworks."

"We got plenty mo' ta pop tomorrow, Fat Fat," Sosa assured her. "But if you don't do what'cha mama says, no mo' fireworks fo' you. You hear me?"

Kia pouted and crossed her little arms across her chest in protest.

"Girl, you betta get'cha ass up those stairs," Cotton said. "Lookin' like a lil' pug."

Kia turned and stomped away.

"Jerrika an' Jenario, y'all make sho' she brushes her teeth good befo' she gets in bed," Cotton added. "I'ma be up there in ten minutes. Y'all butts better be in those sheets by then. An' no phones."

"Ai'ight, I'm out," Sosa declared. "I gotta meet up wit Wes at da Red Roof Inn on 45th by da interstate, count da bread real quick, then make da transaction."

"I hear all that, but I wanna know *exactly* where this transaction gonna be at an' how long you gonna be gone."

"I told ya I dunno. Da plug gonna gimme turn-by-turn directions. I guess he doin' it that way as a precaution."

Cotton pouted and crossed her little arms across her chest, looking like a bigger version of Kia. "Ai'ight. You good... as long as you keep ya location on."

"That's a no-brainer." He kissed Cotton on the lips, then retrieved his YSL duffel bag and stepped out of the house.

Once Sosa left, Cotton spent ten minutes straightening up the kitchen and living room. She then went upstairs and made sure the kids were situated. She finally retired to her bedroom. There, she got on her phone and powered up the TV with it. She pulled up a particular app next and, a few seconds later, said to herself, "I see you, nigga. An' as usual, I ain't goin' ta bed till I see you're on ya way home."

Chapter 19

July, 5 2020 - 12:14am
Somewhere in Martin County, FL

"...Ee, er... Ee, er... Pullin' out da coupe at da lot/ Told 'em fuck twelve, fuck SWAT/ Bustin' all da bales out da box/ I just hit a lick wit da box/ Had ta put da stick in a box ..." Roddy Ricch's verse pumped through the speakers.

"Bro, are ya sho' we goin' da rite way?" Wes asked, his voice colored with aggravation. "Cuz we been on this road a long fuckin' time an' ain't nuttin'... I mean NOTHING... is out here."

Sosa grabbed his phone from the cup holder again to see if his phone's signal bounced back. "I still ain't got no bars ta pull up Google Maps, but this da road he told me ta take in his last text."

"Eva since we crossed ova into this county my phone been fuckin' up. Bullshit 5G."

"Mine, too. An' my ol' lady gon' kill me cuz my location ain't bein' shared wit her now." He let out a guttural sound. "But at least, I can text back an' forth wit Lucifer."

"Lucifer," Wes said mockingly with a laugh. "I ain't neva met or heard of a nigga wit that name. You'd think buddy name would be rangin' like a telethon in da streets if he was really that nigga."

Sosa took his eyes off the empty road and looked over at Wes for a second. "How you know he ain't really that nigga? Cuz how I see it, I'm that nigga 'round my way just like you feel you're that nigga 'round yo' way. But ta er'body else, we're nobodies. Personally, tho', I don't mind bein' a nobody now in niggaz eyes. Keeps me off da radar. I ain't gotta worry that much 'bout hot niggaz tryna five-kay-one on me or jack boyz plottin' on me or da feds gettin' on my line cuz of anotha nigga conspiracy. So, Lil Wayne said it best: Real Gz move in silence like lasagna."

"Facts. But wit a standout name like Lucifer, an' wit all da work he gettin' off at a slashed price durin' a drought, me, you, one of our homeboyz or associates, shoulda heard of him. Cuz believe me, once I accepted da name Lucifer, I'll be livin' up ta that name by terrorizin' shit er'day of da week. That's on God."

"You dunno how he got that name. It might be his real name." Sosa shrugged. "Or he might'a got it from da shit he did way back when an' usin' his past ruthlessness ta get ta da bag at ease now."

"Possibly." *Silence.* "Bro, where da fuck we at? When was da last time ya text buddy?"

Sosa picked up his phone from his lap. "It's been a minute. I'ma hit him now, tho'." With one hand gripping the wheel he began typing a message as he zoomed down the dark, empty highway in his Maserati. After he sent the short message he felt as if he took a shotgun blast to the gut.

He'd be lying to himself if he said he wasn't on edge. Yes, he had a strapped-up Wes with him and his own firearm. But he was slightly suspicious of how fast things unfolded. He hadn't known Lucifer a whole month yet, so with good reason he felt uneasy. He was merely taking a chance this buy because if the remarkable deal panned out, his and Wes' bag would be back on its way to where it was prior to their feud.

And the prospect of going beyond his peak made him live with his discomfort and stay on course.

"Who that up ahead? Is that trol?" Wes exclaimed, sitting up straight and fastening his seatbelt.

Buckling up himself, Sosa said, "I dunno. They too far ta say rite now."

"Slow down just in case that's dem boyz. We're unsure where we're at, in da middle of nowhere, surrounded by sugar cane an' shit, so we're trapped out here. I ain't tryna go ta a unfamiliar jail tonite fo' ridin' dirty wit fire an' a half M in da trunk."

Sosa looked at the speedometer. "I'm doin' a lil' ova da fifty-five mile per hour speed limit."

Holding the steering wheel correctly, as well as holding his breath, he passed by the Lincoln Continental that was pulled over on the side of the road with its headlights on and hazard lights flashing. The car was unoccupied, and yet he still gazed intently into his rearview mirror for a while "We good," he eventually said.

Bing.

"Please, let that be buddy," Wes prayed. "If it ain't, we turnin' back an' goin' home. Fuck this shit."

Sosa looked at his phone. He was prepared to call off and reschedule this deal if it was not the plug.

Lucifer had texted back with further directions.

***

Approximately forty minutes later...

"Goldurn, Harden," Noah piped up, slapping his neck in an attempt to kill the latest insect that bit him, "for the past three hours we've been driving on this road, pulling over every now and then when you feel like it, and canvassing the area. Moreover, we've been in Martin County without approval the last hour or so. And the entire time you've been unspecific about what we're doing. I'm getting bit by all types of things while looking around blindly. So, please tell me exactly what we're looking for."

To Noah, aimlessly knocking about on the fifty-seven-mile-long State Road 710, aka Beeline Highway, was wasteful, and he wanted to know the reason right now.

Harden, poking along in the illumination of the headlights near a canal with his rosary beads in hand, said, "I'm not looking for anything."

"What?" Noah waved a hand in front of his face to shoo away the annoying bugs. "If you're not looking for anything, why are we even out here?"

"You're out here, in fact, because you chose to tag along. I'm out here, however, waiting for the moment I get a funny feeling. Once that happens, I will look for sign."

Noah was confused. He thought for sure they were periodically pulling over on the side of the highway for a reason, even if he didn't know what that reason was. But knowing now that Harden was counting on an extraordinary feeling to lead him to a sign was mind-boggling. *I'm going to talk to the chief tomorrow about reassigning me already,* Noah said to himself as he kept in step behind Harden, *because Harden has clearly lost his sense of what's what over this case.*

Low grumbling

"What's that noise?" asked Noah, holding up.

Harden knew precisely what generated that disturbing noise, for he was staring at its glowing eyes.

"Run... for... the... car... NOW!"

They made a break for it just as a humongous alligator burst out of the canal. They scrambled into the vehicle. Both breathing heavily, they watched the alligator's glowing eyes until it turned tail and crawled back into the water.

"Whew! That there was a close shave," Noah insisted from the driver's seat. He turned on the interior light and looked over at Harden. "Does being frightened half to death by a prehistoric animal count as both the feeling and sign you were waiting for?"

A smile unexpectedly formed on Harden's face.

Low humming

"Now what's that noise?"

This time Harden had not the slightest idea what caused the noise.

But he felt the hairs on the back of his neck stand up.

The humming grew louder and louder inside of the car. It was as if a bumblebee was growing rapidly in the car.

Then... VROOM!

A white luxury car flew past them at nearly double the speed limit. It was also zigzagging slightly.

"Follow that car," Harden instructed.

"Huh? Why? Are we out of our jurisdiction tonight just to pull over and ticket speeders?"

"Do what I say or get out of my car and dance back to the station."

Noah wasn't sure if the speeding car was the feeling and sign Harden was looking for, but he put the car in gear and sped off after the lone racer.

***

In the intervening time...

"What da fuck? Ain't no way buddy live on this street," Wes said seconds after Sosa turned at the sign he was told to. "These houses so raggedy not even da poorest guats would live in them."

"You ain't lied 'bout that one," Sosa replied, observing and leaning forward so far that his chest was on the center of the steering wheel. "This shit gettin' weirder an' weirder by da second."

"Yeah, so let's make this quick an' get da fuck off of Elm Street."

Five big yellow signs, with the middle one reading DEAD END, soon appeared in front of them. Following the instructions in the last text, they turned into the driveway at the end of the block. Creepingly, the Maserati's headlights lit up the house.

Once every inch of the front of the place was in view, the center of Sosa's chest began to feel strange.

"I'ma keep it a buck wit'cha, Sosa. My heart ain't neva beat this hard in my life," Wes confessed once the car was in park. "Er'thang 'bout this whole situation feels... off."

"I feel it, too, bro. My heart ain't beatin' fast, but my chest is burnin'," Sosa admitted, cutting off the engine but keeping the headlights on. "So, you still wanna go through wit this?"

Zeroed in on the house, Wes replied, "I'm sittin' here, homie, tryna figga out why buddy chose ta paint his crib black. Plus, why does it look like it got hella clearcoat on it?"

Sosa wondered the same.

But instead of lingering in the car wondering about that, or anything else, he reiterated, "Wes, what'chu tryna do?"

"Maaannnn... Fuck it! We here now. Let's do this." He reached between his legs, grabbed the MAC-10 off the floorboard and exited the car confidently.

Sosa pushed the button that popped the trunk before killing the headlights. He got out of the car and walked to the trunk where Wes was.

Wes took out the duffel bag, then Sosa pulled out his Draco. While remaining alert of their surroundings, they gave their weapons a quick inspection. Once they saw the coast was (creepily) clear, they headed toward the house.

"Damn, this Buick cleaner than a bitch," Wes pointed out as they stepped past the Regal parked backwards in the driveway with their guns ready to bust anything that moved.

"Keep ya eyes off my baby," Sosa replied.

"Yo' baby?" Wes said, looking at Sosa suspiciously.

"You ain't gotta look at me like that, nigga. I said my baby cuz Lucifer gonna sell it ta me next time I cop."

Bing

come in. door open, read the text message on Sosa's phone.

Though it was a muggy night, the sensation in Sosa's chest intensified to a burning feeling with every stride. *Is this strange feeling telling me that I'm putting my life on the line over my greed?* Sosa pondered after making it to the door. *Or am I just overreacting?*

Sosa grabbed the doorknob, which was abnormally warm but not cause for alarm, and rotated it. He pushed the door in slowly with his Draco raised. Noticeable warmth smashed into him.

"Why is it so fuckin' hot in there?" Wes asked.

"I dunno. But my best guess is that this a grow house," Sosa answered while pushing the door open more.

"I don't smell no weed, tho'."

Sosa didn't either.

"Lucifer," Sosa shouted into the dark house.

"Big dawg, c'mon in," Lucifer yelled back from deep in the rear of the place. "Ya brought ya homie wit'cha, rite?"

"Yeah," Sosa responded, Draco ready to fire.

"Ai'ight. I'm solo dolo. Now, make y'all way to da back. I'm makin' sho' da pack straight in da master bedroom. Er'thang copacetic, big dawg."

"Copacetic?" Wes said, playfulness in his tone. "That shit so 1990s."

Sosa smirked because, in the short time he'd known Lucifer, he thought Lucifer was indeed behind the times. He wasn't sure if Lucifer refused to follow the latest trends or if Martin County niggas had their own swag. Either way it went, he understood quickly that Lucifer was an oddball... with *mucho* drugs.

"Yo', Lucifer, let's double time this," Sosa said as they cautiously slipped into the toasty house. "I gotta get back to a area where I can getta signal on my phone ASAP or my ol' lady gonna kill me. Plus, I ain't tryna be on da road droppin' off this—"

All of a sudden both Sosa and Wes blacked out.

Chapter 20

July 5, 2020 - 1:23am
Somewhere in Martin County, FL
Noah was tired, in every sense of the word.

He couldn't believe he threw away a night of fun with his family for this.

"I think we've fooled around long enough, Harden." He yawned again. "I say we turn it in and return tomorrow or pursue another game plan, if—"

"I say shut up and keep following that car," Harden horned in.

That was it.

Noah was done being Mr. Nice Guy.

"You're a miserable, spiteful, ornery asshole, Harden, and I refuse to put up with your… your assholeness one more second. The first thing tomorrow I'm asking Chief Brewster to reassign me because being your partner is counterproductive. So, bravo, Harden, you've succeeded in your secondary mission and have officially made me bow out in record time. Now, I'm turning around because following this Lexus is—"

"Slow down. They're turning," Harden interrupted him once more.

Just as fast as Noah's inner fire arose, it abated when he saw the car's blinker on. His mind executed a U-turn instead of the one he was planning to do with the car and heading home.

Noah took his foot off the gas and let the Lexus, which was roughly two football fields ahead of them, turn.

"Don't lose them," Harden said like a boss.

Noah soon came to the street the car took. He saw the car's taillights not too far down the road.

"Hurry and turn off the lights before you hang that corner," Harden instructed.

Noah did as he was told, then turned onto the street.

They rolled forward at a slow pace, hoping the driver of the car ahead hadn't detected them. They simultaneously kept an eye on the car and appraised the terrain.

"I don't know where we're at, but this place is giving me the heebie-jeebies," Noah disclosed. "I can't see nothing because it's so dark. Can you?"

Harden couldn't see a damn thing, either. However, he tingled. He tugged his phone from the clip on his waist. He flipped it open and saw he had no service. "Do you have a signal?"

Noah got his smartphone out of the holder on his hip. He, too, had no signal. "This must be a dead zone."

A dead zone? Harden thought. *What a coincidence?*

"Look they're coming to a stop," Noah said, noticing the brake lights brightening. "From their headlights I can see this is a dead-end road."

"Great, a dead-end road," Harden sarcastically said aloud.

"They've pulled up to a house, which seems to be the only habitable structure on the block. There are two vehicles at the house."

Harden saw it all. Habitually observant, he noticed something else.

"That light-colored car parked behind that Buick passed by us on Beeline Highway about an hour ago." He pointed. "Pull over there and let's see who gets out the car."

***

Meanwhile, inside of the house...

"I didn't make this trip for nothing," he growled. "I can't believe your keen perception didn't reveal to you that he was protected. Since it didn't, you're going out there this minute and bringing back someone else before the sun rises. Or else."

ZooMan never encountered someone that was protected by such a powerful spell. At least he now knew why he itched in their presence.

"I'm not going anywhere because, in actuality, I fulfilled my mission," ZooMan barked at Francois in defiance before adding, "How was I supposed to know that an itchy sensation was a sign that he was protected through the special gris gris around his neck? So, if you want someone else, you go out and risk being burnt to death by the sun because you did a full transformation and couldn't make it back to your skin in time. Or you can just use your supreme powers to remove his protection so we can proceed before daybreak."

"The gris gris was given to him by someone just as powerful, if not more powerful, than I am. I can feel it." Francois' face contorted in anger. *This buffoon's screwup won't postpone my personal aspiration tonight,* he concluded as he balled his fists, *so I'll improvise.*

Knock knock knock

"Who can that be?" Francois asked ZooMan

"Hell, I don't know," ZooMan said. "Besides you and I, every person that knows about this place is in a *govi.*"

ZooMan walked off to see who the first ever unexpected visitor was at the door.

Bang Bang Bang

Is that the police? thought ZooMan due to the urgency of the pounding. But then again, he knew if it were the police, the door would be in a million pieces by now.

"I know yo' dawg ass up in here so open da door!" *Thunk Thunk Thunk.* "An' if you in there wit a bitch, I'ma kill you *and* her ass. Now, open up." *Clonk Clonk Clonk Clonk.*

"Which one of these loser's spurned lover has stupidly followed them here?" ZooMan said aloud to himself. He opened the door. Standing before him was a little white woman dressed inelegantly in an oversized white t-shirt and fuzzy Fendi slippers.

"Who you? An' where is my fiancé?" she snapped, looking ZooMan up and down.

ZooMan did a quick scan beyond her before saying, "Who you? An' who invited you ova here?"

"Don' t worry 'bout all that, nigga. But if you don't tell my man Sosa ta get his ass out here rite now I'ma really spazz out, out this bitch."

Dogs barking

ZooMan inconspicuously observed the manic canines in the Lexus parked crookedly in the yard. With them, he saw the heads of what appeared to be children. "C'mon in real quick. Me an' Sosa wrappin' up some bizness."

Cotton leaned to one side and peeked past ZooMan. The interior of the house was too dark for her liking. Yet, the thought of Sosa doing something he wasn't supposed to compelled her to rudely push her way by ZooMan. "Sosa, where yo' ass at? Yo' ass betta be up in here handlin' bizness an' not fuckin' wit no hoes," she yelled. "Why is it so fuckin' hot in here?"

ZooMan shut the door and locked it. *I'll deal with those mangy mutts and kids in a bit,* he thought. Then a lightbulb lit up in his head. *I'm in luck as a matter of fact, because she can fill in for the protected one we can't use.*

***

Back outside…

"Those dogs in that car are really excited about something. I think we should go investigate," Noah insisted.

They'd been sitting there for at least five minutes now, and those dogs hadn't stopped barking yet. Rumor had it that dogs could sense fear and evil, so their incessant barking was a sign for Harden. Thus, he opened the door and got out of the car to check things out.

Harden walked softly toward the passenger side, while Noah took the driver side. They approached the car with their hands on their sidearms. The two distinct barks let them know there was a big dog and a little one in the vehicle.

Noah pulled a small flashlight out once he arrived at the trunk. He switched it on and shone it through the clear back window. Three small figures in the backseat, as well as the dogs in the passenger seat, reacted to the light. "Let me see your hands," Noah commanded.

"They're kids," Harden said. "That's not necessary. They're no threats." He tapped on the rear window until he got the attention of the child closest to him. "Is everything okay?" he said loudly because the barking dogs had turned their attention to him. Disregarding the dogs, he saw both fear and confusion in the boy's eyes. "Can you control those dogs and open the door?"

The boy shook his head no. "My mama said to not get out of the car for nothing."

"Well, can you tell me who lives here?"

The boy shrugged. "I don't—"

Muffled screaming

Both Noah and Harden looked at the house, which was where the scream came from.

Harden quickly said, "Stay in here and keep the doors locked. We'll be right back." He then ran back to his vehicle and grabbed something that may come in handy. Thereafter, he rejoined Noah.

"I tried to call for backup," Noah said, "but I have no signal still."

"It's all up to us then," responded Harden. "Now, let's get a move on it."

On their toes, they stalked toward the house with guns drawn.

***

Inside of the house...

"I call upon Papa Legba, the Gatekeeper...

The distant chanting woke Sosa up. He batted his eyes a few times. He saw nothing but black. He subsequently realized he was laying down on his back and couldn't move. *What's going on?* he said to himself as the chanting continued. "Hello," he yelled, struggling to move.

The house began to vibrate. The vibration was shallow at first, but it deepened with every passing second.

Sosa strained some more against the restraints. Before long, he miraculously was able to free a hand. Not long after that he untied his other hand. He was freed completely in no time. He swiftly got to his feet. He didn't know where he was so he put his arms straight out and moved through the darkness carefully. He eventually touched a wall. He ran his hands up and down the wall's surface as he moved along it. He soon came to the frame of a door. He found the door's knob and opened it an inch and snuck a look through the crack. He saw more darkness. Unsure if it was safe to go forward, he entered and did the only logical thing there was to do: he walked toward the weird chanting.

Feeling his way through the dark, Sosa's heart began to beat faster and faster the closer he got to the chanting. He came upon another door after a while. Beyond the door he heard the chanting. Again, he was unsure if it was safe to advance, especially without firepower.

The chanting suddenly stopped, and someone started talking.

Sosa recognized the voice immediately.

The familiar voice caused him to burst through the door, weapon be damned. What he saw in the candle-lit room sunk his pounding heart to the bottom of his stomach.

Two strange individuals caught his attention first. One was standing over a thrashing and hollering Cotton in what seemed to be a trance and the other was kneeling next to an out-cold Wes. The one standing was mumbling lowly and the kneeling one was scratching an emblem into Wes' bare chest. Around them were a lot of clay pots, and coming out of those pots was a mist.

And that mist was infiltrating Wes' body as the house continued vibrating.

Sosa then noticed that the one standing resembled Lucifer, if he were older, and he had on Lucifer's chain. Without thinking, he rushed Lucifer's look-alike and tackled the man.

"Julius," screamed Cotton the moment she sighted Sosa. "Help me!"

Sosa heard Cotton's cry for help but he couldn't do nothing for her that second. He was occupied trying to bash the man's face in; he would get to her as soon as he could.

The other individual ceased carving the symbol into Wes' torso because of the abrupt skirmish nearby. He swiftly hopped onto Sosa's back.

The trio tussled on the floor. In the process of trying to overpower each other, they kicked over the clay pots and candles.

The toppled clay pots were still smoking. However, the mist was dissipating in the air instead of entering Wes' body. And the knocked over candles had set the floor afire.

"Julius, help," Cotton cried out some more as small flames licked at her heels. She squirmed until she got a few feet away from the fire. "The floor is on fire!"

The house shook violently.

All of a sudden, Wes sat up. He arose, without using his hands. He briefly examined himself, then said, "I breathe again at last."

Baron Samedi, a 32nd degree-initiated Mason and Grand Master of the Celestial Masonic Lodge of Vodou Spirits, had successfully been reincarnated. He celebrated the moment by doing his usual: dancing and laughing.

His celebration was cut short, though, by the erratic movement he detected in the corner of his eye. He waved a hand at the entangled trio. His motion sent them flying in separate directions until they crashed hard into a wall. He levitated about a foot off the ground and slid over to a dazed Sosa first. He waved his hand again, which caused Sosa to float vertically. "You... I can feel and smell your protection. But it will be of no use for what's due now. You will be eradicated just like everybody else on this planet." He erupted in laughter after tossing Sosa aside with a flick of his wrist.

Baron waved his hand at ZooMan next. ZooMan floated up and drifted towards him. "Euclide Vilsaint, you have performed excellently. I will honor my pledge to you." He gently set ZooMan on his feet. "At dawn, we travel to the next dwelling that houses souls. Once I have accumulated all souls from all storehouses, the commencement of the purge will take place at last. So, prepare for our journey at once."

ZooMan, a little woozy, left the room to do what he was told.

Baron Samedi sailed over to Francois. Looking down at his once worthy servant, he said, "And you, you believed you could outwit me and commandeer this body once the souls occupied it. You desired to shut down my coming and become ruler of this world. Well, your paltry spell didn't work, and your plan failed terribly. Now you will never see glory."

Baron Samedi waved his hand again. A clay pot came to him. He reeled off a few words in a gothic language, and Francois Gedeon's screaming soul was sucked out of him and placed into the *govi*. Once Francois was in the *govi*, he sealed it permanently with a spell and heaved it into the spreading fire.

Lastly, Baron Samedi calmly went over to Cotton.

Eyes wide with fear, she screamed, "Julius! Julius, get up! Please, help me!"

Baron Samedi ogled her. "You're beautiful. You remind me of my love Erzulie." He smiled. "You will come with us. I will reincarnate my betrothed in your body at the next storehouse and together we will lord over the remaining enslaved."

"You can't have my body," Cotton protested.

Baron Samedi frowned. He raised his hand and another clay pot came to him, then said, "I have no use for your soul. I will take your corpse with—"

* BOOM! *

Harden and Noah barged into the smoky room.

"OH MY GOD!" Noah blurted out instead of saying freeze. Seeing the person floating prompted his reaction.

"Freeze!" Harden yelled before coughing.

Baron Samedi quickly waved his hand their way. The guns flew out of their hands, and he laughed. "You fools. I am Baron Samedi. Your primitive weapons are no match for me! Now, experience real power."

Out of nowhere, Dinky and Mondo shot through the door.

Dinky readily lunged at Baron Samedi's midsection, while Mondo jumped and latched onto an ankle. Baron Samedi immediately kicked little Mondo off, sending the chihuahua soaring across the room and into the flames. Mondo's bloodcurdling yelps sent Dinky into a frenzy. Thereupon, Dinky hysterically tried to rip open Baron Samedi's center.

Baron Samedi eventually grabbed Dinky's snapping jaws. Using his supernatural strength, he pulled the Cane Corso's jaws apart until they snapped.

"Nooooo," Cotton wailed as the fire engulfed one side of the room.

Baron Samedi flung the dog away. "That felt amazing. Yet, it's going to feel even better when I exterminate all iniquitous scum." He continued laughing maniacally.

Baron Samedi turned to ZooMan, who had returned to the room. "No worries, my loyal one. All has been taken care of. Now take her and prepare for our departure."

As the last words left his mouth, a large hypodermic syringe was plunged into Baron Samedi's chest.

"Got'cha."

Baron Samedi fell to the floor. He touched his chest, and it began to hurt... intensely. "This... This can't be. What did you do to me?"

"Pumped you full of saline," Harden professed.

After talking with his mother about voodoo, Harden decided to read up on the bizarre belief. Most of what he discovered on the internet was too far-fetched for him to believe. However, he remained receptive. He retained all practical info, namely how salt was a deterrent to the spirits. And because of that bit of knowledge, he surmised that salt could be lethal if injected into a spirit-occupied body.

And, it seems, his intuition was dead-on point.

Flames climbed the walls as ZooMan ran to Baron Samedi's side. "My Master, what do I do? Tell me how to fix it."

"There… There is nothing… you can do for me now," Baron Samedi stammered as his insides liquefied. "You… You are my number one now. So go… and obtain more souls at once… Bring me into existence once more."

Mist began spewing from Wes' body.

"Euclide Vilsaint, put your hands up and walk this way. Now!" Noah ordered with his recovered service weapon fixed on ZooMan.

ZooMan looked around. The fire had encircled him, and it was closing in on him fast.

Besides the doorway, he had no way out…

…except for…

"Stop!" Noah opened fire. He emptied the clip. "Harden," he yelled next, "the suspect jumped out of the window!"

"Forget him for the time being. Help me get these people out of here before it's too late."

Harden and Noah helped Cotton and Sosa get out of the blaze just before it consumed the room. They assembled on the front lawn. As all but an incoherent Sosa watched the fire overtake the house, the agonizing squeals of hogs and other animals could be heard coming from the back of the house.

Pitiful yowling

"Is that… That's Mondo," Cotton shrieked. She soon spotted Mondo near the front door, and he was hobbling considerably. She ran and scooped him up with tears of joy running down her face. She kissed the singed dog several times. "You mama's hero, Mondo."

The harsh heat from the fire and the piercing wailing from the animals ultimately brought Sosa back to his senses. He looked beside him and saw Cotton, his kids and Mondo huddled up and tending to him with tears on their faces.

Where's Dinky? he wondered as his family held him close and kissed him, including wet licks to his face by Mondo.

"You've come around finally," Harden said, walking up to the nestled family. "I think you inhaled some smoke while dazed and that left you disoriented."

Seeing the white man caused Sosa to tense up. "Who you?" he countered while getting to his feet as quick as he could. His back hurt like hell.

"At ease, sir. You and your family are safe now," assured Noah as he joined Harden.

"We're officers from the Boynton Beach Police Department," Harden let Sosa know. "And before you rattle off a thousand questions, I'll fill you in on what just took place. You just survived... Let's just say you made it through a horrifying event."

The white officer's words had it all coming back to him now: the deal, the chanting that woke him up in the darkness, the smoking clay jars, the ring of candles Cotton was in the middle of, and... Wes floating?

"Wes? What happened ta my dawg, Wes?"

"I'm sorry to say your friend perished," Noah said with a sigh. "And your dog... I'm assuming it was your dog... perished, too. But that courageous dog died rescuing all of us tonight."

Dinky died saving our lives. Sosa said to himself with watery eyes. *That's my girl.*

"Now, I'd like to know what you were doing out here?" Harden asked.

Sosa wasn't prepared for that question. "Uh... I was out here... I was—"

"Cut the bullshit, liar," Noah interjected. "We know you came here to do something illegal, like a drug deal or to buy guns."

Sosa swallowed. "You can't prove that. Where's ya evidence?"

Noah saw red, and it wasn't the fire of the house. He was all set to lash out, but...

"You're correct, son," Harden said. "So, don't worry. After what we experienced tonight, I'll write up a report that excludes you and your family. You don't ever have to worry about this tragic night again. You just give me your contact info and I'll call you with the facts about what occurred tonight, okay?"

"Wait a minute, Harden," Noah began his complaint. "You can't do that. You can't let this... this lowlife off the hook so easy."

"I can do what I want because I'm the senior officer here. And besides, we're out of our jurisdiction. We have no arrest powers here. I'm only authorized to catch Euclide Vilsaint wherever. But since he has fled again, *we* are just investigators."

"I'm calling this in," Noah said, retrieving his phone. "I got a signal finally. Thank God."

"That's twice in a matter of minutes you called God's name, Mr. Nonbeliever." He shrugged. "Anyhow, you tell the Martin County sheriff to send all available units so we can initiate a manhunt for that two-legged monster. He couldn't have gotten too far."

Noah walked off once he got dispatch on the line.

"Now give me your info and get out of here," Harden told Sosa.

Sosa quickly recited his number and gathered his family, and they began to leave.

"Remember what happened here tonight, son," Harden added. "Next time, karma may not let you off the hook."

Sosa nodded. His family then climbed into Cotton's Lexus, which had a busted out passenger window, while he got into his Maserati, and they cleared the scene.

Noah rushed to Harden's side. "What the hell, Harden? You really let them go? Backup is on the way."

"The scales of justice can't always be weighed. Sometimes you have to accept imbalance... Partner."

Noah wasn't buying that profound crap right now. And since he wasn't, he stormed off.

Harden turned to observe the burning house. He no longer heard the animal's woeful screams, but the rolling flames and floating embers dazzled him. The spectacle soon brought to his mind the map in his office. *Although my prayer of simultaneously tacking a white and black pin on my layout tonight wasn't answered, I can conclusively close all the RISING SUN cases,* he deduced.

"Carol."

Harden instaneously looked around. He clearly heard his name called, and he undeniably placed whose voice it was. But he saw nobody.

"Carol."

He did a three-sixty while surveying the scene.

"I'm here, Carol."

He spun around hectically until he saw her. "Mackenzie?"

The vapor came out of the burning house and materialized in the form of his sister. She glid his way and stopped mere inches from his face. She stared into his now wet baby blues for a while. Then, in a heavenly reverberation, *"Little brother, I knew you'd be the one to free me and the others before it was too late. Thank you."* She smiled.

Harden wanted to say a million things to Mackenzie. But he was too astounded to utter a syllable.

"Carol, you must let go now. What happened to me was not your fault. Or mom's. I love you both. And rest assured, I'll be going to a much better place now." She floated towards him until she passed into his body.

When she entered Harden's body, he smelled her, felt her love and gratitude, and, finally, he felt liberated.

Yes, Euclide Vilsaint had got away from him yet again, but he wasn't as distraught as he should've been. Because he stopped (or delayed?) the end of the world from happening, he was walking on air. He planned to enjoy this victory. *I'll find him again,* he promised himself as an image of Mackenzie surrounded by angels popped into his head. *And when I do, I'm killing him on sight, for I am God's weapon.*

He grinned while tinkering with his rosary beads.

Epilogue

July 7, 2020 - 5:13pm
West Palm Beach, FL

"… an' I wanna turn our old place on 14th into my doll house since you still got'cha man cave on Truman."

"Ai'ight," he said without quite understanding what he'd said yes to because something else had breezed into his mind moments ago. "I been meanin' ta ask ya sumthin'."

"What?"

"How'd y'know where ta find me that nite?"

"Ummm… You shared yo' location wit me, duh." Cotton blushed as she pushed the shopping cart.

"See, there ya lil' hobbit ass go lyin'. Wasn't no signal out there so my location couldn't have been on at da time. If you wanna go back ta lyin' ta each otha, I'm wit that. Cuz believe me, I got new excuses I'm dyin' ta use."

She sucked her teeth with emphasis. "Damn, nigga." She inhaled and exhaled melodramatically. "Okay, don't get mad… I went on *CHEATERS* website, bought a tracking device an' put it on ya car. There. Ya happy now? You betta be, nigga, becuz if it wasn't fo' that tracker, yo' Haitian ass would be dead. So, be thankful I did that."

Sosa was shocked, but not too shocked. He knew that was just typical Cotton, the insecure woman he loved to death do them part.

"Yo' slick ass sho' know how ta flip shit 'round." He shook his head with a cheerful expression. "I told ya I been done fuckin' around. An' after what we went through da otha nite, I'm done wit all da bullshit, even husslin'. So, altho' I should be cussin' you out for puttin' a tracker on my car, I'm glad ya did. Ya neva-endin' fear of me cheatin' on ya saved my life. Thanks, bae."

Cotton blushed again, but for a different reason this time.

"But you takin' that shit off my car ASAP!"

The couple went on with their small talk while shopping for essentials in the just about sold-out Sam's Club. It was only the two of them. They dropped the kids off at Cotton's parent's house earlier so they could run errands in peace. They shopped for nearly an hour before paying for their purchases and making their way out.

As they walked to the car, Cotton said, "Bae, did you decide when we gonna get anotha dog? Da house feels empty witout Dinky. Me an' da kids miss her."

"Yeah, it don't feel da same witout her. I miss my boo, too." He took a few seconds to mourn Dinky. "I'll decide after we get back from vacation."

"About that. Whereva we decide ta go once Covid eases up, it's my treat."

"Yo' treat?"

"You heard correctly, nigga. It's my treat."

"Well, if it's like that, I wanna go… I want'chu ta take da fam ta Saint Tropez after we visit my grandparents in Louisiana. You got that?"

Cotton pulled her phone out of her bag that was in the shopping cart and Googled Saint Tropez. After she saw that it was one of the liveliest towns nestled along the French Riviera, she said, "No problem. I got it."

With suspicion, Sosa eyed Cotton.

"Okay okay okay. Just stop lookin' at me like that." When he didn't, she turned her head instead. "I was gonna tell ya da otha day that three PPP loan checks totalin' close ta a million came in da mail recently. I was 'posed ta split it wit Slater, but after I told him what happened da otha nite, he told me ta keep it all."

"I thought I told ya hardheaded ass ta quit? You just—"

"I did quit!" she screamed in defense while looking him dead in the eyes. She didn't care that she got extra loud in the parking lot, but she toned it down and continued, "Those checks were already bein' processed when we last talked 'bout it. What was I 'posed ta do? Cancel them? An' on top of that, it helps make up fo' da money you lost in da fire an' fo' our future since you givin' up husslin', which I think is good."

Sosa sighed frustratedly.

They reached the car. They began loading their purchases into it.

All the while, a black vehicle with extremely dark tint crept past them.

Sosa, more aware than ever now, noticed the black car had doubled back just as Cotton and he finished filling the trunk and backseat. He wasn't butt-naked, but he prayed it was nothing to be concerned with. *I hope Da HOL Boyz not trying to pull a fast one on me after my story matched the one that the police gave,* he thought, watching the car with his hand on his fire at his waist.

Time seemed to pass in slow-motion once the eyes of the driver and Sosa's locked.

Then, right as the car got within five yards of Sosa, he saw something through the windshield so familiar that it provoked him to up his H&K 9mm and squeeze the trigger.

Nothing.

The driver of the Dodge Demon, wearing a customized Jesus piece, winked at Sosa before burning rubber and vanishing in the smoke.

HEROES OF HAITI

In Haiti, the slaves were foreigners, and it was their suffering that brought about the vision of Boukman Dutty.

He was a slave from Jamaica who had long been held captive for offenses he'd never committed. He was also a Vodou priest, and it was he who gave slaves their liberty.

Enraged at the oppression he saw around him, Boukman passed into Vodou history when he rounded up a group of escaped slaves called Maroons at Bois-Caman in the hills about Cap Haitian in north Haiti. On August 14, 1791, Boukman made an offering to the gods. That offering launched the Bois-Caman ceremony, which was a uncomplex ritual that soon led to the only victorious slave insurgency in history.

Entitled the new Spartacus, Boukman's ceremony sparked a revolution that began on August 22. That day almost two thousand coffee plantations and two hundred sugar farms were burned to the ground and the plantation slaves were freed.

The Frenchman Napoleon Bonaparte hit back by demanding thirty-four thousand of his troops, who were en route to New Orleans, to detour to Haiti so as to shut down the rebels. Napoleon believed his troops would be plentiful enough to brink back structure to Haiti. Only two thousand of Napoleon's men survived, despite their military experience and artillery and the fact that they notably outnumbered the barehanded slaves. The Haitians, however, had something far more dynamic than guns on their side.

Invoking the lwa to watch over them, the slaves, many of them deep in the trance of a spirit possession, ran at the French. Whole magazines of bullets were emptied into the bodies of the possessed slaves, but they still kept charging. There were tales of Houngans going into the battle fitted out only with magical horse tails with which they steered a cavalry of the dead and the spirits of war. The French army mysteriously fell dead in front of them, with no proof at all of bodily damage.

The uprising progressed in this way for nearly two years until, on August 29, 1793, the French government surrendered and put an end to slavery on the island.

The victory was half won, but the battle was not done. Upset that white men had been overpowered by black slaves, England decided to assist the French in order to reinstate slave ownership. The English troops struck but was immediately beat back by a new hero of the black movement, Toussaint-Louverture. Toussaint-Louverture was the grandson of the king of Arada and he was born to slavery on a plantation in the north of the island. Empowered by his triumph, Toussaint-Louverture went on to vanquish the entire island, declaring it a free black nation in 1801.

The heroes of the revolution died proudly. Boukman was killed in an ambush. Toussaint-Louverture passed away in a French jail after being captured. Together they liberated thousands of slaves who had committed no other crime than having a particular skin color and belief. The autonomy of Haiti was confirmed on January 1, 1804, almost thirteen years after the ceremony at Bois-Caman, where the priests had called for the intervention of the gods.

To be conditioned... maybe.

Lock Down Publications and Ca$h Presents
Assisted Publishing Packages

BASIC PACKAGE	UPGRADED PACKAGE
$499	$800
Editing	Typing
Cover Design	Editing
Formatting	Cover Design
	Formatting
ADVANCE PACKAGE	**LDP SUPREME PACKAGE**
$1,200	$1,500
Typing	Typing
Editing	Editing
Cover Design	Cover Design
Formatting	Formatting
Copyright registration	Copyright registration
Proofreading	Proofreading
Upload book to Amazon	Set up Amazon account
	Upload book to Amazon
	Advertise on LDP, Amazon and Facebook Page

***Other services available upon request.
Additional charges may apply

Lock Down Publications
P.O. Box 944
Stockbridge, GA 30281-9998
Phone: 470 303-9761

Submission Guideline

Submit the first three chapters of your completed manuscript to ldpsubmissions@gmail.com. In the subject line add **Your Book's Title**. The manuscript must be in a Word Doc file and sent as an attachment. Document should be in Times New Roman, double spaced, and in size 12 font. Also, provide your synopsis and full contact information. If sending multiple submissions, they must each be in a separate email.

Have a story but no way to send it electronically? You can still submit to LDP/Ca$h Presents. Send in the first three chapters, written or typed, of your completed manuscript to:

LDP: Submissions Dept
P.O. Box 944
Stockbridge, GA 30281-9998

DO NOT send original manuscript. Must be a duplicate. Provide your synopsis and a cover letter containing your full contact information.

Thanks for considering LDP and Ca$h Presents.

NEW RELEASES

BLOODLINE OF A SAVAGE **BY PRINCE A. TAUHID**

THE MURDER QUEENS 4 **BY MICHAEL GALLON**

THE BUTTERFLY MAFIA **BY FUMIYA PAYNE**

KING KILLA 2 **BY VINCENT "VITTO" HOLLOWAY**

BABY, I'M WINTERTIME COLD 3 **BY MEESHA**

THESE VICIOUS STREETS **BY PRINCE A. TAUHID**

TIL DEATH 2 **BY ARYANNA**

CITY OF SMOKE 2 **BY MOLOTTI**

STEPPERS **BY KING RIO**

THE LANE **BY KEN-KEN SPENCE**

MONEY GAME 2 **BY SMOOVE DOLLA**

THE BLACK DIAMOND CARTEL **BY SAYNOMORE**

CRIME BOSS 2 **BY PLAYA RAY**

THUG OF SPADES **BY COREY ROBINSON**

LOVE IN THE TRENCHES 2 **BY COREY ROBINSON**

TIL DEATH 3 **BY ARYANNA**

THE BIRTH OF A GANGSTER 4 **BY DELMONT PLAYER**

PRODUCT OF THE STREETS **BY DEMOND "MONEY"**
ANDERSON

Coming Soon from Lock Down Publications/Ca$h Presents

BLOOD OF A BOSS VI
SHADOWS OF THE GAME II
TRAP BASTARD II
By **Askari**

LOYAL TO THE GAME IV
By **T.J. & Jelissa**

TRUE SAVAGE VIII
MIDNIGHT CARTEL IV
DOPE BOY MAGIC IV
CITY OF KINGZ III
NIGHTMARE ON SILENT AVE II
THE PLUG OF LIL MEXICO II
CLASSIC CITY II
By **Chris Green**

BLAST FOR ME III
A SAVAGE DOPEBOY III
CUTTHROAT MAFIA III
DUFFLE BAG CARTEL VII
HEARTLESS GOON VI
By **Ghost**

A HUSTLER'S DECEIT III
KILL ZONE II
BAE BELONGS TO ME III
TIL DEATH II
By **Aryanna**

KING OF THE TRAP III
By **T.J. Edwards**

GORILLAZ IN THE BAY V
3X KRAZY III
STRAIGHT BEAST MODE III
By **De'Kari**

KINGPIN KILLAZ IV
STREET KINGS III
PAID IN BLOOD III
CARTEL KILLAZ IV
DOPE GODS III
By **Hood Rich**

SINS OF A HUSTLA II
By **ASAD**

YAYO V
BRED IN THE GAME 2
By **S. Allen**

THE STREETS WILL TALK II
By **Yolanda Moore**

SON OF A DOPE FIEND III
HEAVEN GOT A GHETTO III
SKI MASK MONEY III
By **Renta**

LOYALTY AIN'T PROMISED III
By **Keith Williams**

A GANGSTA'S KARMA 4 | FLAME

I'M NOTHING WITHOUT HIS LOVE II
SINS OF A THUG II
TO THE THUG I LOVED BEFORE II
IN A HUSTLER I TRUST II
By **Monet Dragun**

QUIET MONEY IV
EXTENDED CLIP III
THUG LIFE IV
By **Trai'Quan**

THE STREETS MADE ME IV
By **Larry D. Wright**

IF YOU CROSS ME ONCE III
ANGEL V
By **Anthony Fields**

THE STREETS WILL NEVER CLOSE IV
By **K'ajji**

HARD AND RUTHLESS III
KILLA KOUNTY IV
By **Khufu**

MONEY GAME III
By **Smoove Dolla**

MURDA WAS THE CASE III
Elijah R. Freeman

AN UNFORESEEN LOVE IV
BABY, I'M WINTERTIME COLD III
By **Meesha**

QUEEN OF THE ZOO III
By **Black Migo**

CONFESSIONS OF A JACKBOY III
By **Nicholas Lock**

JACK BOYS VS DOPE BOYS IV
A GANGSTA'S QUR'AN V
COKE GIRLZ II
COKE BOYS II
LIFE OF A SAVAGE V
CHI'RAQ GANGSTAS V
SOSA GANG III
BRONX SAVAGES II
BODYMORE KINGPINS II
By **Romell Tukes**

KING KILLA II
By **Vincent "Vitto" Holloway**

BETRAYAL OF A THUG III
By **Fre$h**

THE MURDER QUEENS III
By **Michael Gallon**

THE BIRTH OF A GANGSTER III
By **Delmont Player**

TREAL LOVE II
By **Le'Monica Jackson**

FOR THE LOVE OF BLOOD III
By **Jamel Mitchell**

RAN OFF ON DA PLUG II
By **Paper Boi Rari**

HOOD CONSIGLIERE III
By **Keese**

PRETTY GIRLS DO NASTY THINGS II
By **Nicole Goosby**

PROTÉGÉ OF A LEGEND III
LOVE IN THE TRENCHES II
By **Corey Robinson**

IT'S JUST ME AND YOU II
By **Ah'Million**

FOREVER GANGSTA III
By **Adrian Dulan**

GORILLAZ IN THE TRENCHES II
By **SayNoMore**

THE COCAINE PRINCESS VIII
By **King Rio**

CRIME BOSS II
By **Playa Ray**

LOYALTY IS EVERYTHING III
By **Molotti**

HERE TODAY GONE TOMORROW II
By **Fly Rock**

REAL G'S MOVE IN SILENCE II
By **Von Diesel**

GRIMEY WAYS IV
By **Ray Vinci**

Available Now

SANCTIFIED AND HORNY
by **XTASY**

THE PLUG OF LIL MEXICO 2
by **CHRIS GREEN**

THE BLACK DIAMOND CARTEL
by **SAYNOMORE**

THE BIRTH OF A GANGSTER 3
by **DELMONT PLAYER**

RESTRAINING ORDER I & II
By **CA$H & Coffee**

LOVE KNOWS NO BOUNDARIES I II & III
By **Coffee**

RAISED AS A GOON I, II, III & IV
BRED BY THE SLUMS I, II, III
BLAST FOR ME I & II
ROTTEN TO THE CORE I II III
A BRONX TALE I, II, III
DUFFLE BAG CARTEL I II III IV V VI
HEARTLESS GOON I II III IV V
A SAVAGE DOPEBOY I II
DRUG LORDS I II III
CUTTHROAT MAFIA I II
KING OF THE TRENCHES
By **Ghost**

LAY IT DOWN I & II
LAST OF A DYING BREED I II
BLOOD STAINS OF A SHOTTA I & II III
By **Jamaica**

LOYAL TO THE GAME I II III
LIFE OF SIN I, II III
By **TJ & Jelissa**

IF LOVING HIM IS WRONG…I & II
LOVE ME EVEN WHEN IT HURTS I II III
By **Jelissa**

BLOODY COMMAS I & II
SKI MASK CARTEL I, II & III
KING OF NEW YORK I II, III IV V
RISE TO POWER I II III
COKE KINGS I II III IV V
BORN HEARTLESS I II III IV
KING OF THE TRAP I II
By **T.J. Edwards**

WHEN THE STREETS CLAP BACK I & II III
THE HEART OF A SAVAGE I II III IV
MONEY MAFIA I II
LOYAL TO THE SOIL I II III
By **Jibril Williams**

BLOOD OF A BOSS I, II, III, IV, V
SHADOWS OF THE GAME
TRAP BASTARD
By **Askari**

A GANGSTA'S KARMA 4 | FLAME

PUSH IT TO THE LIMIT
By **Bre' Hayes**

A DISTINGUISHED THUG STOLE MY HEART I II & III
LOVE SHOULDN'T HURT I II III IV
RENEGADE BOYS I II III IV
PAID IN KARMA I II III
SAVAGE STORMS I II III
AN UNFORESEEN LOVE I II III
BABY, I'M WINTERTIME COLD I II
By **Meesha**

A GANGSTER'S CODE I &, II III
A GANGSTER'S SYN I II III
THE SAVAGE LIFE I II III
CHAINED TO THE STREETS I II III
BLOOD ON THE MONEY I II III
A GANGSTA'S PAIN I II III
By **J-Blunt**

THE STREETS BLEED MURDER I, II & III
THE HEART OF A GANGSTA I II& III
By **Jerry Jackson**

CUM FOR ME I II III IV V VI VII VIII
An **LDP Erotica Collaboration**

BRIDE OF A HUSTLA I II & II
THE FETTI GIRLS I, II& III
CORRUPTED BY A GANGSTA I, II III, IV
BLINDED BY HIS LOVE
THE PRICE YOU PAY FOR LOVE I, II ,III
DOPE GIRL MAGIC I II III
By **Destiny Skai**

A GANGSTA'S KARMA 4 | FLAME

WHEN A GOOD GIRL GOES BAD
By **Adrienne**

A GANGSTER'S REVENGE I II III & IV
THE BOSS MAN'S DAUGHTERS I II III IV V
A SAVAGE LOVE I & II
BAE BELONGS TO ME I II
A HUSTLER'S DECEIT I, II, III
WHAT BAD BITCHES DO I, II, III
SOUL OF A MONSTER I II III
KILL ZONE
A DOPE BOY'S QUEEN I II III
TIL DEATH
By **Aryanna**

THE COST OF LOYALTY I II III
By Kweli

A KINGPIN'S AMBITION
A KINGPIN'S AMBITION **II**
I MURDER FOR THE DOUGH
By **Ambitious**

TRUE SAVAGE I II III IV V VI VII
DOPE BOY MAGIC I, II, III
MIDNIGHT CARTEL I II III
CITY OF KINGZ I II
NIGHTMARE ON SILENT AVE
THE PLUG OF LIL MEXICO II
CLASSIC CITY
By **Chris Green**

A DOPEBOY'S PRAYER
By **Eddie "Wolf" Lee**

A GANGSTA'S KARMA 4 | FLAME

THE KING CARTEL I, II & III
By **Frank Gresham**

THESE NIGGAS AIN'T LOYAL I, II & III
By **Nikki Tee**

GANGSTA SHYT I II &III
By **CATO**

THE ULTIMATE BETRAYAL
By **Phoenix**

BOSS'N UP I, II & III
By **Royal Nicole**

I LOVE YOU TO DEATH
By **Destiny J**

I RIDE FOR MY HITTA
I STILL RIDE FOR MY HITTA
By **Misty Holt**

LOVE & CHASIN' PAPER
By **Qay Crockett**

TO DIE IN VAIN
SINS OF A HUSTLA
By **ASAD**

BROOKLYN HUSTLAZ
By **Boogsy Morina**

BROOKLYN ON LOCK I & II
By **Sonovia**

GANGSTA CITY
By **Teddy Duke**

A DRUG KING AND HIS DIAMOND I & II III
A DOPEMAN'S RICHES
HER MAN, MINE'S TOO I, II
CASH MONEY HO'S
THE WIFEY I USED TO BE I II
PRETTY GIRLS DO NASTY THINGS
By Nicole Goosby

LIPSTICK KILLAH I, II, III
CRIME OF PASSION I II & III
FRIEND OR FOE I II III
By **Mimi**

TRAPHOUSE KING I II & III
KINGPIN KILLAZ I II III
STREET KINGS I II
PAID IN BLOOD I II
CARTEL KILLAZ I II III
DOPE GODS I II
By **Hood Rich**

STEADY MOBBN' I, II, III
THE STREETS STAINED MY SOUL I II III
By **Marcellus Allen**

WHO SHOT YA I, II, III
SON OF A DOPE FIEND I II
HEAVEN GOT A GHETTO I II
SKI MASK MONEY I II
By **Renta**

GORILLAZ IN THE BAY I II III IV
TEARS OF A GANGSTA I II
3X KRAZY I II
STRAIGHT BEAST MODE I II
By **DE'KARI**

TRIGGADALE I II III
MURDA WAS THE CASE I II
By **Elijah R. Freeman**

THE STREETS ARE CALLING
By **Duquie Wilson**

SLAUGHTER GANG I II III
RUTHLESS HEART I II III
By **Willie Slaughter**

GOD BLESS THE TRAPPERS I, II, III
THESE SCANDALOUS STREETS I, II, III
FEAR MY GANGSTA I, II, III IV, V
THESE STREETS DON'T LOVE NOBODY I, II
BURY ME A G I, II, III, IV, V
A GANGSTA'S EMPIRE I, II, III, IV
THE DOPEMAN'S BODYGAURD I II
THE REALEST KILLAZ I II III
THE LAST OF THE OGS I II III
By **Tranay Adams**

MARRIED TO A BOSS I II III
By **Destiny Skai & Chris Green**

KINGZ OF THE GAME I II III IV V VI VII
CRIME BOSS
By **Playa Ray**

FUK SHYT
By **Blakk Diamond**

DON'T F#CK WITH MY HEART I II
By **Linnea**

ADDICTED TO THE DRAMA I II III
IN THE ARM OF HIS BOSS II
By **Jamila**

YAYO I II III IV
A SHOOTER'S AMBITION I II
BRED IN THE GAME
By **S. Allen**

LOYALTY AIN'T PROMISED I II
By **Keith Williams**

TRAP GOD I II III
RICH $AVAGE I II III
MONEY IN THE GRAVE I II III
By **Martell Troublesome Bolden**

FOREVER GANGSTA I II
GLOCKS ON SATIN SHEETS I II
By **Adrian Dulan**

TOE TAGZ I II III IV
LEVELS TO THIS SHYT I II
IT'S JUST ME AND YOU
By **Ah'Million**

THE STREETS MADE ME I II III
By **Larry D. Wright**

KINGPIN DREAMS I II III
RAN OFF ON DA PLUG
By **Paper Boi Rari**

CONFESSIONS OF A GANGSTA I II III IV
CONFESSIONS OF A JACKBOY I II
By **Nicholas Lock**

I'M NOTHING WITHOUT HIS LOVE
SINS OF A THUG
TO THE THUG I LOVED BEFORE
A GANGSTA SAVED XMAS
IN A HUSTLER I TRUST
By **Monet Dragun**

QUIET MONEY I II III
THUG LIFE I II III
EXTENDED CLIP I II
A GANGSTA'S PARADISE
By **Trai'Quan**

CAUGHT UP IN THE LIFE I II III
THE STREETS NEVER LET GO I II III
By **Robert Baptiste**

NEW TO THE GAME I II III
MONEY, MURDER & MEMORIES I II III
By **Malik D. Rice**

CREAM I II III
THE STREETS WILL TALK
By **Yolanda Moore**

LIFE OF A SAVAGE I II III IV
A GANGSTA'S QUR'AN I II III IV
MURDA SEASON I II III
GANGLAND CARTEL I II III
CHI'RAQ GANGSTAS I II III IV
KILLERS ON ELM STREET I II III
JACK BOYZ N DA BRONX I II III
A DOPEBOY'S DREAM I II III
JACK BOYS VS DOPE BOYS I II III
COKE GIRLZ
COKE BOYS
SOSA GANG I II
BRONX SAVAGES
BODYMORE KINGPINS
By **Romell Tukes**

CONCRETE KILLA I II III
VICIOUS LOYALTY I II III
By **Kingpen**

THE ULTIMATE SACRIFICE I, II, III, IV, V, VI
KHADIFI
IF YOU CROSS ME ONCE I II
ANGEL I II III IV
IN THE BLINK OF AN EYE
By **Anthony Fields**

THE LIFE OF A HOOD STAR
By **Ca$h & Rashia Wilson**

THE STREETS WILL NEVER CLOSE I II III
By **K'ajji**

A GANGSTA'S KARMA 4 | FLAME

NIGHTMARES OF A HUSTLA I II III
By **King Dream**

HARD AND RUTHLESS I II
MOB TOWN 251
THE BILLIONAIRE BENTLEYS I II III
REAL G'S MOVE IN SILENCE
By **Von Diesel**

GHOST MOB
By **Stilloan Robinson**

MOB TIES I II III IV V VI
SOUL OF A HUSTLER, HEART OF A KILLER I II
GORILLAZ IN THE TRENCHES
By **SayNoMore**

BODYMORE MURDERLAND I II III
THE BIRTH OF A GANGSTER I II
By **Delmont Player**

FOR THE LOVE OF A BOSS
By **C. D. Blue**

KILLA KOUNTY I II III IV
By Khufu

MOBBED UP I II III IV
THE BRICK MAN I II III IV V
THE COCAINE PRINCESS I II III IV V VI VII
By **King Rio**

MONEY GAME I II
By **Smoove Dolla**

A GANGSTA'S KARMA 4 | FLAME

A GANGSTA'S KARMA I II III
By **FLAME**

KING OF THE TRENCHES I II III
By **GHOST & TRANAY ADAMS**

QUEEN OF THE ZOO I II
By **Black Migo**

GRIMEY WAYS I II III
By **Ray Vinci**

XMAS WITH AN ATL SHOOTER
By **Ca$h & Destiny Skai**

KING KILLA
By **Vincent "Vitto" Holloway**

BETRAYAL OF A THUG I II
By **Fre$h**

THE MURDER QUEENS I II
By **Michael Gallon**

TREAL LOVE
By **Le'Monica Jackson**

FOR THE LOVE OF BLOOD I II
By **Jamel Mitchell**

HOOD CONSIGLIERE I II
By **Keese**

A GANGSTA'S KARMA 4 | FLAME

PROTÉGÉ OF A LEGEND I II
LOVE IN THE TRENCHES
By **Corey Robinson**

BORN IN THE GRAVE I II III
By **Self Made Tay**

MOAN IN MY MOUTH
By **XTASY**

TORN BETWEEN A GANGSTER AND A
GENTLEMAN
By **J-BLUNT & Miss Kim**

LOYALTY IS EVERYTHING I II
By **Molotti**

HERE TODAY GONE TOMORROW
By **Fly Rock**

PILLOW PRINCESS
By **S. Hawkins**

BOOKS BY LDP'S CEO, CA$H

TRUST IN NO MAN
TRUST IN NO MAN 2
TRUST IN NO MAN 3
BONDED BY BLOOD
SHORTY GOT A THUG
THUGS CRY
THUGS CRY 2
THUGS CRY 3
TRUST NO BITCH
TRUST NO BITCH 2
TRUST NO BITCH 3
TIL MY CASKET DROPS
RESTRAINING ORDER
RESTRAINING ORDER 2
IN LOVE WITH A CONVICT
LIFE OF A HOOD STAR
XMAS WITH AN ATL SHOOTER